Decl ay
new s his
first novel.

All The People
All The Time

Declan Lynch

POCKET BOOKS

TOWNHOUSE

First published in Great Britain and Ireland by Pocket/TownHouse, 2003
An imprint of Simon & Schuster UK Ltd, and TownHouse and
CountryHouse Ltd, Dublin

Simon & Schuster UK is a Viacom company

1 3 5 7 9 10 8 6 4 2

Simon & Schuster UK Ltd
Africa House
64–78 Kingsway
London WC2B 6AH

Simon & Schuster Australia
Sydney

TownHouse and CountryHouse Ltd
Trinity House
Charlestown Road
Ranelagh
Dublin 6
Ireland

A CIP catalogue record for this book is available from the British Library

ISBN 1 903 65028 3

Typeset by SX composing DTP, Rayleigh, Essex
printed and bound in Great Britain by
Cox & Wyman Ltd, Reading, Berkshire

All the People All the Time

Chapter 1

They stopped talking to Victor after he got the plate in his head. Families are like that, he reasons. Friends too.

And Victor can see their point. Really he can. He considers leaving a message on Simon's answering machine, saying it's all right, that people are odd. But he doesn't do it. In fact, Victor hasn't rung Simon since the night before he went under the knife, the night Simon said Victor was no brother of his any more, as though the head operation was to remove the last vestige of his humanity.

It was a good thing not to do, not to call Drumbolus with a message, an exercise in restraint that Victor wishes he could manage more often.

The son would be proud of him. Paul Bartley frequently advises his father to seek professional help, because counselling helps Paul a lot, and in particular, it might help rid Victor of the notion that close friends and family would abandon him over a bit of metal in his head. The metal is fine, according to Paul. It's all the other shit that needs seeing to.

Paul is about to appear on television now, in the late afternoon, the sun streaming through the one big window of Victor's flat, mocking him as it illuminates billions of specks

1

of dust. Are they there all the time or does the sun just bring them out? He would have tea to mull on this, then draw the curtains and sit looking at his son on television.

Who else in a Rathmines flat has a son on television? Victor surprises himself that he can still get the butterflies, having been in the business so long, having perhaps stayed in too long.

Paul presents a gameshow, a bad one. His son, his only son, is laughed at all over Ireland. He comes across more gay than he is in real life, where you'd need to know him to suss it. Too gay, Victor thinks, for the peasants. Victor is proud of his liberal attitude to homosexuality. Tells himself it's all the same to him, fellows rogering fellows.

Paul will be coming around after the show. He will want an opinion. If Victor has one regret about his son being gay, it is that the flat must look even worse to one of them. The routine is, Paul passes no remarks on the flat and Victor lies, telling Paul he was great but the format needs tightening. Paul would talk about a second series, how they might crack it next time.

Who else in a Rathmines flat has a son dying the death on television? The old self-pity. He has to watch it or it will chew him up. He has his monogrammed shirt on. The business left him with the odd bauble. The business that they were in and that the bastards who jeered at Paul would never be in.

He has to stop comparing himself with others. Paul is big into this theory that everyone is depressed these days because they know too much about other people who are better off than them. If you say you're better off than the fellow in the flat below, it follows that you're worse off than Tony O'Reilly by some distance. Paul is right, up to a point. But the Bartleys are still in the business and those bastards are still not in it.

Forrest Fucking Gump. The word is that Simon is calling him Forrest Fucking Gump since he got the plate in his head. Cannon keeps him abreast. An old soldier from the showband days, Cannon. A man who is loyal and true and who will always have a bed for Victor down in Drumbolus, when the others have nothing but scorn.

The show. Paul's show, his shot at the title. Victor steels himself. Ah, it's useless. Useless. And Paul will take the fall for it, not the RTÉ clowns who put him out there, not them. Now the butterflies, the bad air, the tension in his gut about Paul, the bad vibes from Simon, he feels he can still handle all that and Forrest Fucking Gump, so it is a profoundly shocking thing to him that as he watches Paul working, Victor Bartley weeps.

He doesn't want to be weeping, he has no intention of weeping at some lousy television show, but weeping he surely is, at something, a weeping that begins somewhere near the centre of his being and spreads horribly through him, a heavy-set man convulsed by a sudden explosion miles inside of him, a wounded bear fearing his head is coming apart, that they gave him a bad plate, and what is really doing Victor's head in is this: he likes the weeping. He can't help liking it for the sensational relief of it, liking it and hating that he likes it, this astounding release. It is going away now. He will live.

'Lemons, that's what we need. Lemons.'

Victor hits Paul with this, just winging it, before Paul is properly in the door. Keep him off-balance until Victor can think straight.

'There's no second series,' Paul says, removing his leather gloves in a way that Victor thinks is definitely gay. 'Fuckers.'

'Fuckers,' Victor adds.

3

He is surprised by Paul's venom. The kid must have thought he was really in with a shout. Paul usually has everything in proportion. His perfectly dark features are perfectly proportioned. They are not meant for venom. They are meant for publicity photographs with a big smile and an autograph.

Victor can see something of his young self in Paul, the same darkness. But all the badness was bred out of Paul somehow, that baleful look of Victor's when he is down, the heavy physical menace that still oozes out of him when he goes to war.

Paul flings a copy of the *Herald* across the room. Very out of character, to throw things. Victor thinks the bastards are sullying Paul. Making him ugly, defiling him with their badness.

And what is this shit in the *Herald*? Richie Earls, rock god, says that since he came back to live in Ireland, he's mad about it, thinks it's really happening at last, apart from his one pet hate, which is Paul's poxy programme.

'What do you need lemons for?'

There's an edge to Paul's question, like he's looking for a row.

'For hot whiskies,' Victor says, businesslike.

Victor doesn't like this. He avoids eye contact. He doesn't fancy Paul like this, thinking there's some meaning in something you said when it might mean nothing at all. Maybe, just maybe, lemons were the first thing that had come into his head, because he felt he needed a drink, and rightly so, and lemons always remind him of drink. The smell of lemons from behind the counter of a pub when they're chopping them up in the morning, lemon mingled with the tang of last night's beer. Lemons remind him of drink more than drink itself. Brings it all back to him every time.

Paul is still pushing it. 'You're still at the moderate drinking thing?' he says.

Let him be, Victor thinks. He must be mortified. He's sitting on the arm of the couch, like this is how he really wants it every week, a flying visit, take off the gloves but not the creamy overcoat.

'Controlled drinking,' Victor says gently. 'They call it controlled drinking. I'm sorry, Paul, I'd offer you a hot one but there's no gargle. Go out?'

Go out? It sounds a bit perky. Paul is in a trance.

'If we had a lemon we could make hot whiskies, if we had whiskey,' Victor says, switching off the television, symbol of rejection.

To hell with it.

Victor keeps talking. 'Maybe I had a feeling. A premonition,' he says. 'You'll never believe this, but I've been bawling like a baby and I don't know why.' He looks Paul in the eye, and feels encouraged to go on. 'Maybe I picked up the bad vibes from RTÉ or something. It's very mysterious. Something set off the waterworks.'

Paul starts to chuckle and Victor is pleased to join in. Paul beckons Victor to come close and goes knock-knock on his father's skull.

'Maybe the plate is picking up messages,' he says.

Is Paul more himself again?

'You look different today, Victor,' he says. 'Less tensed up.'

Victor fears that Paul will start on about counselling again. Paul is at the shower unit in the corner now, messing with it, starting to lecture. 'This isn't fixed is it?'

'Sorry, chum,' Victor says.

'You must be far gone to crack up like that. Even us queers. . .'

But Paul's heart isn't in the lecture. Victor thought Paul

would be overjoyed about the weeping, seeing it as a sign that Victor is getting in touch with his demons. Victor thinks it's a funny thing that if a man starts bawling these days, his people rejoice, where once they would have put him away.

But nothing is any good for Paul today. Perhaps Victor hasn't made it clear enough that the fit of hysterics was not a direct result of Paul's line of TV patter. Paul still doesn't look gay, queer, whatever. Maybe if he did, he could do a Graham Norton, a pure camp thing. Something that the public could latch on to.

'I'm way ahead of you, boy,' says Victor. 'With all your psychobabble.'

Paul is quiet now. Victor needs to keep going. He needs Paul to snap out of it.

'Paul,' he says quietly, 'Professional time. A-weepin' and a-wailin' aside, I was actually thinking, and it's nothing to do with you, but in fairness the show is shite. It does you no favours.'

Paul switches the shower on and draws the curtain from the outside.

'That'll heat up now,' he says. He sounds calm.

Victor is becoming giddy now, straying beyond his usual limits of candour. But Paul is owed some truth. Paul can handle this stuff, with his counselling. And Victor is, after all, a professional. Victor brandishes the *Herald*.

'This bastard rock star is not wrong to think this. But he is totally wrong to *say* it and hurt a fellow-professional. I am personally acquainted with three members of U2 and I will ask them to let Richie Earls know in no uncertain terms that he is a bollocks, and that he needs to atone for this.'

Paul switches off the shower.

'I've already fucked Johnny Oregon out of it on the mobile,' he says. He seems now to be talking to himself. 'I

6

know Johnny. He's Richie's mate. He lives in Richie's house when Richie is away. I like Johnny. I feel bad about it now.'

Paul isn't exactly snapping out if it. Victor thinks it's probably too strange for him to have to listen to the old boy's wisdom for a change, to take this battering on top of everything else.

'Let's get out of this hole and hit one of these new bars I hear about. That place with the palm trees. I am Forrest Fucking Gump and I need out of here,' Victor says, as heartily as he can.

Paul laughs. 'So you heard what Simon is calling you?'

Victor's impulse is to keep moving now that Paul is laughing, so the overcoats are buttoned up and they're out on Leinster Road quickly, hailing a taxi, Victor still wearing runners which clash with his black Crombie.

It was Cannon who told Paul about the Forrest Gump crack. They go back a long way.

Dublin City Centre

Father and son are sitting at a marble table in Zanzibar. It's not a bad time in Ireland's history to be controlling your drink, Victor thinks, as Dublin's new style of bar is not to his taste. Too much daylight, too many noisy wooden floors, making him pine for the gloom of a lounge darkened at noon, and the bit of carpet.

The rest of the evening is free of the afternoon's emotions. Both of them complain of being washed out. Victor is so drained, he has no anger left even for the flash punters in this bar. But he can't help seeing Paul's rejection as a symptom of some new tyranny, the shape of which is still forming in his brain. Not the axing of the show itself, which was hard but fair, but the way they can't see that it was no worse shite than what Richie Bastard Earls is putting out there, Richie Kilbrittan Fucking Hill Earls who sold eighteen million albums to eighteen million tossers, stuff that Earls himself would have jeered when he started out, when he really was a bit special, a bit mystical, when the guy could rock.

The Irish have put away begrudgery, Victor reckons, but they would still have a good laugh at Paul for failing. They haven't lost their ability to jeer at a poor man's misfortune. Victor will definitely sort out the rock god Richie Earls, definitely.

Paul apologises more than once for being in a bad mood at the flat, and Victor says it's only worth mentioning because Paul's bad moods were so rare. And in this case, thoroughly justified.

Victor's fit of weeping is completely off the agenda. Each seems to need time for the latest developments to settle. Though right to the end, Victor is expecting Paul to pursue the weeping, proof positive that the gay man is right, that Victor is becoming human again, human enough to have his head examined in a progressive manner.

They drink glasses of Guinness slowly and make general resolutions to stick at it, because the bastards would be made up altogether if they drove you out of the business.

As Victor sits into his taxi on Dame Street, he pulls down the window and says to Paul, 'Keep the faith, chum.'

Paul tries to say something back to him, but the wind is getting up, and it doesn't seem worth the effort, shouting over the elements. Paul says he might drop into Renard's, and as he walks away, Victor scans the taxi-rank to see if any punter is smirking at his son.

Like the crowd in Zanzibar, they are indifferent. But he isn't really looking properly. And Paul doesn't really look gay at all in the long coat, walking towards the corner of

Kapp & Peterson like a gentleman, and in the direction of Grafton Street, shoulder against the wind, round the corner and gone.

As he feels the first stirrings of another catastrophic eruption within, Victor says to the taxi driver, 'Rathmines for fuck's sake.'

Does everyone not know that he is reduced to a fucking bedsitter in Rathmines? But he puts the stopper on it this time, with a furious monologue about property prices that gets him home in the one piece.

Rathmines

The nine o'clock news runs it fourth, how the body was washed up in Dún Laoghaire. An RTÉ spokesman mourns the loss of a promising talent, and nothing about the show about to be axed. Nothing about Victor, the young reporter never heard of him. They say that Paul was twenty-seven but he was only twenty-five. 'Foul play is not suspected.'

Chapter 2

Drumbolus, County Westmeath

Poor Paul is dead, there will be a funeral, is Simon to go or what?

'Oh, for the wings, for the wings of a dove. . .'

The voice of the boy soprano evokes for Simon Bartley special things, a cold and lovely dawn in the countryside, always in the countryside, as they call it in England. Not down the country, as it is in Ireland.

He feels guilty that he prefers the artificial chocolate-box quality of the English countryside to his own place. The gorgeous music ends and the presenter on Lyric FM, the new classical station that Simon finds soothing in the car, says that the soloist and choir are from the Rockingham School in Leicestershire.

Now Simon's pleasure is intense. Parked outside Nulty's bungalow on a fresh Monday morning, he can take in his own rough country and add to it that exquisite vision of civilisation to which the presenter has just alluded. The pure sound of the soprano and the beauty of its contemplation brings a sweet ache to the gut made sweeter by what went into making that sound, the thousand years of learning and of making people learn to do algebra and to translate Latin

10

and to play cricket and at the end of the day, at the top of the range, to train a young lad to stand out from the choir and to sing 'Oh, for the wings, for the wings of a dove.'

The Rockingham School in Leicestershire. You'd need to be up early for those boys. But rather than resent the English for their cultivation, Simon admires the way they hold fast to their heritage, even if the Rockingham School is out of bounds for most. And he hopes that Ireland will be as tenacious in holding on to her own traditions, through these dangerous years. Who was he to talk, he scolds himself, sitting pretty in a new silver Mercedes, listening to classical sounds on Lyric FM on the super-sensitive speakers?

Victor despises him. He'll have a go at the creature comforts, the big car, as though it were a crime to have nice things, and to keep them nice.

But Victor made more money than Simon ever made, he just pissed it away and then sneered at the brother for making himself comfortable. But listen, once Simon starts running these speeches about Victor in his head, the idyll of Rockingham School and the wings of the dove gets away from him, and this man's country, this hardy spot in Westmeath, looks a little less special, a bit more lonesome. He switches off the radio. There would always be struggles, no matter how you took care of business.

About Paul and the funeral. He will ask Nulty for counsel on this, on their way to the Drumbolus Golf and Country Club. Oh Lord Jaysus, Victor cut rashers out of him over that one. Golf and Country Club? Fuck's sake.

Vic is the one with the talent, no mistake. Simon has no problem admitting that Victor has a great ear for an up-and-coming group, that he could hear promise where Simon could only hear noise. Every group they managed, without exception, had been groomed and brought to the table by Victor. Yes, but what careers would they have had if they had listened to the mad bastard the way he became, ranting at them to produce their own material?

Listen, the bands out of this stable were never going to produce new material that any sane person would want to hear, but thanks to Simon, they had fruitful if modest careers which had raised families. Victor would fall out of love with the groups after three weeks and leave Simon to do the business, then show up drunk at dancehalls calling them all a shower of useless pricks. Still on his ten per cent though. Still taking his cut, just the same as muggins here.

He has no feel for the country, Victor. He thought he had too much taste for the muck-savages around these parts, but up in Dublin, the pop types thought Victor was a bit of a bumpkin. So he was getting the shitty end of it every way. And he would never be happy now.

Here is Nulty now, with his golf bag. He is blond, very slim and pretty in a sixties style, and speaks in a Cork murmur that hints at permanent amusement. He wears a black polo-neck top and jeans, virtually a uniform that suggests an old photo of The Kinks.

'You caught me in a bit of a dream,' says Simon out of the electronic window of the silver-bodied beauty.

'Lovely day for it,' Nulty murmurs, his golf mantra. 'Gorgeous.'

Nulty joined the Hare Krishnas once for about two weeks, and is regarded by Simon as perhaps the last remaining socialist in the Republic of Ireland. Nulty dumps his clubs in the boot and sits beside Simon in a series of actions which Simon seems to be orchestrating from the master dashboard of the Merc.

'All the toys like Greg Norman,' says Nulty, his traditional weekly salute to Simon's lifestyle.

In addition to being Simon's regular golf partner, Nulty is a sort of employee of his, due to his rambling Saturday evening show on the local radio station run by Simon, Midlands Community. And that, thinks Simon, in addition to Nulty's various disc-jockeying gigs, you could call a lifestyle too, big on excitement if low on finance.

Perhaps things will change now between the two men, because Simon is going to raise a private matter. Until now, they have been silent about all emotional controversies, especially on Mondays. The golf, with its Byzantine etiquette, its ancient bonds of male empathy, bars guilty talk about hammerheaded brothers and dead gay nephews. But now this might change, and Simon doesn't like relationships to change. That's Victor's thing.

Simon wants to do this now, and so he starts the car and cruises away from the little bungalow, figuring he will have it done and dusted by the time they reach the sanctuary of the club. He puts it like this to his golf buddy:

'Nulty, I would like to go to my nephew's funeral but I want to avoid Victor. What to do?'

Nulty is amused by how Simon looks to him for spiritual guidance, just because he was in the Hare Krishnas for two weeks. But Simon wants an answer, a yes or a no. Simon wants the old trouble out of his life now. He will not agree to any personal contact with Victor if he can possibly avoid it. The image of a grieving Victor comes to his mind, making him wince. If there is hope at all of averting some chaotic episode, it'll be if the formalities of the funeral somehow drain all the hysteria out of the air.

'Sorry, Simon,' says Nulty, aware of Simon's anxiety. 'Sorry about the slow start. I've been thinking about the funeral too.'

'The press gave the lad a hard time, there was some slagging on the part of Richie Earls no less,' says Simon. 'But, Jaysus, if my fellas started topping themselves over a bad press the bodies would be piled high.'

Simon is driving into the car park of the Golf and Country Club, which is still mainly a building site, the clubhouse no more than a pile of bricks, but all full of promise, all business even early on a Monday morning. You wouldn't know this country any more.

'Nulty,' says Simon, parking the car, 'if I don't go to him, then he'll come to me.'

Then he thumps the window, like some perfectly groomed waxwork becoming emotional.

'If I don't go to him, then he'll come to me,' Simon says again, quietly.

Nulty pitches it man to man. 'You want to know the right thing to do?' Nulty says.

'I can't talk to anyone else about this,' Simon says.

Since Simon is unmarried, childless, and unlikely to do anything rash in this department in his late forties, Victor is all the family he has now to tell his troubles to. And Simon can hardly reveal any personal weakness to the locals, half of whom work for him. He needs Nulty to say the right thing, now.

'Don't go to it,' Nulty says. ' You didn't really know the lad. It would be a sham.'

Simon likes what Nulty says and the decisive way he says it.

'You're the man,' Simon says, touching a switch that opens the boot.

The golf course is still a scrawny thing, the greens will never be magnificent, the club in its mature state will never be a match for Athlone or Mullingar, but this latest project gives Simon an enormous feeling of accomplishment, which returns to him now at the thought of a morning's play.

'That lad will be going up anyway,' Simon says of Cannon, who is arriving now to work on the clubhouse. He blows the horn and Cannon salutes him with an enormous hand which he then uses to adjust the black woollen cap that he wears at all times in public.

'Cannon will be looking for the lift to Dublin,' Simon says, saluting Cannon back. 'Cannon knew Paul.'

'Cannon knows everyone,' Nulty says.

'He was like a father to Paul,' Simon says. 'He'll be very cut up about it.'

'He's working away,' Nulty says, watching Cannon in overalls slathering wet cement on a building block, getting a rhythm going, like his massive frame needs all the action it can get. His friendly giant's face now looks intense under the black cap, lost in concentration.

'Cannon's a worker,' Simon says.

'No golf for Cannon,' Nulty says.

'Forty different jobs from musicianing to labouring, and he never learned how to drive a car,' Simon says.

Nulty is getting the hint in full. 'I'll go instead of you, like the aide-de-camp,' he says. 'What do you say, Simon? Would that be the constructive thing?'

Simon feels bound to say that Nulty doesn't know the man Victor, wouldn't be up to his tricks. But he is fine now after his little attack of the Victors, and he wants to be done with it.

'Tell you what,' he says. 'You can take this car if you want.'

When they are well out on the course, he speaks freely about the plate in Victor's head and about Forrest Gump.

Chapter 3

Dublin, North Side

Victor Bartley is keeping vigil at Jennings's funeral parlour on the Oscar Traynor Road when Johnny Oregon walks in. Johnny Oregon, that bastard Richie Earls's mate. He is tall and muscular, his jeans and black leather jacket are rock 'n' roll regulation, but his red hair is the outstanding feature, still long and thick and newly washed, swept back from his face and bouncing off his shoulders in the heroic mode of the windswept warrior.

Victor recognises a true colour and calculates that Johnny might be fifty years old, given how far back he goes into the mists of Irish rock. Johnny is a frontiersman. No-one could have guessed how the original Irish rockers would look in middle age, because no such people existed before the likes of Johnny, and none of them envisaged being around anyway at fifty. Victor is impressed by how well Johnny is wearing it, by his gypsy spirit that never surrendered to the rat race, and that kept him young, always up for rolling a joint with some rock chick, Victor surmises, listening to Tim Buckley or Richard and Linda Thompson, joss sticks and candles for that mellow mood.

The rock chicks had never come Victor's way. His aura

repelled them. He was too fucked up. He had defied his own better instincts and whored around the business doing all sorts, while Johnny went one way and one way only, to the rock and the rock chicks. Johnny knew who Johnny was. But even he was not to know that Ireland would one day have its own rock gods, who would sit at Johnny's feet while he filled them in about what a lovely man Captain Beefheart was.

But this is no time at all for the old self-pity. Paul is lying dead a yard away, and Victor suspects he is madder than he has ever been before, because he is coping so well. So professionally. He received the news of Paul's drowning with such calm, the bastard cop at the door had his suspicions. Definitely, there are little spasms of terror about what will become of him when it all sinks in. But he is on top of it for now, he tells himself, organising everything, doing the business for Paul. Catastrophe seems to come easy to him. Big trouble he can manage. It's some asshole on the radio on a wet September morning that will set him off. Something small like that.

They know each other a bit, Victor and Johnny, to say hello at ligs. Maybe they had a drunken conversation one night in a Leeson Street club. Could have gone to the Manhattan Café afterwards for a fry, the mixed grill.

Johnny Oregon comes straight over to Victor and shakes his hand.

'Sorry for your trouble, mate.'

He takes in the surroundings, the sparse dignity of the scented parlour with the dead entertainer lying in state, but no crowds filing past, just the square-shouldered father in a long black coat and now Johnny Oregon, representing the spirit of rock 'n' roll.

Yes, they had gone on to the Manhattan for a mixed grill. Victor is sure of it. A mad night.

The two men look down on the perfect face of Paul in the coffin, 'sent back to his Maker in top nick,' exchanging whispers as though they know one another a bit better than they do.

He has a gift for intimacy, Johnny Oregon. People tell him things after five minutes' acquaintanceship that they wouldn't tell close friends ever. Victor himself is sure that he spewed out a few state secrets in Leeson Street, whenever, but something about Johnny tells you that he is not going to judge you too harshly. Which is probably why all of rock 'n' roll loves Johnny Oregon. They just like having him around, to tell their troubles to. He is no mere ligger, but a genuine confidant of rock's aristocracy.

Victor can't help feeling flattered by Johnny showing up, knowing where he has been, and considering the blithe contempt with which Ireland's rockstar élite views an all-rounder with showband roots, a warhorse like Victor Bartley.

'I spoke to him, mate,' Johnny says. 'Spoke to him on the phone the day he died.'

Johnny is from some dank Dublin suburb, but from the moment he discovered rock 'n' roll, he spoke in a soft London accent and never stopped speaking like that, and never bothered explaining it. His real name is Johnny O'Regan, but Philip Lynott christened him Johnny Oregon when Lizzy were on tour in England and a hotel receptionist mispronounced O'Regan on the register. Johnny O'Regan became Johnny Oregon from that moment on, an Ellis Island vibe he called it.

What was he doing on the road with Lizzy? There was no name for what Johnny did back then, but these days, he'd probably be called a 'publicist' or a 'personal assistant'. It amounted to more or less the same thing, keeping up morale with good vibes and the best spliff, in an accent not quite your own.

'I'm very calm now,' Victor says. 'I've been very calm all through it.'

Johnny looks at him with just the right amount of sympathy, not too much to be pathetic, enough to convey the fact that he'd stood over a few coffins himself, the bodies of famous mates who flew one too many missions in the great acid wars, or just the unsung corpses of road crew.

'We've all been there, Vic,' he says.

Victor ushers Johnny away from the coffin and over to some chairs lined up against the wall.

'What did he say to you?' Victor says.

They sit down, and Johnny tells Victor that Paul gave him a bollocking over being dissed by Richie Earls in the paper, and told him to pass it on. He tells it just as Paul told Victor.

'I'll need to talk to Earls myself now,' Victor says. 'As part of the grieving process.'

The grieving process. That was Paul's line of patter.

'Richie is away right now,' Johnny says. 'But a meeting might be set up at a future date.'

Victor takes this as Johnny just saying the decent thing.

'I'm living up in Muscle Shoals, looking after it,' Johnny says.

'Muscle Shoals?' Victor says.

'That's what Richie calls the place up on Kilbrittan Hill,' Johnny says, 'the place I'm looking after for him. He called it after the Muscle Shoals recording studio, where all that good shit came out of. He's actually an OK geezer.'

Victor considers this calmly.

'No, Johnny, I don't think so,' he says. 'I don't think he's an OK geezer.'

'Fair enough, mate,' Johnny says.

'Richie Earls is entitled to think whatever he likes about Paul's poxy show, but he was all wrong to abuse a fellow-professional,' Victor says.

He considers some philosophical remarks about one man ending up in a mansion on the hill, and another man drowning, seeing the lights in the big houses as he loses the will to live, but he keeps it professional.

'I can't figure this out, Johnny,' he says. 'I don't know why Paul would do himself in, like he was making a protest, like that monk who set fire to himself. Paul didn't go in for that shite. He was psychobabbled up to the gills. Sure I told him myself that the show stank. He was irate about it, he was most irate. But what do you think, Johnny? You who knows fellows who did themselves in. Did Paul look like a candidate to your expert eye?'

Johnny thinks it's better if Victor doesn't get vexed now. 'Have a drink later in the week, mate?'

Victor certainly might have a drink later in the week to reward himself for his exemplary attitude to the drink of late. He is determined to get through this sober, and now maybe he has something to look forward to, a target, a few civilised drinks waiting for him at the end.

He shouldn't be thinking like that over his son's dead body, but Johnny's visit has soothed his soul. A man so cool gives you a handle on things, helps you to find that bit of grace that always gets away from you, because you are Victor Bartley, and you are not cool. In his own head, maybe, years ago, but he never stuck at it like Johnny Oregon. He never believed he could get to where they are hip to the tip, all the way through. But Johnny is giving him respect anyway, and he feels a bit lighter for it, and he sees some small advantages to being Victor Bartley, like having a few wisps of hair himself, from dodging the nine to five.

And maybe, if he can get his head around it, there's a life in front of him. For a few moments of clarity he sees himself repairing some of the damage he has done and even burying the hatchet with Simon, as a tribute, yes that's the way to look at it, as a tribute to Paul, and his Trojan work for peace and love amongst all who are fucked up.

But first, he must bury Paul. He must be a good boy at the removal and the requiem mass and while they wheel the coffin out the church gates and slide Paul into the hearse and then out to be lowered into the grave beside his mother. Big trouble he could handle.

They promise to meet in The Jester, just down the road from where Johnny Oregon is living the life of Richie Earls until Earls comes home.

Chapter 4

Drumbolus, County Westmeath

Nulty won't take Simon's car. Not for comfort, not for speed, not for fun or as a favour from one golf buddy to another. He fears contact with big silver cars and fancy goods in general. He would sooner be photographed by the *Westmeath Examiner* making love all night long in Simon's big silver car than be seen driving it to Dublin like it was his.

Sex is not his thing, he tells himself. It was enough of a thing to help him leave the Hare Krishnas sharpish, but he doesn't have it on the brain. Drink is not his thing. The North is not his thing, and sport is not his thing. Golf isn't really sport, he reckons. He makes his occasional living as a disc-jockey, but he has no strong views on the subject, none that would distract him from his pursuit of one thing above all these, this thing called social justice. That's his thing.

He joined the Communist Party in Cork once, and he left university after one term to devote himself to full-time political activity. But in his heart he knew that he had gone mad. So he rented a shack, a bungalow-shack, in which to get his head together. Rented it from Simon, of course. Six years ago. So he plays golf, so what? So he plays it with the most acquisitive man possibly in all of Westmeath?

Fanaticism will get you nowhere, and a healthy mind can live with the odd contradiction. Bob Dylan plays golf, off a handicap of seventeen.

And as for Simon, the socialist approves of none of his politics but gives him his due for the radio show, in which Nulty can mutter about the redistribution of wealth as long as he does it with dry Corkonian wit and some easy-listenin' sounds.

Nulty is forgiven a lot because he is so good-looking. Somewhere in the silence between Nulty and Simon is a kind of dread, there-but-for-the-grace. They feel sorry for one another, Nulty reckons. He can sense fathoms of isolation in Simon, who has a gift for making money, who couldn't help making money if he tried. And he assumes that Simon feels sorry for any man trying to do down the manifest evils of Irish capitalism from the strategic heights of Drumbolus, which is hardly even a town, more a townland, a locality.

Simon once told him he had about twenty different sides to his personality but he might be better off with just the one. He told Nulty he was a chameleon, pronouncing the 'ch' as in 'chancer', which Nulty found quite touching. In the war against greed, Nulty can live with these feelings of compassion for one so greedy, because he does not sneer at compassion, but is at times floored by the weight of his sympathy for endeavour gone wrong, for the awful exposure of humans to rejection. It does him in sometimes, to see people rise one more time, and again, above these searing little cruelties. So he can live with a bit of tolerance for Simon Bartley and his empire.

He also lives with a weakness that shows no sign of leaving him, a weakness for stealing. He has a gift for it. In college, he ran what amounted to a small business, shop-lifting and selling the gear at knockdown prices to other students. Bottles of whiskey, books, once he just walked out of a shop with a painting under his arm. He still keeps his hand in, nicking ridiculous things, like a banana or a cream bun. And it isn't greed or badness that drives him to it, he is sure. Being rigorously honest, he can look at photos of Formula One ace Eddie Irvine festooned in Ferraris outside his Dalkey mansion in *VIP* magazine, Ireland's answer to *Hello!*, and genuinely feel no envy in his heart. But then he robbed the copy of *VIP* from Mrs Grogan in the Drumbolus Stores.

In his heyday, he ripped off yards of silk from a material shop in Cork that had a ninety-nine point nine per cent female clientele, because a girlfriend passed a remark that she fancied it. Then her friends paid him to swipe plenty more yards. And perhaps his personal favourite was the time that he really needed money for a night's drinking, so he knocked off several albums from a second-hand record shop, and sold them all back to the same shop two hours later.

He has some quality of stealth about him, something elusive that makes people leave him alone even when he is walking out of their shop with a large watercolour. They sort of assume that he has paid for it, that no thief could be so blatant.

He cherishes his talent. But he also regards it as a basic character flaw, a mysterious defect miles inside of him that could at least partly explain why his life ran aground so early. It never enters his head that ripping off shopkeepers might deprive them of their share of social justice. To Nulty, stealing is a form of self-expression. In the past week, for pleasure that merely coincided with need, he pinched from the Drumbolus Stores a tin of John West red salmon, a packet of Vesta curry, two bars of Fruit 'n' Nut chocolate, a tub of peach yogurt, a copy of the *Westmeath Examiner* with *VIP* magazine tucked inside it, and a small statue of the Emperor Napoleon for no reason at all.

But the big silver car is barred. When the boom goes bust, they will look back and see those thousands of big silver cars as the poignant emblems of a nation gone briefly berserk. So he is ferrying kettles of boiling water to his old green Ford Fiesta early on the morning of Paul Bartley's funeral, melting the frost from the windows, warming her up for what always feels like one last journey.

Cannon is on time, answering his own description of 'a big lump', wearing a thick anorak and respectable black trousers and the black cap. Nulty and he do a lot of drinking together in Malone's, owned by Simon, where Nulty plays records on slack nights. Nulty likes the old showband stories that Cannon tells him when the drink brings it all back.

He steers the Fiesta towards the motorway, its first run on the highway where it must maintain its dignity among the Porsches, the Jags, and the Alfa Romeos, tooling up the new dual carriageway in a heap of junk with a registration number of interest to archaeologists.

The Fiesta can hardly contain Cannon's bulk. It occurs to Nulty that Cannon never learned to drive due to the sheer physical discomfort of it, for the simple reason that his feet were too big for the pedals. He'll raise it another time, because today they are both short of chat.

Cannon is reading a paragraph in the *Irish Independent* about Paul. It seems to be taking a long time.

'It must be great to have talent,' Cannon says. And then he thinks about it. 'I have no talent.'

He hands Nulty a Don Williams cassette.

'He liked listening to a bit of Don Williams. He liked that song "Gypsy Woman", Paul did.'

Nulty sees images of Paul as a child coming down to

Drumbolus for the summer and Cannon taking pity on the city boy.

'I hear you practically reared him, Cannon,' says Nulty. 'Taught him the guitar and everything.'

Nulty is aware that the big lump next to him had once been a figure of some glamour on the showband scene, a guitarist. It is said that he played a fluent lick and that he shagged like a lion.

'I taught him "Gypsy Woman",' Cannon says. 'That's all.'

The motorway reduces the journey from the midlands to Dublin so that it feels more like a commuter ride, with small towns along the way starting to look like suburbs of the city, new houses going up in a frenzy of development, big money being paid. Sometimes Nulty feels a part of this fantasy when he thinks that his little bungalow, his shack seventy miles from Dublin, convenient to all amenities including golf, might go for over a hundred, hundred-and-fifty grand. If it was his to sell. Still, it's always something to talk about in a country where most other forms of conversation are dying out.

They are about five minutes' drive from their scheduled stop at Mother Hubbard's, big fries, and a lie-down for the Fiesta.

'Simon walked me into this,' Nulty says. 'The way he talks about Victor. . .'

Nulty slips Don Williams into the machine. He'd forgotten that he likes this song. Maybe he'll play it on his radio show as a tribute to Paul. It might even sound classy. Simon wants the station to sound more classy, but he probably means smarmy. Simon is hoping to get a full radio licence for the midlands region. He wants classic hits and super sounds, interspersed with some harmless local content, and absolutely no chat about gay young entertainers killing themselves. Nulty hears him speak disparagingly about 'political correctness' and 'the poverty industry'. Nulty reckons that this means him. A sign has gone up in the studio, 'Who The Hell Is Tom Waits?'

Nulty still feels an impostor on the motorway. He parks the Fiesta alongside a jumbo Range Rover outside the glass front of Mother Hubbard's and says what he wants to say before the day gets complicated.

'While we're all still sober,' he says, 'what is it with Simon? What did Victor ever do on him?'

Cannon doesn't want to talk about it. Nulty doesn't push it. They get out, stretching themselves like grown-ups climbing out of a kiddie's ride.

It's the Full Irish twice. There is a natural silence now, Nulty and Cannon quietly looking forward to their fries amid the bustle of the motorway restaurant, famous for its solid grub and swift service, endorsed by the several truckers at their ease, connoisseurs of the Full Irish, alone with their trucker thoughts, men apart from the busy family groups, alert to the imminent invasion of a coach party.

Pots of tea and coffee arrive.

'Are you seriously telling us you don't know about Victor?' Cannon says. 'It was all over the papers.'

Nulty feels a nervous rush. He tears a paper napkin into long strips.

'Victor killed his wife,' Cannon says. 'He drove himself and herself off the end of a pier somewhere up in Louth. Except he got out of it somehow, maybe thought better of it. Manslaughter. Did a couple of years for it eventually.'

The waitress brings the fries.

Cannon pauses before he eats. 'It's great to have talent,' he says. 'I have no talent.'

Nulty needs to go to the toilet. He is trying to work out how he missed such a story. He hopes it was during his

27

Krishna days, because otherwise there's no knowing what other vital events of the century he has missed. In the mirror above the urinal he sees a pretty boy who knows nothing of a world in which men drive their women off the edge of a pier, and go to jail for it, and are now waiting to bury an only child that the sea took too. He knows nothing about all that.

Dublin is upon them, sucking them in. They gain speed in the heavier traffic. Now it's all roundabouts, flyovers, the Fiesta is touching 70 and Nulty is glad to give himself up to the highway. They say no more about Victor, and why people have finished with him. Cannon has directions that will take them to the north side.

Chapter 5

Kinsale, West Cork

The rock god Richie Earls is the first customer of the day in The Neptune pub and restaurant. He asks for a whiskey and takes it to a table by the window along with his *Irish Times*. A scan reveals no mention of him, which is good. He will probably search the paper again later, looking in sections where he couldn't possibly be, a hero of rock rummaging through the sports section and the theatre reviews, riddled with fear that anyone might be paying any attention to him.

He will probably be sick later, back at the lodge two miles outside of town, where he has taken to retching for the afternoon. Richie Earls has gone off his food since the night that he did away with Paul Bartley. Maybe it was something less than plain killing, something technically short of murder, and surely he can find a superstar barrister to plead for his ass if it comes to that.

But he doesn't want to think that far ahead. All he knows is that Paul Bartley is being buried today and that he has brought this about. The Neptune has become a kind of campaign headquarters since he raced down to Kinsale in the middle of the night on his Harley, three insane hours from Dublin to West Cork in a howling gale, the big Harley once a symbol of paydirt and freedom, now of demented escape.

This is the third day running he comes into town and buys *The Irish Times* and has a whiskey breakfast beside this window, digging in for what might be all hell. He thinks that the barman recognises him, but he's not sure. It's that Irish thing again of leaving the stars a bit of space. Usually it suits Richie Earls to be given space. But in his present predicament he would settle for something less enigmatic.

This morning he will take his fame for a walk through Kinsale's narrow little streets, wanting to be noticed as he studies the menu in the window of a gourmet restaurant or is charmed by a painting in an art shop, or an antique, or as he calls for fish 'n' chips down by the marina in Dino's, where they give you a slice of lemon and tartare sauce with your takeaway, because this is Kinsale. He will welcome being accosted by some asshole who doesn't know the etiquette of the region, who may be so crass as to ask for an autograph while Richie Earls dallies at the bureau-de-change, receiving odd looks from passing German yachtsmen. He wants it to be known, without having to talk to anyone, that he is in residence up the road, acting relatively normal for a rock star in West Cork retreat, the morning sharpener, *The Irish Times*, the constitutional.

'Morning, Mr Earls,' says the barman, emptying the ashtray.

Recognition.

Earls thinks that this day has at least started according to plan. He is sporting his best-known look, the black beret, the four-day growth of beard, the plain denim jacket and jeans evoking the hobo of American legend, that freewheeling muse which had been his inpsiration, Woody Guthrie and Dylan, Steinbeck and Kerouac.

He is smoking again. Marlboro, not the roll-ups of old,

which in his present state of anxiety just take too long to skin up. Smoking again at thirty-six. Another melancholy footnote to this abysmal turn of events. He gave them up at thirty, when he made the breakthrough, figuring that a man who was now in the business of collecting homes in Dublin, Kinsale, Antibes, Manhattan and Kensington would feel a bit of a chump if he started croaking from emphysema.

'Staying for lunch today?' says the barman, nodding to the fish-tank beside the bar containing lobsters which are taken straight from there to the kitchen pot and the dining table. Richie has been diverted by this daily performance, by the nonchalance with which the staff carry the living crustacean into the kitchen, holding it in some vital part of its middle so that it is paralysed, its claws powerless for the struggle.

He is going to take a risk here, a big risk, given the depths of his misery. He has spoken only to Johnny Oregon since he arrived, acting normal, informing him over the mobile that Muscle Shoals was all his for a few weeks, as calmly and as quickly as he could manage it on the day after the shit-rain. Now he is going to break his silence to a member of the general public. He has to try something if only to see the reaction, to learn whether decent people run away and hide when they hear him speak, now that he is languishing among the damned. For a man whose voice made him, he really is not sure of what will emerge, some satanic growl or some merry banter, the banter of a-man-clearly-innocent-of-all-wrongdoing.

'Would you do me a favour, amigo?' Richie says in his soft Dundalk accent with a splash of the Americas. 'Show me one of the big bastards?'

The barman is warm, respectful. He selects a lobster by poking through the tank with a rod that grips the fiend as it idles in the water and hauls it out, then the trick to immobilise it, and here is the beast now, its snappers a yard away from Richie Earls's vital parts, in the casual custody of a smiling youth.

'Let this one go, amigo,' Richie says, taking a fifty-pound note slowly from his wallet lest there be any sudden movements. 'And buy the poor bastard a bourbon.'

He is amazed at how strong and smooth his voice sounds, a bit too much on the Dundalk side perhaps, but then he's not talking to David Letterman here. Is it the whiskey bringing him back to his Dundalk beginnings, helping him improvise? He had made a general resolution to say nothing to nobody for fear of what gibberish his fevered brain might disgorge. Instead he's rapping, and he could not sound more affable and charming if he was explaining to Letterman the plight of the white rhino, how the Rhino Aid extravaganza will raise awareness and several million dollars, and how much he is looking forward to working with The Chieftains.

He might just come out the other side of this yet. Foul play was not suspected after all, it said on the news that the body was washed up in Dún Laoghaire, and they're burying the kid today. Jesus Christ he sounds like some mobster thug, but he is starting to work on this small change of mood that he has found, a promise that he might feel slightly less nauseous this afternoon, and that maybe if he is very good and never even thinks about doing that proposed duet with the ghostly voice of the dead John Denver, even if it's just for charity, he might feel a whole lot better after about twenty years. He can feel his star's survival instincts coming through, enabling him to quip good-naturedly after three days of the fullest agony he has known. For a minute he is himself again, he knows that he is special, that his gifts will always emerge to raise him high above the crowd.

He is out the door now as the kid babbles his thank-yous, a kid who will tell anyone who wants to know that this guy

Richie Earls is a nice guy, very down-to-earth, a big tipper, and in top form today. And as he strides up towards the main street, he waves to the kid and the kid waves back, first with his free hand, then with the lobster. Others are seeing this celebrity vignette, and will speak approvingly if it comes to that.

He knows where he is going now, out through the town and up towards Charles Fort, a good walk away from these cramped little streets and past all the boats to the top of the harbour. Let the fresh air stir up the whiskey in his blood. He can't help it. He is a star.

He must have what it takes, because he never even wanted to be a star from the beginning. All he had wanted was to make great records, to be respected as a musician by men like Van Morrison and John Martyn and Christy Moore. He could have had a solid audience for life, with a deal from some record company who wanted him on the label for the credibility. He had gained a sound international reputation as a white soul singer with a special feel for the southern style, for numbers like 'The Dark End of the Street' and 'Do Right Woman, Do Right Man', the sound of Muscle Shoals and the sublime songs of Dan Penn and Spooner Oldham, and a few of his own in that vein. He had been sustained by the tributes of critics and the loyalty of acolytes, and was largely untroubled by the affections of the masses.

In the old Ireland where Richie Earls was born, a promoter told him there were three types of music, country-and-western, pop and mad pop. And he advised Richie to get out of the mad pop if he ever wanted to make a shilling. That was all before he sleepwalked into singing the title track for some Hollywood weepie, a dreary big power ballad called 'The Loving Cup', which became number one in twenty-eight territories including Britain and the United

33

States, and which launched him into the stratosphere, three mega-platinum albums so far, disturbingly close to the musical neighbourhood where Michael Bolton lives, but with Joe Cocker and Stevie Winwood close enough by for emergencies. It also re-located him to neighbourhoods where only legends live, to the homes in Dublin, Antibes, Manhattan and Kensington, and to possibly the most cosmopolitan of the lot, the lodge here in West Cork.

He had sincerely not pursued any of it, he tells himself as he marches down through Summer Cove and up the hill to Charles Fort. Stardom found him because it was his destiny, and he had taken on the trappings with grace. And now he feels it is good for humanity all round that he is a star. The first year, he pretended to resent it for the mewling critics, but now he will say to them that a guy like him who speaks out strongly against French nuclear testing and against Sellafield can use his position to influence the young, to fuck with the mainstream. And hey, after a year the cheques started to arrive, and that gave him bags of confidence too.

The sea air has pumped another few ounces of well-being back into his system as he pays his three pounds to the lad at the entrance to the restored fort. Recognition. A knowing smirk from the lad.

Johnny Oregon introduced him to this place years ago, took him up here to smoke and to reason. Business is slack now in early September, making him feel in charge of the premises, as though he were indeed walking a property of his, or one that was soon to be in his portfolio. He walks straight to the sea-facing side of the monument, a star-shaped, seventeenth-century wonder of fortification, where you can still hear the cannonade as you look out to the Atlantic or back to Kinsale and imagine all that costumed bollocks about the Flight of the Earls. He is getting giddier with this new rush of hope, his imagination pumped up by the sheer fuck-you-all brilliance of the battlements, the scale of the hexagon, and then a feeling of humility, of his own smallness in the great scheme, he this icon who is yet flesh and blood, who has suffered so much these three days, a man, just a man from Dundalk, blown back by this sea breeze getting up now and making him retreat from the ramparts until he is running down the hill from the grass to the gravel path and on at a quickening gallop towards a nice sheltered nook where he falls to his knees and splatters the old stones with a gush of whiskey-scented puke.

So it was the drink talking after all. The whiskey, leading to a crazy rush of optimism and now this supreme emptiness. He can see a couple in yellow windcheaters thirty yards away, ambling through the shell of the married quarters occupied by the Brits up until the 1920s. Their sluggishness brings a kind of comfort. If they had seen his dash for cover and heard his horrible retching, they would surely be at his side now, agog that they had come from Wilmington, Delaware, to check out the monuments, only to find the great Richie Earls throwing his ring up over four centuries of Irish, British and European history.

He reckons he must be very close to madness now, or maybe over the line. New visions are forming in his head as he sits in the foetal position at the entrance to his new sanctuary, the restored magazine which once housed the fort's supply of gunpowder. He remembers a local telling him that restoration began on Charles Fort as a response to its occupation by a hippie colony, or what seemed like that to the town worthies. Free spirits taking drugs and humping, no doubt, making their own hare-brained connections. Shades of the Manson family to the good burghers. Could he find his bearings in this vision of pagan love and excess? There was something about this place that drew the hippies to it, its beauty of course, but some other stuff too that eventually brought all exotic beings to West Cork, something that cured a delicate head whether you were an original settler like Noel Redding of the Jimi Hendrix Experience, or some celebrity chef working on his latest divorce. Something that you might eventually crack if you sat for long enough in the foetal position in this place which has seen so much fighting and fucking.

Dee, his lady, is in Antibes. She loves the sun. He will phone her now, right now, to tell her everything. She is so wise. She knows too much to argue or to judge. Did Dylan write that about Dee? He takes a mobile phone from the top pocket of his denim jacket and is ready to dial when the couple in windcheaters pass by. Recognition. They laugh but say nothing. Too dreary, these students. Good news is, they've seen him brandishing a mobile phone like any mega-star would be doing.

Now he knows it isn't Dee he should be ringing, but his man, Johnny Oregon. It's not that he's worried about Dee hauling him down to the pigs in Dalkey, in fact he has not wasted a minute worrying whether she will come through for him. It's just you don't want talking about this shit on a mobile phone with every creep and spook listening in, guys on trawlers, probably David Puttnam up the road will get a crossed line. He'll tell Dee when she gets back from Antibes. Maybe she knows about it anyway with her sixth sense. But she'll be cool about it, he has no doubt.

This is what people who were outside the loop did not understand about people like him and Dee who were on the inside. When you're on the inside, the only people you respect are people like you, and mostly the only people you meet are people like you. If someone who doesn't belong ends up hurt, it only shows that they shouldn't have been there in the first place. You have no responsibility to anything or anyone except your vocation. You didn't get to this higher ground by just wanting it, you are called to this higher ground, and your calling demands eternal vigilance towards any asshole who barges in looking to take you down to their level. This is what happened to Paul Bartley.

But you have to have a feel for it, a feel for what gives the artiste a stiffy and what is all wrong for him. Dee has a feel for it. She'll be cool. Richie Earls feels sufficiently in charge of his emotions to call his man, Johnny Oregon. He stands up as he presses the buttons, and is finding his stride near the front gate when Johnny answers.

'Johnny Oregon?'

'Richie.'

'Richie. Oh, you cunt.'

'Sorry?'

'Sorry, mate, I nearly ran over a punter. I'm taking the Daimler out.'

'All good?'

'Yeah. Walked the dogs. Fixed up the security den.'

'Right. I mean, that Victor Bartley stuff, the thing in the paper we were bothered about. The son?'

'Got Victor on his own last night. Made the right noises. He'd still like to meet you as, eh, a fellow-professional. To clear the air.'

'Right.'

'If I catch him later, will I set up something?'

'Don't talk shite, Johnny.'

'He really wants to talk to you mate.'

'Don't talk shite.'

Richie Earls makes for the town where he feels he might be able to swallow a Guinness and a plate of oysters in a quiet corner of the famous Blue Haven, with a bit of luck. Johnny gave him a bit of bad with that cunt riff. Probably just the surprise of hearing Johnny use the word, not Johnny's style at all. Johnny is almost incapable of losing his cool about anything, Richie reckons. Dee had a thing going with Johnny once and when she split, he'd still come over to put a bit of Charlie up her hooter, expecting nothing in return. A real gent.

Richie Earls slips into The Blue Haven. He feels the better for that phone call, it has calmed his spirit, and now his gut is willing to take on a nourishing glass of stout with oysters on the side, if only to look at them. He claims a window table for one. The Guinness and the oysters are brought to him by young Ciara. Recognition.

'Enjoy your seafood, Mr Earls.'

Look, he's getting away with it all ends up. No-one knows a damn thing. The first sip of Guinness hits home and settles. He lights a Marlboro. The next taste of Guinness makes him feel right in the head for the first time since Paul Bartley came banging on his front door, making it past a dead security system and into the hall, berating him under his own roof, screaming at him, abusing Richie Earls who had let him in out of pity, dissing Richie Earls after midnight up on Kilbrittan Hill. Maybe the beer was making Bartley brave but Richie Earls had a head full of Charlie and three Dobermans. The dogs ran Bartley down the back garden, and ran him all the way down on to the beach and into the sea, and when Richie finally stopped hooting and whooping at the total mad dog frenzy of the scene, it became clear that Bartley wasn't coming out of there. Fuck him.

Richie Earls signals for another glass of Guinness. He will have a crack at the oysters now. It is lovely to be back in West Cork.

Chapter 6

Dublin, North Side

They're paging Victor Bartley in the Forte Dublin Airport hotel. He is in the lobby with Nulty and Cannon when the announcement is made. He goes straight to reception. It is Mary Jones from the *Evening Herald* on the phone for him. Sorry she couldn't make it out.

He tells her that it was a small private funeral with some old friends up from Westmeath, a few RTÉ types, Mr Johnny Oregon representing the music industry.

Sorry she had to ask this, but was Paul depressed by recent adverse media comment?

No, says Victor, he never read the critics. He was just a creative young man who decided to say goodbye. Victor tells her he understands she is only doing her job. He too is trying to cope in a professional manner.

Cannon is greatly amused as Victor returns, in quiet convulsions as they proceed down the hall towards the bar.

Victor puts an arm around his shoulder. 'This fella's laughing at me,' he says. 'He's thinking I set it up to be paged.'

Cannon is free to roar laughing.

Victor shepherds them to a booth.

39

'The big guy is having a go at me over an incident in the Berkeley Court Hotel a long time ago,' he says.

Cannon's laughter goes on, sounding like a-hin-a-hin-a-hin-a-hin, as he settles into the booth, and Nulty sits opposite him. In this giddy mood, Nulty half-expects Cannon's black cap to come off, but it stays on through the funeral and now the afters.

Victor pulls up a chair.

'I better tell this myself or the big guy will spoil it,' Victor says.

He closes his eyes and massages his temples with the thumb and forefinger of his right hand, like an old man saying his prayers. It's a technique that Paul told him about, if you're on a radio programme and you don't want to be distracted from your flow.

'About ten years ago, the Revenue Commissioners had a crow to pluck with Victor Bartley,' he begins, a storyteller evidently in command of his material. 'So I tell this taxman who's on my back that I'll meet him in the Berkeley Court, no less, in order to outline my affairs. These fellas aren't used to the big time, you see, so I'm thinking that just sitting there in the foyer, the taxman'll pass out with the smell of money coming off the clients, and he'll think better of coming the heavy with an important man like Victor Bartley. But to throw him altogether, I have Cannon standing over at a payphone, and any time I'm feeling the heat, the big guy here gets the high sign and puts the call through to the desk, and instead of wrestling with this lad over the VAT, Mr Victor Bartley is being paged. It worked too.'

Cannon wants more. A-hin-a-hin-a-hin-a-hin-a-hin.

'You want to hang me in front of this man?' Victor says.

The waitress arrives with a big pot of tea. Cannon orders a pint of stout, Nulty will have a rum-and-black, a bad call straight away it seems to him, like he's having the kiddies' portion, a nervous boy in the company of big men.

Victor continues. 'I bamboozled this poor taxman. Victor Bartley did the one thing that the excise men just do not understand. He told the truth.'

Victor pours his tea, savouring the attention.

'He had me under the gun. He said there was no way around it, I had made huge money for the last ten years, and not a dickie-bird to the Revenue. Now it was payback time. They could pick a number between one and a million and hit me with that, or we could go through the gory details and arrive at a fair settlement. So I say we can do anything he likes but the end result is still the same. Victor Bartley has no money. Zero pounds and zero pence.'

The girl comes back with the drinks. Nulty gives her a tenner.

'It's all looked after,' the girl says.

'Good luck, Vic,' says Cannon, draining a good third of his pint in one swallow.

Victor goes on. '"But Mr Bartley," says the little man from the Revenue, "you must have money." And I say to him, "I most certainly did have money, but let me illustrate to you what happened to it." And so I told him that every Monday afternoon, I would get paid by the artistes in my charge. Good money it was too. Very good money, like you say. Some weeks I'd be looking at a thousand pounds, and that was a thousand pounds in 1979. So I'd call up my good friend Matt Brogan, and Matt would call up some of our mutual friends, and we'd have what we called the Monday Club. Up first to the Palace Bar for afternoon pints. Loads of pints. We'd be fighting each other to buy drink, fighting each other. Then maybe down to Mulligan's to hit up with a couple of the press lads and more pints. Fighting each other to get them in, fighting each other.

41

'Off down to O'Donoghue's then, I would let no other man put his hand in his pocket, still on the pints mind you, but now we'd be looking for some dry filling. So it's a taxi-cab out to Sandycove, to the Mirabeau, the best nosebag in the city, no prices on the menu, and good wine, maybe brandies, what have you. We might divide up the bill, but then again we might not. Big-hearted Arthur here would always be first on the draw when the bill arrived.

'So the Monday Club would ride back into Leeson Street. Bottles of wine all night, and I don't mean Blue Nun. Bottles of champagne. Bottles of wine and bottles of champagne being sent over to other tables with my compliments, and at night-club prices mind, at night-club prices. So what I'm saying here is that you could be down six hundred pounds no bother and you'd be none the wiser.

'Well, the taxman is scribbling all this down, his two eyes are out on sticks. So I put my arm around him, there in the Berkeley Court, and I said, "Six hundred pounds, my friend, all gone, wasted . . . And that was only Monday."'

Victor opens his eyes and takes his hand away from his face. He gets big laughs. A few years seem to have drained away from him with this small success, he seems less heavy in the black Crombie. Blood has returned to his cheeks after the cold graveyard, and for a flush moment he could be mistaken for a businessman who is still in business.

Actually, six months later the taxman sticks Victor with a bill for £175,000 that is still outstanding, but for the story to work fully, in the mind's eye he has to shuffle away a broken man. For today, that's how the story sits.

They have just buried Paul Bartley in the graveyard beside the airport, but a stranger might wonder why these people are carousing so early in the day. They are not exactly embarrassed by it, but agree that one big laugh and one only is probably just about right, just for the relief of it. Victor reckons there is something to be said for a small Dublin funeral, the indifference of the city to the misfortune of the few. The priest at the service was professional but no more than that. When you've taken to weeping for no reason that you can fathom, like Victor has, maybe you appreciate the low-key approach.

Johnny Oregon didn't go for the big production number either, just paid his respects and peeled away southbound in the big car. No cemetery for Johnny, no mumbling the rosary with a few culchies and RTÉ types. The city just wants you and your funeral out of the road, and maybe this is right. Today is not the day for weeping. There would be a year for that, a bad year that might get better or it might not. That's what they said, others who had lost a son like this. One dirty rotten year, guaranteed. Today might just be as good as it gets for some time. There's a routine to be followed, you are given respect whether you deserve it or not. There's really not a lot that can go wrong for you at a funeral, no new shit at any rate. Especially if you are on top of your drink situation.

'And that was only Monday,' Cannon says, still savouring the line.

'Maybe you were the only honest man in Ireland at the time,' Nulty says. 'You could have done like everyone else and gone off shore.'

'I would have done,' Victor says. 'Except I don't care about money.'

The others are waiting for Victor to elaborate, but he leaves it there.

For weeks the country has been waking up to stories about tax evasion on a vast scale during the 1980s and into the early 1990s, of rural shopkeepers and publicans opening bogus non-resident bank accounts to dodge tax, of the banks themselves running vast revenue scams, of rampant fraud among the respectable classes, an alternative Irish economy in the Cayman Islands, and big-time black-guardism in general.

Nulty is engrossed in all these stories of shady practices. He reckons that Victor is probably acquainted with most of the big stars of the latest round of scandals. But Nulty is brooding. He has none of the usual words of comfort for Victor. He can't even say 'Sorry for your trouble.' Everyone else could say it, and mean it, but not him. He is full of compassion for the class of people who were getting screwed by the Cayman Islands types, but he can't say he is sorry for Victor's trouble. Such words should flow from him like syrup. But syrup doesn't agree with him. He is all blocked up about syrup. Then again, they are just civilities, and they work. He just can't say them.

He drinks his rum-and-black. Across the table from him Cannon is basking, at peace. Victor signals to the waitress. The same again.

'Anyway it's not me paying,' Victor chuckles. 'It's Simon. He sent up a few bob to look after us all. A lovely gesture there from Simon. Simon pays no more tax than is good for him.'

Then Victor yelps. 'Tax, tax, tax, everyone talks about tax these days like it was a great thing, and you were a bad bastard if you didn't pay your tax. No harm to you, Nulty, but you seem like the sort of man who thinks it's immoral not to pay tax.'

Nulty mumbles, agreeing that he is that sort of man.

'That's all my arse, chum,' Victor growls. 'What's immoral is paying tax to these fuckers so they can waste it. I would no more give thousands of pounds to the government than I would give it to a ten-year-old child. And I mean that. A ten-year-old child.'

Victor closes his eyes again and massages his temples.

44

'There are men who can take a fiver and grow another fiver beside it, because they have the magic touch. None of these men are there to take your tax and do something useful with it, grow another fiver alongside your fiver. The way it is, you might as well be giving it to a simpleton. Now that's immoral.'

Nulty murmurs. 'Still . . .'

Victor feels like he might never stop talking when he starts like this. He takes a breath and holds it while he formulates a reply.

'I don't care about my own money,' he says at last. 'If it belongs to me, I treat it with the contempt it deserves. But not the total contempt you'd need to be paying tax on it. What I really care about is other people's money, and the way they waste it buying shite and paying tax. Does that make any sense, Nulty?'

'I think so,' Nulty says.

Victor rubs his right temple, which is the side that the plate is on. He knows what he means, he's just not getting it across right. He has another go.

'In the heel of the hunt, I am not interested in money itself, because what I am interested in is music. You could say that music is my life. You might say that I personally let a lot of bad bands loose on the public, and that I personally made Ireland a worse place, me and Simon below. But I always knew better, do you hear me? I always knew the difference. Do you understand?'

'Absolutely,' Cannon says.

Victor is composed now.

'My belief, you see, is that the more money there is around, the worse the music gets. It's supposed to work the other way around. When the few bob arrives, what you have is *Cats* at The Point, with the suits in all their glory. You don't get the next Beethoven, you get the boy bands.

Richie Earls.' Victor seems weary all of a sudden. ' I'm some snob, me. A showband type. The lowest of the low. But you have to let me think these things. Inside my own head. You have to give me that much.'

Victor closes his eyes again, rubbing the plate. He loves being with his old butty, Cannon. He's talking his head off but he's not completely ga-ga.

Cannon is laughing. He wants to say something, but he wants to whisper it to Victor first.

After some negotiations, Victor puts it like this: 'Cannon wants it to be known, on the day that is in it, that he was the holder of a non-resident bank account in the Allied Irish Bank of Drumbolus. He got twenty-two thousand pounds in compo when a suitcase fell on him from the luggage rack of a CIÉ train. So he brought along his lump to the manager of the AIB, our mutual friend, and soon they had established to their mutual satisfaction that Cannon here is actually a resident of Mauritius, and therefore not a resident of Ireland for tax purposes. That's about it.'

Nulty decides this is one scandal too big for him. What's he to do, give Cannon a lecture on his social responsibilities? He watches Cannon sucking his pint of stout, savouring the banter, this man who has done forty different jobs and paid tax on none of them. But then if Nulty's shack got flooded in the middle of the night he would call Cannon straight away and show him the damage. Then Cannon would fix it while Nulty would stand around looking cool. And Cannon would do it for free.

Victor, after all his talk, has begun to detect warning signs, the fatigue which follows a burst of nervous energy. He loves the way that people up from the country made him forget a lot of bullshit, but he can't risk too long of an innings, not the way that he is. Nulty is a good lad, he figures. A bit political. Gives him a piece of paper with some writing on it, maybe a poem. Victor tells them he'll be down in Drumbolus to see them all soon, and he means it. They agree to keep in touch and they all mean it.

The Fiesta pulls away, the large figure of Cannon hunched in the front seat, Cannon the tax exile. Victor sits into the back of his taxi. Cannon gave him this Don Williams cassette, muttering that he'd know what it was about.

He asks the taxi-driver to play 'Gypsy Woman' on the eight-track as the car starts towards Rathmines. He knows what it's about.

Chapter 7

Muscle Shoals, Kilbrittan Hill, South Dublin

The Dobermans are serene now, stretched on the back lawn of Muscle Shoals. Johnny Oregon can see them from the vast black leather sofa where he lies smoking a joint, his jobs done for the morning. Or he can look at them on video, chasing Paul Bartley down the lawn and over the back wall and down towards the beach, Bartley stumbling and getting up again, the hounds coursing him for a hundred yards, maybe two hundred or more, until the cameras lose the pursuit in the black sea below, swallowed up by the high tide.

Then there is a wicked five minutes to wait until the dogs come back into camera, shaking the spray from their flanks, welcomed and fondled and taken inside by their grinning master, the rock star Richie Earls, defying the storm like King Lear in leather strides.

In the two days since the funeral, Johnny Oregon has become addicted to this short snuff movie, running it a hundred times, his very own Zapruder tape, and like Zapruder's footage of JFK's head getting blown apart, it's a fucker every time.

This is the Big Boys' Room, so the television is huge, with

a sound system to match. There's a full bar where often Johnny would be pulling pints and pouring shorts for Richie Earls and his celebrity mates as they watch Super Sunday football on Sky, and shoot pool, oblivious to the ravishing view of Kilbrittan Bay. He is welcome to join the stars on the acres of leather upholstery, he just prefers it behind the bar, does Johnny. He likes helping out. So he has travelled a long way in one week, from a guy who likes helping out, to a guy who can barely keep his lunch down looking at the catastrophe that the curse of the Charlie has brought on the house of Richie Earls.

Richie calls him every day now from West Cork, twice, maybe three times. He might sound cool and calm or he might sound out of his box, like when he called at seven in the morning to scream that the dogs need castrating.

The whole point of having someone reliable like Johnny living in your house for you is that you can forget about these things. Johnny hopes he sounds cool to Richie, telling him nothing much. Johnny Oregon has big decisions to make now, bigger than the judgement calls he is accustomed to making, the usual stuff like who can be allowed in Richie's orbit when he is clubbing in Lillie's Bordello, and more to the point, what assholes must be kept away from Richie when he is hanging out in the famous Library of Lillie's, and any other place, public or private, where Richie might be exposed to foolishness.

Johnny is highly rated in rock 'n' roll for his screening skills, that masterly intuition which means that a top rocker rarely has to meet anyone who displeases him, even in obscure ways that the offending party would never understand, some unknowing remark that forfeits the affection of the star for all time. But all the nuances learned over a lifetime of star-minding are useless to Johnny now. These are the ugliest days he has known. He could stand an awful lot of shit from Richie, because Richie, though he could be such a prick, was eventually a friend of the vibe. Even when Johnny's lady Dee had taken up with Richie, they were all still friends of the vibe. Even though they had been together for so long that Dee had graduated to being Johnny's old lady, let alone his lady, it all somehow came under the broad heading of the vibe, to which they all subscribed.

To live outside the law you must be honest and all that. But fuck me, this is different. This movie never gets any prettier, even when Johnny is extremely stoned, as he is getting to be now, taking intense blasts on the thick joint. He knows enough about drugs to realise that anything can seem funny at the time. So he allows for the fact that Richie on the devil's dandruff might have found the scene funny from some weird angle. The frantic scurrying of Paul Bartley has a cartoon quality, or it might remind you of some Buster Keaton routine if you were really, really out of it. But this was an actual bloke who had come to this actual door, and even if you have forty platinum discs on the wall, and Richie doesn't even have that many, there is right and there is wrong.

And still he is in agony. Johnny all his life has judged no man. Still, even still, even after a week looking at this monstrosity, some tiny part of Johnny holds out on making the ultimate call. Not yet. He is not yet one million per cent sure about this business of right and wrong. And he is not proud of his own performance.

Johnny had not been expected up in Muscle Shoals that night. He was supposed to be back in the Monkstown mews which he rents, two miles up the coast. Richie was in residence, and did not require Johnny at this time, but Johnny came up anyway. He came up even though it was one of his official days off, a holy roadie ritual, a day just for Johnny, on which he would don the white silk shirt, the freshly-pressed jeans, the two-hundred-dollar Texas boots and go hunting for beaver in a waft of Brut.

In this mode he had gone drinking in The Jester that day, where he was recognised by a fan of Richie's, a young Dutch lady called Greta, who said she worked in the film business, and who was keen enough to make out with the old retainer after a few lager and limes. Past closing time, when the wind was getting up and the nearest safe house beckoned, they dawdled unsteadily up towards Muscle Shoals, up along the tight little roads, and past the high walls, the forbidding gates where the grandeur of the properties within seemed to induce some eerie quietude in Greta. The soft London voice of Johnny Oregon held its own against the gusts of wind battering the old oak trees, Johnny with his ginger mane blowing wild providing a midnight commentary on the homes of the stars, the class acts of the industry of human happiness who had unseated some of the oldest money in town and colonised this stretch of the bay with their own kind. Soon, perhaps, they would simply erect huge electric fences around the whole neighbourhood, guarded by their own police force, as the top brass of rock 'n' roll bought it all up. The South of France was starting to sound tacky next to south Dublin, where the houses have bags of character and wagonloads of old decency, and a chopper can get you down to West Cork within the hour.

BP Fallon, the vibemeister, said that the act of love is the third-leg boogie, and Johnny was looking for no more than the third-leg boogie on this night, with a bit of sightseeing on the side for the lady. Richie Earls got to live in the mansion on the hill, but Johnny got some good living too, without the hassle of strutting onstage like a big tart to accept an MTV award.

Greta was cool. They would not disturb the master in the

51

main building. They would boogie on down in the extension that housed the security gear, a beautiful pad in itself, a mixture of mission control and a high-class bachelor's den, though the mirror on the ceiling above the bed was a tad crass.

Johnny had all the keys and combinations, but the front gates had been open anyway. The coke was making Richie careless. It had made him paranoid enough to have an awesome surveillance system fitted, but not necessarily to stroll across and switch it on. Johnny guided his companion quietly into the security den, hush-hush even though it was blowing up a storm now, noting as he turned the dimmer switch up low that with her corkscrew hair and tinted glasses, she bore a crazy resemblance to his mate Ian Hunter of Mott The Hoople.

The fridge had been full of beer, a fine sight after the howling wind had briefly chilled their lust. Johnny uncorked two Heinekens, and Greta said, 'I cannot believe I am here with the great Johnny Oregon.' She meant it too. Sure, being close to the big names gave Johnny a lot of access, but hey, he was no mean conquest in his own right. He was as celebrated in the business as most of the nutters he minded. Like Philo said, the chicks go for the sideman.

The loving cup was stopped right there by the Dobermans barking, and in a reflex, Johnny turned off the dimmer and switched on the surveillance system from what looked like Led Zeppelin's mixing desk. The cameras were running now, for the record, and Johnny on any other night would have switched on the screen to be sure to be sure. But something in the old roadie's heart made him gamble for this night only rather than keep the lady waiting. A roadie's night off is a precious thing. They listened to the dogs, and then the silence. They finished their Heinekens, still listening.

'You think that Richie is OK?' Greta said.

'I guess the dogs heard us coming in,' Johnny said.

He didn't really think that. He felt a pang of unease, a bad vibe. And this is why he is not proud. Because he let it pass. He felt the presence of danger and he lay low. He heard the blasts of wind rattling the windowpane and he didn't fancy it. Did he hear the voice of Paul Bartley too, or is that just his imagination, twisted by these terrible scenes on the tape?

He let it pass because Greta had started to unbutton his 501s and had fallen to her knees in the classical mode, ready to feast a while on Johnny Oregon's highly rated tool. He let it pass for the promise of the third-leg boogie. But first, he had to get Greta up off her knees. Johnny doesn't like it like that. Virtually alone among the rock 'n' roll legions of the night, Johnny eschews oral sex. He thinks he has spent half of his life manouevring ladies away from his crotch, which tends to be their first port of call, since he is, after all, a rocker. But Johnny reckons the head vibe is over-rated. He wants to fuck, with any prelims you like apart from this one exception, the old blowjob.

'Tell you what,' he said to Greta, lifting her away and making her look up at him. 'Put this on.'

He took out a condom and gave it to Greta and brought her over to the bed with the mirrored ceiling where they both undressed quickly. Greta took off her glasses and put them carefully away in their case.

Still Johnny was anxious about Richie, but seeing how together Greta was with the condom, how she rolled it over his erection with an air of quiet absorption which he could only class as very Dutch, he was now past the point of sincere concern. He was in fact sure it was a false alarm as their bodies locked, and they rolled madly across the bed, Greta finally on top, her large breasts and those abandoned specs leaving Johnny Oregon free of that lingering image of Ian Hunter.

He could see it all now in the mirror above them, Greta screwing away while the old rocker lay rigid underneath her, his seniority dictating that the female did most of the heavy work, but his experience keeping him hard until they were both ready to come. That's how sex these days made him see himself, like some old aficionado breaking in a new generation. Johnny had the makings of a joint.

'I want to tie you up,' Greta had said. And Johnny was game as long as they had a smoke during the interval.

'You think I'm an old geezer?' he said, sprinkling the grass on to the tobacco.

'You have not one grey hair,' Greta said, taking a ribbon from her curls.

It was true. Johnny's red head was known all over the world, a beacon of liberty all along the endless highway.

'For a moment there, I felt old,' Johnny said. 'At least I felt a lot older than you. But in a nice way you know? In a nice way.'

He knows now that while he was indulging himself in these reflections, Paul Bartley was struggling for life a few hundred yards away. While they shared a smoke, Bartley was surrendering to the sea. And while Greta bound his hands with the ribbon, and Johnny lay back on the bed ready to go again, the gale was pounding and Richie was starting to freak.

When they heard the Harley starting up and roaring out the front gate, he and Greta froze, though he remained stiff inside her, true to his rocker's code. And they fucked to a conclusion too, spectacularly this time for Greta, just great for Johnny, as great as any he'd known, and hell, what is all this voodoo about the chick getting down on her knees?

Johnny rolls off the leather sofa now and ejects the video from the machine. It has been in there for a week, since the morning he came back from the DART train station where he had escorted Greta, who again understood perfectly that she couldn't just wander around the big gaffe on a first date. This lady just might have the right stuff, Johnny thought.

He tries to calculate what the tape must be worth to Richie. All the houses and all the money, for sure. He'd trade Dee for it, if it came to that. Maybe he'd do away with Johnny Oregon, if that was what it took. Johnny takes a copy of *Richie Earls Unplugged* from the video library next to the bar. He substitutes the *Unplugged* tape with the one of Richie Earls unhinged, and replaces it on the shelf. He is meeting Victor Bartley at The Jester this evening.

He puts his head down on the arm of the leather sofa, and tries to sleep. Johnny all his life has judged no man. He switches the phone to the answering machine, and as he starts to dream, he can hear Richie Earls calling from West Cork, saying he's had this idea for a bunch of rock personalities to visit Tony Blair and to call for the withdrawal of British troops from Northern Ireland.

Chapter 8

Drumbolus, County Westmeath

Nulty has no trouble believing that Paul Bartley killed himself. There was no evidence that he had done anything but drown, none of that forensic stuff where they discover a few hairline fractures to deepen the mystery. He just walked into the sea somewhere, they reckon, and fetched up in Dún Laoghaire, dead.

The cops asked Victor a couple of hard questions, since he had been with Paul all that night, and he had form in this department. They settled for suicide.

Nulty has no quarrel with this. He can see hundreds of reasons for it, in everyone.

When they get back to Drumbolus the night of the funeral, Nulty and Cannon troop into Malone's. At the second drink stage a lovely buzz goes around the table. They're in for the night, releasing all the strange emotions of the funeral, looking forward to some more showband stories as the lamps are lit in the warm little lounge. Up ahead, Nulty might look back and think that he was happy here for a while, on autumn evenings with a third rum-and-black coming and so many airheads far away in Dublin looking for the perfect cappuccino.

'I want to say something about the roads,' Cannon says. He pauses, as though he needs Nulty's permission to air this controversial topic. 'You're very hard on the roads I feel,' Cannon says. 'But did you ever see one of them roads being built?'

Nulty did not.

'It's unbelievable,' Cannon says. 'Just unbelievable. It's a work of art.'

'Taxpayers' money,' Nulty mumbles.

'A work of art,' Cannon says. 'It must be great to have talent. I have no . . .'

'Yes you have,' Nulty interrupts. 'There's about forty different jobs you can do, from musicianing to labouring.'

'Shit jobs,' Cannon says.

'You taught Paul how to play the guitar,' Nulty pushes. 'You taught him that song "Gypsy Woman".'

'It didn't work,' Cannon says. He takes a long draught of stout and then settles his enormous hands on the knees of his respectable trousers, a pose like that of a footballer in the front row of a team photo.

'It didn't work,' Cannon continues, 'because we spent weeks learning the song when Paul was down here on his summer holidays. And he had a fine voice too before it broke. But the big thing was, Victor was supposed to come by on one of his flying visits, and this was to be the treat, to hear Paul playing this song that was popular at the time. So Vic comes by all right, and Paul does his bit, but of course Vic is jarred to fuck. Bad, bad smell of drink off him after days and nights on the piss. I'll never forget it, Victor dancing around to the song like a clown, and Paul gutted because he knew it was all wrong. Paul was very down about that. I don't think they ever got over that.'

Cannon looks lost in the memory of it.

'You did your bit,' Nulty says.

Cannon swirls around the last third of his pint.

'The way I see it,' he says, 'talent is not about being able to do things. Any eejit can do things. Talent is doing it in the right place at the right time . . . for the right money.'

'That's just luck,' Nulty says.

'Then that's what I don't have, whatever you call it,' Cannon says.

Nulty shakes his head.

'The only thing I can do is rob,' he says.

'And drive a car,' Cannon reminds him.

'Why did you never learn?' Nulty asks.

'It's a superstition,' Cannon says. 'I have a very strong suspicion that if I'm going to die, I'll die in a car crash. And for some reason, I don't want to die.'

He relaxes again, swilling the dregs of his stout.

'And the cap? Is that a superstition?' Nulty says.

'My wife likes it on me,' Cannon says.

Simon sends over two drinks, the fourth round of the night, not counting the refreshments sponsored by him at the airport hotel. He comes in through the bar and sees them in the lounge and he wants to join them, anxious to know how the day went without him.

Simon is wearing a Slazenger jumper with a yellow diamond pattern, like he's just off the course.

'How was he?' he says.

'He was a gentleman,' Nulty says. 'Great company. Loads of funny stories.'

'I sent him a letter and a few quid,' Simon says. 'I biked them up. Guilt, I suppose.'

'We hear you're a bit shy about paying tax,' Nulty says.

'He probably had you in stitches. He was always a talented fellow, Victor.'

Nulty is perturbed by Simon's golfing regalia on this day, how he bursts with well-being after a day's sport, rich and plump and pink and turning just a tad silver about the temples, too much the fat-cat on the day that is in it.

'Victor swears he's coming down here,' Nulty says. 'He wants to see us all again. Soon. Next week is it?'

'I better tell you, Nulty, that I have very good reason to want Victor out of my life,' Simon says.

Cannon cuts in. 'Nulty knows. He knows what Victor did. He knows about Sheila.'

Simon flounders. 'I'd better explain, Nulty,' he says. 'I was trying to be fair to everyone, not telling you all the gory details. I mean if I told you he'd killed the wife you might have been prejudiced. Not that you're prejudiced . . .'

'Forrest Fucking Gump, eh? '

'That's the drink talking, Nulty.' Simon gets up to leave. He makes for the bar, all business, rattling a set of keys. He turns back to speak to Nulty. 'I do trust you, Nulty. I want to see you Saturday about a massive project. Massive.'

'I'll be around the station Saturday,' Nulty says.

'Ciao,' Simon says.

Cannon splutters into his pint.

'Ciao!' he mimics.

'A massive project,' Nulty mutters. He has a feeling that on Saturday, Simon will just close the old station down. He is concentrating now on the big pitch. He fancies the classic hits formula, with a few bits and bobs of local nonsense to satisfy the regulators. It is good for appearances to have culchies talking to one another about local customs that are dying out, mourning the lost arts of small-town Ireland, but in the real world, there isn't much money in it. Around the table in Malone's, they assume that this is what Simon means by the massive project.

Simon calls another round to be sent to the table. He disappears through the bar.

Nulty doesn't like the sound of the massive bit, or

indeed the project bit. He suspects that Simon is developing a lisp.

Cannon and Nulty drink with the gentle rhythm of cattle at the trough.

Chapter 9

Rathmines

Donal McCann is dead. Victor knew him a bit in the days when the Monday Club was hopping and McCann was starring as a dashing Irishman in some BBC costume drama. Victor sits in his mean little chair reading the tributes in *The Irish Times*. Victor reckons that he looked like McCann back in about 1970, a thought which brings on a wave of melancholia. Victor sometimes regrets that they didn't slice away his frontal lobes when they were putting in the plate, and have done with it, because every stray thought seems to invite these ripples of memory. Everything good that happened to him, like drinking with Donal McCann, has the same effect when called to mind as all the bad shit. Every damn thing brings a jab of grief for the way it all worked out, and a final swipe when he rebukes himself for the old self-pity, still expecting Paul to arrive in and chastise him for that.

Victor is still numb about Paul. It is two days since Paul was buried, and Victor is still being professional about it. He feels worse about Donal McCann than about Paul. Because it's not over yet. He needs something from Richie Earls. The funeral was on Tuesday. He's been sitting in this armchair all day Wednesday, and all Thursday so far. The curtains are drawn on the big window for fear a shaft of sunlight will illuminate the billions of specks of dust.

Sitting in this mean little chair, Victor has been thinking a lot about what he would like to do to Richie Earls. Maybe he will weep then, maybe he will have a hideous fit of weeping worse than the last one. But until he has decided what to do about Richie Earls, the part of him where Paul lives will stay on ice. He needs something, a gesture. He just can't let Earls get away with this. These guys get away with everything. He heard that some night-club bouncer took the rap for Earls on a cocaine charge. The bouncer did about eighteen months, and when he came out, he had his own club.

Victor will pour himself a glass of wine soon. There is a bottle of Chilean red wine on the counter which fences in the kitchen area to Victor's left. Between the armchair and the window is the television that will be screening Paul's show in five minutes, a final tribute from RTÉ. Victor sits close enough to it to lean forward and switch it on. The television is on a stool with no back to it, so he doesn't want to press hard.

He gets up and goes to the window, opening the curtain an inch. He can see down into the flat at the back of the house, just a small part of it where the television is. The student is at home this afternoon but the television is off. The show is called *Goin' Nuts!* Three members of the public are invited to tell the audience how nutty they are, citing various examples of lunatic behaviour on their part, verified by friends and relations in the audience. Paul in his yellow satin suit jollies it all along, munching nuts from a bag, offering them to contestants as a sign that they are truly bonkers. The final decision rests with him as to who is the maddest bastard of them all. Monkey costumes are awarded to the two losers, members of the audience are flinging nuts at them, and then the big moment arrives. A sackful of peanuts is dumped on to the studio floor, and the maddest one must guess how many nuts are in the pile, to the nearest hundred. A correct guess wins the grand prize, a trip to Manhattan.

Victor is getting the butterflies. The show holds no tension for him now, but he is going to drink wine after it, the first drink he has had since those glasses of Guinness with Paul in Zanzibar. He is hoping to have an evening of controlled drinking. He is meeting Johnny Oregon this evening for more drinks in The Jester. A glass or two of wine will calm him down, get him settled, deaden these nerves that are gnawing at him now, watching the last episode of *Goin' Nuts!*

One of the contestants is describing how he goes to every Republic of Ireland match home and away, how this cost him his job, and then his home, and very nearly the wife and kids. Victor realises what is wrong with the show. He was not able to articulate this to Paul, but now the nature of the structural flaw is clear to him. These people are all assholes. It is an insult to the genuinely unstable to bracket them along with these buffoons, these unfunny egomaniacs, these fucking idiots. If he had been able to make this clear to Paul, to convince him that it really was the show that was useless and not the host, that no man could survive an association with these pricks, would it have made any difference? He suspects not. Victor sincerely feels that his words did not wound Paul, and certainly not enough to send him over the edge. Frankly, he reckoned that Paul didn't rate his judgement any more, good or bad.

But he rated the judgement of a top man like Richie Earls. Victor understands how an artiste feels when he is unjustly shafted, especially by someone who counts. He knows how it can fuck with their heads, how it can destroy them. He also knows that just because Paul was quiet in Zanzibar, just because he looked calm as he turned the corner at Kapp & Peterson, it didn't mean that he could handle it.

Victor will be making these issues clear to Richie Earls, whether Richie likes it or not. There will be a reckoning. The programme ends with a photograph and the legend, Paul Bartley, 1974–1999.

Victor goes to the wardrobe, holding back the agonies of nostalgia as he takes out his monogrammed shirt, crisp and white with 'VB' in royal blue, Louis Copeland's best. It is the one quality shirt that remains in his possession, and putting it on gives him a buzz.

He is ready for a glass of wine. It gets dark early now, but Victor has no lamps, just the main bulb. He takes down a tumbler from the cupboard, and sits in the dark sipping his Chilean wine, wondering why he never tried controlled drinking until now, cursing the horrors that the drink brought on him for all that time when he showed it no respect. Why does it take so long to learn how to take it easy?

He starts a second glass, calculating that the taxi comes in twenty minutes, enough sipping time to take the edge off his anxiety, but not to make him silly for the meeting with Richie Earls's minder, Johnny Oregon. That little block of ice in his head must not melt until the job is done, until Richie Earls holds his hands up like a man. Sending Johnny to the funeral had been a gesture, but it wasn't enough. These guys couldn't pawn every damn thing off on the hired hands.

Victor will get to Simon eventually. Simon has not covered himself in glory either. He biked up three grand in cash for the funeral and to get Victor through this difficult time. Those were his exact words on the covering note. 'To get you through this difficult time.' A covering note, not a personal note, let alone a letter of condolence to say sorry that your only beloved son has gone and fucking killed himself. Simon will soon know that this situation demands much more than a motorcycle courier handing over a bagful of used tenners. He will soon know all about it.

The cash will pay for taxis for a while, until Victor figures out what Simon really owes him, in business and in brotherhood. The doorbell rings and Victor drains the tumbler. He is in no rush. The taxi can wait as he buttons up his old black Crombie, old but distinguished. He is about to leave when he remembers that he is still wearing runners, and not the good pair of black shoes. He sees it as a healthy reminder that there is drink on board. Victor pauses at the door of the dark flat, taking in the chipped tiles on the fireplace, the television unsteady on the stool, the single bed, the busted shower in the far corner, the mean little armchair, the empty kitchen cupboard and the bottle of Chilean wine on the kitchen counter, the stale smell that never goes away. He actually thought that this was quite a nice place when he moved in.

Victor sees a picture of Donal McCann looking back at him from *The Irish Times*, Donal *circa* 1970. He leaves quickly for fear that he will fall apart.

The Jester, South Dublin

Johnny Oregon sits on a high stool at the bar with his back to a partition, pouring Carlsberg Special into a glass. Carlsberg Special reminds him of Motorhead, how Lemmy and Phil(thy) Animal Taylor strode into the bar of the Montrose Hotel the morning after a big metal gig in Belfield and ordered up a round of Carlsberg Specials, chased by a couple of Southern Comforts, for breakfast. Those guys were for real.

Johnny's body-clock is confused after his daytime sleep, so the special brew feels like an early evening breakfast vibe. Not that it will make much difference to Johnny's unchanging constitution. He is as hardy now as when he bounded around Europe with the Horslips, arranging press for guys with a natural feel for it anyway. A super gig.

He is early for his appointment with Victor. Johnny is always early. He is ten minutes early but he would prefer half-an-hour to set up the gear, as it were. He would have preferred a fast walk down from Muscle Shoals but he woke up late on the couch and took the Daimler instead. He fancies himself as a gourmet, but Johnny doesn't eat much any more since Richie did the dog on it, and made Johnny feel suddenly like Robert Oppenheimer, the guy who made the H-bomb and realised that he had become a destroyer of worlds. With that video up on the shelf in the Big Boys' Room, he is Johnny Oregon, destroyer of rock.

Once, it would have been an easier call to make. Richie had fucked up but he wouldn't do it again. Just bury it. Once, it was us against them, the rockers versus the rest. But these days, the rockers had no claim to the high moral ground, unless you meant those palaces up on the hill. These days you couldn't say that Richie Earls was doing something totally different to Mantovani. They were all just flogging product. No-one put themselves on the line any more.

Johnny sincerely does not welcome this terrible power over the life of Richie Earls. It gives him a grip on Dee into the bargain, and he had once let go of Dee with great difficulty. And as the days go by, and he feels no better about it, Johnny wonders if he could destroy Dee along with Richie. He wonders if losing faith in Dee was what really made him think again about Richie. This sick vibe was brewing for some time before Paul Bartley got the shitty end of it. He wonders if it was all about Dee, all the time, over there in Antibes wrapped up in a power haze on the yacht, no principles left to dump overboard. None, at least, that would cost her a quid.

So it's nice to think of Lemmy and Phil(thy) Animal skulling Carlsberg Specials and Southern Comforts for breakfast. It's nice to remember the dying days of that whole way of life. Maybe the dead times that replaced it are going for a Burton too. Maybe Johnny Oregon can make it all go away with his magic movie show.

The Jester is a bit top-of-the-world-ma for Victor's liking, there's too much of that bright wood, the ceiling is too high, and he would question the chequered floor. But overall it's not the worst of the trendy places on the south side. The barmen wear a uniform of white shirt and black bow-tie, but at least there's no marble, nothing tropical, no fountains. There's a great fire going, and the Sky Sports crowd are away in the far corner. The bar is the size of a parade-ring.

Johnny Oregon signals from just a few yards inside the door. He offers his hand to Victor and they shake.

'Good to see you mate,' Johnny says.

Victor settles himself on a high stool. 'I don't know, Johnny, if you have to wear a tie in this place, or if you'd be thrown out for it. You know that kind of way?'

'You called it right, mate. Casual.'

'I used to never leave the house without putting on a tie. I suppose I'm more relaxed about it these days.'

'Drink?'

'I'll have a snipe of red wine with you, Johnny.'

Johnny orders a Carlsberg Special and a snipe of red wine.

'How are you, mate?'

'I'm nervous, Johnny. You saw about Donal McCann? Everyone that dies now is either a friend or a relation.'

'I know that one, mate. I know that one.'

The drinks come, and Victor draws a tenner.

'I never got you at the funeral,' Victor says.

'Cheers, mate. It goes like that, you know. I firmly believe that people die in threes.'

Victor chews on this. 'Paul's gone,' he says. 'And McCann's gone . . . So there's one left to go.'

Johnny touches Victor's arm. 'How are you, mate? How are you keeping?'

'I'm trying to be businesslike about it, Johnny. Until I get a few answers.'

'Like, something in his childhood, something like that?'

'Fuck that, Johnny. I'm still trying to figure out where he jumped in. I need to know that, for some reason.'

'What do the rozzers think?' Johnny says, lowering his voice.

'Sandymount. They reckon that would be the nearest jumping-off point to where I last saw him. The tide was in.'

'Maybe that's it then.'

'Except they didn't give a shite, Johnny. They were pissed off that they couldn't pin it on me. They . . . eh . . . they brought up my wife Sheila.'

'These people . . .' Johnny says, with righteousness.

'I suppose you know, Johnny, what happened to my wife Sheila?'

'I may have heard something. A rumour.'

'It was all over the papers, Johnny.'

'Maybe you mentioned it in Leeson Street.'

'I was very down. I just wanted Sheila and me to end it.'

'Tell me about it . . .'

'Did you ever meet my wife Sheila?'

'Never did.'

'I wanted the two of us to go,' Victor says, looking straight into Johnny's eyes.

Johnny doesn't buckle. 'One minute of madness,' he says. 'That's all it takes. The red mist.'

'The cops blame me for this one too,' Victor says. 'They blame me just for being alive. They did the business with no class, took me to the morgue like they were bringing me to the sorting office to pick up a parcel.'

'Fucking fuzz.'

'I think it pissed them off that I had an alibi. This taxi-driver in the Dame Street rank. But the hoors blame me anyway, for being a mad bastard. For passing the mad shit on to Paul. They were very cold, Johnny. Very unfeeling.'

Johnny signals for another round.

'You'll stay on the wine, Vic?'

'Just a snipe, Johnny.'

'How many bottles did we get through in Leeson Street?'

'I'm learning how to drink, Johnny. Drink like a gentleman.'

'You're hanging in there, mate. If this had happened to me, fucking hell . . .'

'I find, my friend, it's the small things that do me in.'

Victor drains his second glass of wine, and opens the new snipe to begin a third. He is keeping count, not in units of alcohol like the quacks say, just bearing in mind that a snipe equals two drinks for the one shout.

Johnny is creating a head on his Carlsberg, pouring the bottle with a barman's touch.

'I thought about what you said in the funeral home, Vic. How Paul was hip to all the psychobabble. Maybe he went easier as a result. Maybe he'd finished what he had to do in this life.'

69

'He hadn't even finished recording the first series of *Goin' Nuts!*' Victor says.

'Sorry, mate,' Johnny says softly.

'No, Johnny, I don't think it was easy for him. My guess is, the flak drove him temporarily insane. I know all about temporary insanity, my friend. I still say it comes down to your man, Richie.'

'He's been very concerned about it, has Richie,' Johnny says. 'He insisted that I attend the funeral. Not knowing that I would have gone anyway . . .'

Victor cuts across him. 'That's another thing about these guys. I mean, who the fuck do they think they are, sending their fucking minions, no offence, Johnny, to do their mourning for them?'

'A lot of these guys are not well, Vic. Richie is not well right now.'

'Ah, Johnny, don't give me that. So they go a bit mad with the money and the fame and all the rest of it. But that's all right. It's natural to go a bit mad when you get success. But there's mad, and then there's bad. And you know, Johnny, I'm starting to think that some of these guys are bad.'

'I could tell you things, Vic.'

'When Victor Bartley started out in this business, he admired the rock 'n' rollers. You needed a bit of bottle at the time, to do your own thing. I never worked with any of them, my fault entirely, but I gave them their due. I stood up for them when the crawthumpers said they were all on drugs, in league with the devil. Now I know they were all on drugs. And as for the other . . .'

'The Horned One,' Johnny says darkly.

'I'll get another one in, Johnny.'

Victor is enjoying this, the wine and the sympathetic company relieving him of his obsessions, all these searing visions that come to him in his armchair. Another snipe, another Carlsberg, The Jester is filling up with the prosperous, and he's away again about the nature of madness and badness.

'Don't get me wrong, Johnny. The crawthumpers were talking through their holes. They couldn't appreciate the rock 'n' roll music. But they felt deep down inside there was something radically wrong with the whole racket. Maybe the badness is only coming out in earnest now. Now that the music has gone completely to shit. Maybe those ignorant people had the right string, Johnny, but the wrong yo-yo.'

Victor downs his wine in one go, and pours himself another, loving it now, feeling it taking the edge off his pain.

'So am I on to something, Johnny? Is the rock 'n' roll getting to be a bit like the paedophile priests? Like, if you are inclined to be an evil fucker, is the rock business the place to be? Tell me, Johnny, how wrong I am.'

Johnny is not about to contradict Victor on any topic this evening, if he can help it. He doesn't want the situation to get gung-ho. He is still like Robert Oppenheimer in awe of the cosmic havoc which his discovery can unleash.

'I've met a few bad'uns, like you say,' Johnny agrees.

Victor puts an arm around Johnny's shoulder. 'No-one shouted stop, eh pal?'

'I hear what you say, mate.'

Victor feels himself coming down a notch, receiving a little jab of panic as he polishes off his wine, and Johnny orders the same again. But he reckons that's the price of a good conversation.

'I admired the rock 'n' roll guys for years,' says Victor. 'Really I did. And I stood up for them. You see, they knew one thing that the showbands never copped. The showbands never copped that you didn't have to be shite. That it wasn't against the law of god to do your own thing. The lads I worked with never sussed that one thing. But your lads, Johnny, they knew it all the time. They knew they were no worse than some ponce over in Los Angeles. Good luck, Johnny.'

Victor opens another snipe. Johnny pours a fresh Carlsberg. The two men clink their glasses. Victor is rolling again.

'It's as easy as that, Johnny. Your fellas had the bit of confidence. And I stood up for them because of that. Because they were taking a chance. And that was no small thing. They were putting themselves on the line and the punters loved it. The punters could always tell if someone was genuine. Gallagher was genuine. Lizzy were genuine. They had the talent to play anything, and the balls to put themselves on the line. I stood up for them all the way.'

'Your guys were making a lot of bread,' Johnny says. 'You can't knock it.'

'Oh yes you can knock it, Johnny. You can knock it all night long. You're only saying the right thing now, but I'm saying the truth. The truth is that money was made but men were broken by it. We started out lovely and innocent, but we got very cynical very quick. The truth is, money was our god. But I'll tell you this, Johnny, I'll tell you how bad it's looking to me these days. I see the same thing happening now with the rock. The same bad-minded shite. But it's worse. It's much, much worse. And I'll tell you why.'

Johnny breaks in with a big apology. 'Hold it just one second, Vic. Really sorry about this mate.'

He sees Greta looking in the front door, scanning the crowd in The Jester through her John Lennon specs. Johnny, close to the door, signals to her with a cough. Greta clocks him, the red hair, and returns a big smile. Victor stands up straight away, offering his stool to Greta as she joins them. She refuses his first offer, but quickly accepts that the big man is up for keeps. There's the old-fashioned code of deference to the lady, but there's also the Victor code of awe in the presence of a rock chick. For this is what she is, in Victor's buzzing brain.

'You are very kind,' she says, taking her perch, giving Johnny's hair an intimate little stroke. Live and dangerous tonight, a rock chick. Though of course Johnny, the fucker, has the call on her, fair play to him.

'This is Greta,' says Johnny. 'Greta is my lady.'

This is no surprise to Victor. But it arrives on Johnny's lips unexpectedly, and it is news to Greta too. Once said, it sounds right to both of them.

Victor draws another tenner. He likes his money in tenners, for the thickness it adds to the bundle.

'What are you drinking, Greta?' he says, a bit perky.

Greta will have a straight Irish whiskey, the same again for the two men, the night ahead of them beginning to feel like a celebration.

Greta squeezes Johnny's hand. It's a deal.

'This gentleman is Victor,' says Johnny. 'We can still talk, Victor. It's cool.'

It was knowing that it would be cool to talk serious business in front of Greta, the instant that Johnny saw her speccing The Jester, that made the dice roll in his head. And he guessed that those big corkscrew curls giving the vaguest hint of Ian Hunter and Mott made the actual words come out in a fanfare of good hope.

'Victor was just saying,' Johnny says to Greta, 'that rock 'n' roll is dead. I've got to confess it's a thought that crossed my mind looking at my man Iggy Pop doing the MTV Awards. Cheers, mate.'

Johnny raises his glass. Victor and Greta clink glasses with him in turn.

'I don't know if it's dead yet,' Victor says. 'I don't think it'll ever die. Not completely. What I'm saying, Greta, is that it's rotten. What I'm saying, Greta, is, I have laid my dreams at your feet.'

Victor takes a swift sip of wine, mindful of the puzzlement he has caused.

Johnny gives Greta a gentle elbow. 'You should hear this guy,' he says admiringly.

Victor gets a blast of energy.

'I have laid my dreams at your feet,' he intones. 'Tread softly, for you tread on my dreams. WB Yeats. You see, the difference between the rock and any other section of the business is that the young people live by it. They believe every word. They're very sincere about it. Jaysus, you wouldn't want to live your life by some of the poor divils that I sent out into the world, but you'd live your life by Bob Dylan. You'd live your life by Bob Dylan and then what the fuck does he do? He goes off to lie down with the fucking Pope. That's what he fucking does.' Victor winces, feeling the first real clout from the drink. 'I'm sorry if I offended anyone. I have no real quarrel with the Pope,' he says, reining himself in.

Greta reassures him with an expression of earnestness, shaking her mass of curls. Johnny feels that Victor is not completely barking, but that he is taking the extremist route.

'I have my own beef from time to time, mate,' he says, pouring another perfect Carlsberg. 'But there's still a lot of top-rate people around. The likes of Beck for instance. And anyway, mate, the business always exploited the young. It's never been a pretty industry. A lot of the old black geezers got screwed right and proper from day one.'

Greta agrees with this line. 'Beck is wonderful,' she says. 'We filmed him recently in Dublin. He's a very interesting guy.'

Victor steadies the ship. 'By all means, fair dues to Beck.

By all means. Through your eyes, Johnny, I am more forgiving. I start to think highly of Bob Dylan again, that he can still get up there and do it at all, and why wouldn't he do it with the Pope, did he not get religion long ago, didn't he go to the Wailing Wall? Yes, Johnny, I can see that now. And I can only say that maybe it's an Irish thing that's wrong with me. Maybe it's just the badness in me, and begrudgery. Maybe I can't take it that these big stars like your fella are living the high life up the road from me, and maybe they're no worse than any that came before them. I just feel it's different now. In my gut. In my gut of guts, I feel it's all gone pure rotten. I feel they're codding the young people now big time. From the top down, they're so crooked, like we say, Greta, and nothing personal, if they swallowed a nail, they'd shit a corkscrew. But maybe it's just me.'

Johnny reaches over and touches Victor on the shoulder.

'You're doing great, Vic. You're holding up really well in my humble. I must tell you, Greta, that Victor had a terrible tragedy, only last week really. You may have read about it in the paper. The young TV personality who passed away? Name of Paul Bartley.'

Greta shakes her head. 'Was it in *The Irish Times*?'

'A small piece,' Johnny says. 'The tabloids ran it a bit bigger. But not too big, out of sympathy with Victor here. You see, it was Victor's son who checked out.'

Greta lets out a soft gasp, and offers her hand to Victor, and he kisses it. Then he takes it again and shakes it as Greta had intended. He is on red alert now for these signs that the drinking is getting uncontrolled, possibly dangerous. But it's just so enjoyable to let off a few rounds in good company. It makes him feel like a fully paid-up human for a change, bantering away at the bar of The Jester with these fine creatures, these exotics, having the same good time that trendy Dublin is having for itself tonight.

75

'You are very strong, Victor,' says Greta, 'to be talking about all these rock stars while you are still so sad.'

Victor figures there is no sarcasm intended. The rock chicks don't cut you like that.

'What must you think of me, Greta? What must you think of Victor Bartley? You must think I have these fellows on the brain. And maybe I do if I'm being totally honest now. Maybe I do, and I'm too sick with hate to give it a rest and my son not gone a week. But it's personal too. It's deeply personal, is it not Johnny?'

Johnny is ordering another round. They're drinking it as fast as it comes. He strokes Greta's corkscrews as he tells her where Victor is coming from.

'Victor is angry, Greta, because our man Richie Earls said some unkind things about Paul. Stuff that hit the young man hard when he read it in the paper. Victor feels what Richie did was unprofessional. He wants Richie to know this.'

'In person,' Victor adds.

Greta begins her second glass of whiskey. The men have stopped counting. She knocks the whiskey back in one sudden movement, and says to Victor, 'You want Richie to say sorry?'

Victor is thinking about a move to the whiskies himself. 'I'll tell you the absolute truth, Greta. I don't know exactly what I want from him. But I need for him to know, man to man, that he has done the dirt on a fellow professional.'

Johnny takes Greta's hand again. 'I'm supposed to be the fixer. I'm supposed to bring these two big geezers together and then skedaddle.'

Greta is signalling to the barman as she considers this. 'It sounds like a good thing for Victor, and for Richie too. I think it is a very good idea to talk.'

Victor intervenes as the barman reaches for the same again. He'd like to try a whiskey. He'd be mixing grape and grain but he thinks, shag it. He presses Greta's fist shut, insisting that she put away her money, so that for a moment Victor has hold of her left hand, while Johnny grips the right. Johnny goes for a Southern Comfort.

'Richie doesn't think this is a good idea right now,' Johnny says. 'But then, Richie never thinks anything is a good idea right now. He's the perfectionist. Needs to know every angle six months in advance. He's in a bit of a state himself if the truth be told.'

The order is now two whiskies and a Southern Comfort as Victor lets go of Greta and holds a tenner up for a young barman's inspection. With some ceremony, he brings the note down towards his mouth and nibbles one corner of it.

'We have a tradition, Greta,' he announces, 'that if you eat a ten-pound note, the drinks are on the house.'

The barman puts the drinks in front of them without a word. Victor winks at him, and calmly begins to chew the note. With one-third of it clearly gone, he gets big laughs from Johnny and Greta, but the barman is unmoved. He looks too young to be wearing the shirt and bow-tie.

'He's thinking, there is some trick. A knack,' Victor says.

And so he bites off another chunk of the green note, leaving the half with James Joyce's head. The young barman turns away with scorn and busies himself at the till. Victor tears up Joyce into small pieces, showering the youth with bits of parchment. A senior barman arrives as Johnny and Greta applaud Victor's feat.

'I was telling this lady about the old tradition,' Victor says. 'Drinks on the house for money eaten.'

The senior man wipes the counter with a cloth. He has the air of a soldier about him, a little corporal. He has a name-tag on his white shirt, 'Chris'.

'Finish up now, sir,' Chris says.

'We're only getting started, pal,' Victor says out of the corner of his mouth.

'It's time to go now,' Chris says. And to Johnny he adds, 'This man has had enough.'

Victor raises the glass of whiskey to his nose and breathes in deeply. He puts it back down gently on the table.

'I'll tell you something about this country,' he says to Greta, ignoring the barmen, speaking with an exaggerated calm.

Johnny wants to throw in some diplomatic words, but Victor talks over him, signalling to him firmly to stay silent. Both barmen are still hovering, unsmiling, as Victor continues to speak.

'I know this man in County Monaghan who fought for Irish freedom. An old-style republican. He wanted to pass the farm on to his only daughter, but she turns around and tells him she wants to marry a Protestant. So the old-style republican, you understand, is on the horns of a dilemma.'

Victor takes a sip of whiskey, and carries on in an even tone.

'One evening, the daughter puts the tea in front of him, and he shoves it aside. He takes out a ten-pound note instead, that he got from the biscuit-tin upstairs, and he eats it in front of her, not a bother on him.'

Victor takes another sip of whiskey. He smiles at Johnny and Greta, but they are both tense. He knocks the rest of the whiskey back in one, and hands the empty glass to corporal Chris, who tosses it into the sink with disdain.

'And this goes on for a long time,' Victor says. 'Every evening meal, the old-style republican makes his protest. And still the daughter will not change her plans to marry the Protestant. She is stubborn like her father.'

His audience is not responding to Victor, but he goes on anyway, the eyes closed now, massaging his temples with thumb and forefinger.

'And then the old boy dies, and the daughter and the Protestant boyfriend go through his things, and they figure out that in total, give or take, the man ate about fourteen thousand pounds.'

Victor takes hold of Chris's lapels, drawing him close until they are face-to-face. 'And you think I've had enough?' he says quietly.

Johnny is beside Victor now, with a friendly arm on his shoulder.

'Steady on, Vic. These geezers don't understand us.'

Greta moves her stool a yard away from the men. She views the scene in a studied fashion, as though researching a thesis on bar-room controversies.

It is still oddly quiet, this joust between Victor and Chris, who like a good soldier stares defiantly back at Victor, though the bigger man clearly has his measure.

'I've got a plate in my head,' Victor murmurs to his captive. 'I'm dangerous with the head.'

'Forgive him, Victor,' Johnny says. 'He's not a friend of the vibe.'

Greta checks in with the junior barman, who seems stunned.

'Victor is in deep mourning,' she says. 'He doesn't need this hassle.'

Victor, through the madness and the shame, can see a road to freedom. He relaxes his grip on Chris and laughs as though it is all a big joke, and laughing straight away feels right. The other way lie ructions and pain. He can let the barman go now and leave with his companions, and maybe not lose face, apart from Greta knowing about the plate.

Victor releases Chris, but stays alert for the backlash. For one glad moment, he thinks his captive is going to see the funny side too, because there is a trace of a grin on Chris's lips as he fixes his dishevelled shirt.

'Get the fuck out of my bar, you mad cunt,' Chris says calmly.

Victor peels off another tenner and throws it to the kid.

'People in this town have no ear for a good story,' he says. 'That's another thing that's gone.'

Merciful, proud that he somehow found the self-control to stop a very ugly scene, Victor leads Johnny and Greta out of The Jester, feeling not exactly a winner, but not beaten either.

Johnny offers to drive him home to Rathmines in the Daimler, and he accepts.

Before the rumble, Johnny had toyed with the idea of inviting Victor up to Muscle Shoals, so he and Greta could have a good poke around and maybe come to a fuller understanding of the great man Richie Earls, but Rathmines seems the more sensible option now, certainly less macabre. Victor would ride again, up on Kilbrittan Hill. For now he cuts a rather stately figure on the soft leather in the back of the Daimler. The three of them feel warm together, bonded by rejection and finally by relief.

Victor insists that the night says something about Ireland. How it is no place any more for men who eat tenners just for fun. How it is definitely no place for men who eat tenners on a point of principle. He has an urge to tell Greta about the Monday Club, and about the taxman who was put in his place, but the heat in the Daimler, the comfort of the big ship, is making him wilt.

Victor steps out of the big maroon car on to Leinster Road. Johnny high-fives him, and says that something will be arranged soon. Greta appears to be drifting off to sleep as the Daimler cruises away, and Victor climbs the steps to the front door, home before midnight with a controlled amount of drink on him, and a few for luck.

He sees the Daimler stopped at the top of the road, and

the two figures inside, Greta close to Johnny. He hopes that she knows that this used to be a more tolerant country. He wants her to know that the story about the old boy eating fourteen grand is true. A true story.

A man needs a cause.

Chapter 10

Kinsale, West Cork

Dee Bellingham figures that, at last, Ireland is getting it right. She can land at Cork Airport and be at the lodge in Kinsale in twenty minutes of motorway bliss. The boreens had their charm in her hippie youth, but when you're trying to run a mega-selling act like Richie Earls, you need infrastructure.

Not that she has junked the bohemian values, or taken to wearing fur, or any perfume, ointment or unguent outside the range approved by her sister in ethical capitalism, Anita Roddick. Ah, but a woman like Dee Bellingham has the true bohemian spirit, some Anglo-Irish way of being in the world that makes a woman like Anita Roddick seem like a farm labourer, and a man like Richie Earls change the way he talks, and maybe even change the way he thinks after about ten desperate years of struggle, trying to find just the right mix between the authentic lingo of the Dundalk backstreets, and the internationally approved cool of the Irish rock 'n' roll magnate, that drawl of a Dee Bellingham and others of her caste who knew members of the Guinness family that the Guinnesses themselves had forgotten all about.

Richie hasn't even had the urge to change his clothes since life landed him with a wallop at the lodge. It is noon and he is stretched on the big old sofa fully dressed after the booze and the fear and the fatigue finally flaked him out. The water is choppy in the lake just fifty yards away from the front window, as Dee is taxied up the lane, a bumpy half-mile in from the beautiful new road.

She can see Richie asleep as the taxi drops her off and reverses down the track, the driver probably taking in the view of the slumbering rock god, beeping his horn as he reverses out of view.

Dee makes a mental note that they will have to make more space for cars to turn around, rather than allowing such unrestricted views of the inside of the lodge. Because from the front, you can see just about everything. The front facing the lake is almost all transparent, a two-storey triangle of glass panels designed to experiment with solar heating. The architect, a local guy just starting out that Dee reckons has a big future, came up with the concept that the house should resemble a ship beside the lake. So there is one large room and a small galley downstairs, and two bed-rooms upstairs, the cute bit being that there is no stairs. Instead, there is a steel ladder that you climb just like a submariner, eight steps straight up and then you swing yourself on to the top floor by grabbing a pole that runs from top to bottom, the mast of the ship, so to speak. To get down, you grab the pole again and swing yourself on to the rungs of the ladder. There is a knack to it that even a nervous guest with vertigo can quickly master, after an initial spasm of fright peering from the bedroom above over the edge of a fifteen-foot drop. Even Richie, who likes to drink a lot at the lodge, has no fear that he will somehow stumble over the edge and become a posthumous legend of rock. It is a fun feature of a fun house, dreamed up out of the ruins of an old police barracks. But Richie sleeps at ground level today.

Dee has flown over from Antibes on an impulse, so she is not expecting a welcome. A major summer gig in Ireland is on the possibles list, and she wants to talk to Richie directly.

She is not one of those callow rock 'n' roll managers who take an exhibitionist pleasure in popping over from Antibes to Kinsale, just because they can. She is Dee Bellingham, powerhouse partner of one of the biggest acts on the planet right now, but she can handle it with the confidence of her breed, a class of people whose genius lies partly in spotting some native talent, and talking it up in a way that the natives never could, in that understated way of theirs that is too arty to be plain posh. Dee sometimes thinks that if Lady Gregory was alive today, she would be spotting raw Irish rockers and explaining them to the world in a way that they could never quite manage themselves.

'Philadelphia,' she says, standing over the prone Richie, senseless as he is to her entrance or to the riot of autumn colour outside that rebukes every moment of unconsciousness.

'Philadelphia,' she intones again, on her way to the galley with some airport whiskey and cigars. Still he sleeps, though 'Philadelphia' is his favourite word. The way that Dee says it, with her understated Trinity College drawl, it has some special music for Richie. It simply reeks of class. He once heard Dee and Adam Clayton and Lord Henry Mountcharles backstage at Slane Castle talking about some rock 'n' roll happening in Philadelphia, and felt almost shamed that he did not fully belong with these golden people who could talk so pretty, and be so aristocratically hip.

But countless generations of bohemian élan are making no impression on Richie this morning, until Dee, irritated now by the utter shambles that he has evidently made of the lodge, gives up on her cool Philadelphia, and bellows straight into Richie's left ear: 'Phila-fucking-delphia!'

Richie Earls, red-eyed and white-faced and whiskery, jolts awake as though touched by an electric prod.

'Philadelphia,' Dee says softly again, all Trinity College now.

Richie is coming to his senses with a familiar, tormenting question. Will he tell Dee? Dee is here. He could tell her the lot right here, right now. He knows she would be cool about it. Not right away, but soon enough. And she'd go to war for him, for them and for all they've got, if it came to that. He knows this as surely as he knew it down at Charles Fort. But now that she's actually here, the gut is giving out on him.

'Morning, Dee,' he mumbles.

He considers a kiss but Dee is already on her way to the galley.

'You stink,' she says. 'I've got some Bushmills here. It'll make you human.'

Richie totters towards the galley, shielding his eyes from the autumn panorama, bracing himself against all that beauty bullying him, mocking his seediness.

'We must widen the top of the road you know,' Dee says, taking down two shot glasses and splashing Bushmills into them. 'Anyone who drives up there can have a good look, coming and going.'

Richie raises the shot glass and knocks it back, flushing some feeling back into his being with the savage blast of the Bush.

'You checked with Johnny Oregon? He told you I was here?' he says, sounding weirdly like Bono in American mode, the bit of Dundalk draining out of him in the presence of his awesome old lady, the duchess Dee.

He vaguely hears her reply that some painter friend of hers in Kinsale had mentioned Richie's day on the town while they were talking on the phone about something else, an exhibition or something. Richie is not really listening. He stares at the lake, engrossed in a hungover reverie that seems of fundamental importance to his survival. The basic problem is, he has forgotten how to talk. He doesn't know what accent to use any more. He is like some Irish movie actor who sounds like half-a-Paddy to the Yanks, and half-a-Yank to the Paddies. He is becoming some terrible hybrid of Dundalk and New Orleans and Trinity College, and when he is not shitting a brick about the killing of Paul Bartley, he is lacerating himself for sounding like some nightmarish mixture of Bono and the Knight of Glin and the guy out of The Corrs. From this moment on, he vows that he will try to be himself, either his original self with an acceptable Dundalk accent, or a smoothie like Dee. It's got to be one or the other. It's his only chance of getting through this. If he can't remember how to talk any more, he will hardly stand up to much interrogation.

You could say that Richie Earls is in a period of transition. In fact that is precisely how Dee would put it. She is still on about widening the top of the track as Richie throws back another whiskey, wondering if and when he should break the bad news, and which accent he should break it in, imagining her telling the world's media with absolute poise that 'Richie is in a period of transition right now.'

Cocaine mania, whiskey hell, hideous murder?

'As an artist, he's been going through some changes.'

Dee is unflappable about the big problems, but she labours like crazy over the piddling details.

'I didn't come over just to discuss the widening of the road,' she says. 'But privacy is everything. How long does some lunatic need to fire a gun?'

Richie pours her another shot. He's got to go for it now. Does he want to sound like a Dundalk person for the rest of his life, or would he rather sound like one of Dee's people? He has nothing against Dundalk, but then again if you can't change your accent after selling records by the gazillion, if that doesn't entitle you to tell the natives to go fuck themselves when they sneer at your refinement, then what's the point? Then again, roots are important. But since Paddy Moloney and The Chieftains already provide a full roots service for the rich and for rock's upper class, maybe a man like Richie Earls should be hiring Paddy too, to do his yelping and his yahooing and his bucklepping and his bones-playing for him.

Fuck it. He is above all this. He feels perfectly comfortable talking like Dee and Adam Clayton and the Guinnesses and their ilk, looking at that lake outside which he personally owns to the last drop of water. Richie drawls.

'You're right. We have to get them to turn around at the top of the track. By the way, welcome home. From Phildelphia. Or wherever.'

'You took the Harley?' she asked.

'Got a bit crazy, you know? Apologies for wrecking the ship.'

'Did the tree arrive?'

'What tree is that, Dee?'

'I ordered a tree, full size, for Muscle Shoals. For that gap in the back garden wall. Anyone passing in a boat can see into the back garden. Just for a few seconds, but that's all you need using a telescopic sight. No point making it easy for them.'

'I suppose that's what it's all about,' Richie says.

'How d'you mean, Richie?'

'That's what success is all about. Sticking a fully-grown

tree in the gap to stop people looking in for three seconds. Then you know you've arrived. Cheers.'

'So did the tree arrive?'

'I honestly don't know, Dee. I honestly don't know. Did you ever think, Dee, that I might be more of a danger to the folks than the folks are to me?'

'I'm thinking ahead of you here. I think your profile is going to get absolutely huge for maybe six months if we go ahead with a certain project. I guess I'm feeling protective of my sweetheart.'

'Sweetheart.' Sounding good, he reckons. Sounding like serious money of the older variety.

They sip more whiskey together, and Richie goes for the full kiss this time. He is never quite sure how Dee will react to his whiskey kisses, but she is starting to get happy herself after a few belts of the Bush, and she receives him with the full Anglo-Irish tongue. Having found his voice once and for all, Richie sees it as perhaps the first truly equal meeting of tongues, a couple of real bigshots getting it on.

'You know what I miss about you?' Dee says. 'I miss that Dundalk accent of yours.'

Richie feels a tremble of pure madness passing across his soul.

'You've never lost it,' Dee says. 'And you must never lose it. I despise these people who start sounding posh when they make it.'

Richie can function merely as an echo. 'Me too,' he whispers.

She's coming on to him, but she's seducing a dead man.

Richie mumbles. 'And I've never lost it?'

Dee seems to want to manoeuvre him on to the galley table, but Richie can't play.

'I hear little traces of posh now and again, little bits of American too,' Dee says, settling for a position on Richie's lap. 'But that's just from mixing with arseholes. I can always hear the mean streets of Dundalk coming through. Hang on to it, Richie. Hang on to it, man. And one more thing . . .'

Dee is straddling Richie now, starting to unbutton his shirt.

'Whiskey doesn't agree with you any more,' she says. 'It used to make you sweet, and funny.'

Richie is a beaten man. 'You're pissed,' he mutters.

He unseats Dee. She regains her composure in seconds, with little more than a shrug.

'We've got stuff to talk about,' she says. 'Business.'

Richie remembers that people like Dee don't turn around and say sorry for acting the fool. It is he who feels like a fool now, a repressed peasant. Dee is moving on to any other business, still in control, just as she was in control when she was drooling over him. No matter what they get up to, these people are always in charge. They inherit these massive levels of self-esteem, while Richie Earls inherited a Dundalk accent. His voice was just luck, and as luck would have it, it allowed him to pursue people like Dee, even though they make him feel like a servant, even while he is giving them the best fuck they ever had. Even while he is paying for everything.

There is hate in Richie at this moment, like the lethal spasms of hate that landed him in this horrible shit. And he is starting to almost enjoy the prospect of hitting Dee with all this trouble, just to see her reeling for a while.

'You're really uptight,' she says, screwing the cap back on the whiskey. 'Doing a lot of coke?'

'I've started smoking again,' Richie says. 'Maybe I'll try one of these cigars. I've run out of Marlboro.'

He breaks open the box of King Edwards and lights up a cigar.

'I actually got them for Jimmy, our architect,' Dee says, as Richie ostentatiously blows rings of smoke.

'Fuck him,' Richie says. 'Or as we say above in Dundalk, fuck him.'

'Doesn't matter,' Dee says. 'But what are you doing smoking? You'll lose a few notes off the top of that beautiful voice.'

Richie feels the edge coming off his rage. He eyes her appreciatively, still a sucker for her ways, always beguiled by her even after rearing up with hate.

'I missed you,' he says. 'It mightn't have felt like it over there at the table, but I missed you.'

'Nice one.'

'We'll do it later,' he says. 'Just get your fucking business out of the way and then I'll get my fucking business out of the way, and if we're fit for it after that, we'll. . . eh. . . we'll ride.'

The bit of Dundalk there. The bit of Irish that the lady loves.

Dee is sitting on the table now in the lotus position, while Richie reclines on the sofa, smoking his cigar.

'Quickly so,' she begins. ' Massive gig at a new venue in July. Somewhere in the midlands, somewhere called Drumbolus I think, could be the new Slane. There's a big house for the VIPs, bigger than Slane Castle, and a natural amphitheatre. A hundred thousand capacity, no problem. The guy I've been talking to has just bought the property. He's been in the Irish music business for years, he's made his money, and he wants to branch out into rock 'n' roll. He's got big ideas and he's pretty upfront about it. He sees this as the new Slane, and I have to say, it looks very exciting. Very, very, exciting.'

Exciting. It is a word that Richie loves almost as much as 'Philadelphia'. He loves to hear the Dee Bellinghams of this world intoning that some project is exciting. They say it in a way that betrays no obvious excitement. They say it low-key, the way that ordinary people say 'interesting'. And as he is now effectively barred from attempting it himself, at least Richie can savour the way that the professionals say it.

'I need to hear you saying that again,' he says. 'I need to hear exactly how excited you are.'

Dee laughs, knowing the routine.

'It's . . . exciting,' she says, with a discreet emphasis known only to the top people, a promise that nothing could be more exciting, except perhaps if it happened in Philadelphia. 'I only spoke to this guy for the first time two days ago, but I have a hunch about it. Money is no object,' she continues. 'Two million minimum but we'll work on the detail. Richie Earls headlining, of course, and we can approve the support acts. I'm thinking that if you do just one gig next year, this looks like the one. We need some live material on video. You're not due to deliver an album until 2001, so the fans need something. And maybe you need it yourself, to stay focussed. It could be a lot of fun.'

'Does this guy know rock 'n' roll?'

'My guess is, he can deliver. He sounds ambitious. Sounds like he's looking for a bit of cred, but who isn't? He's been through all that old showband stuff. Name of Simon Bartley.'

Richie feels his brain go numb. He eases himself slowly off his back, and sits on the sofa rubbing his face hard. Dee rambles on about rock 'n' roll, but Richie has tuned in to the showband channel.

'Simon Fucking Bartley,' he says, breaking into Dee's pitch. 'You don't mean Simon Fucking Bartley?'

'Can we do business with him?'

Dee is still in the lotus position. Richie strides over to her in slow motion, pimp-rolling, circling the table. He stubs out his cigar, crushing it in a full ashtray.

'We can never do business with these people,' he says. 'Never.'

Dee laughs. 'Just think about it.'

Richie is thinking of it essentially as a case of the star murdering the promoter's nephew. But the words of confession will not come right now. He may not be able to lay this shit on Dee after all, if he can't spit it out now. And he can't spit it out now because he is wondering what Dee and her ilk would do in his position. If he can't be like them, he can at least try to think like them. And it seems to Richie Earls that Dee and her type might have murdered half the country, and still keep quiet about it. Fuck it, it's only the peasants who spill the beans. The Bellinghams don't feel the need. They are free from petty-bourgeois notions of guilt. They have killed before and they will kill again, and they don't get their sense of style by blubbering about it, unable to live with their terrible secret. Living with some terrible secret is probably the first lesson that nanny taught them.

'It would take a lot for me to do this,' Richie says quietly, fondling the back of Dee's neck, admiring the profile that allows her to dress like a baglady and still knock 'em out. She has on her usual assortment of denim with so many holes in the jacket and jeans, it looks like she has been savaged by the Dobermans and still remained somehow aloof.

'I am against these people on principle,' he says. 'Musical differences.'

Dee arches her neck to allow more stroking. 'Don't stop,' she says.

Simon Bastard Bartley, that's what the lady said. Richie hated without exception all the bands that Simon and Victor sent out. As an idealistic kid, he went to see shit band after shit band in the ballrooms, standing at the front studying the musicians and hating the compromises they made, and vowing that he would bring the people some decent music some day. Yes, he would wipe out these bastards. And eventually he did. He and Bono and Philo and Rory and Van the Man eventually won the war. They showed the world that Irish people had a special handle on rock 'n' roll, that they could take this great American music and put their own signature on it, instead of sucking the life out of it like these fucking hacks. He would leave the ballrooms cursing the showbands and the cynical swine who sent them out, the Bartleys top of the list. He would do away with them all, he promised the night, walking home alone again. He would make himself sing like the great ones in his record collection, soul and blues and gospel, only the finest, the legacy of an American father who stayed in his life for about a month, making Richie one of ten people in Ireland who knew about this music. They were hopelessly outnumbered. Their loneliness was immense. But, somehow, they would wipe out these bastards.

And eventually they did. Eventually it all happened. And twenty years on, they are still giving him grief.

'I know,' Dee says. 'I know where you're coming from with the showbands. But that's all over now. I think all that negative energy is just . . . If a guy comes to me with an exciting idea, even if he put out a few shitty records, I'll run with his idea.'

Richie wonders if he has the bottle to brazen it out, if he and Dee have humped so often that some of that grade-A juice has entered his system, freeing him from fear.

'A couple of things bother me,' he says. 'But maybe that's just me.'

Dee turns to face him, her eyes full of sincerity. 'I've got it,' she says, slithering off the table and clutching the whiskey bottle for emphasis. 'We're supposed to meet this Simon guy tomorrow. He's willing to come down here if we're interested. So I say we'll put it to him that he writes a big cheque for Sarajevo. Between you and me, it's his punishment for being what he is. But the cred will be exceptional.'

'Sellafield. Not Sarajevo. I think I'm campaigning against Sellafield at the moment.'

'There's politics in Sellafield. This guy mightn't buy it.'

'There's no fucking politics in Sellafield. Everyone hates it. No Sellafield, no gig.'

'Sellafield so.'

'I think it won't be enough to meet him. I'll have to meet his brother too. His brother Victor,' Richie says.

He takes the bottle from Dee, and pours them both a shot. He is going to face them all down, and he will be a better man at the end of it. This is it. This is the only way to go for someone of his calibre. He will meet Victor and brazen it out, and then he will cavort in front of a hundred thousand people at Simon Bartley's place, with the blood of Paul Bartley on his hands and not a soul who knows a damn thing, and then he will probably spend the rest of the summer in Antibes on the boat with the bould Dee and maybe Leonardo Di Caprio if Leo happens to drop by the South of France, because what else would a serious person do in the circumstances? In passing, he will lob a few hundred grand into the struggle against the nuclear menace. All things considered, what Richie Earls will do, is he will hold his fucking nerve.

'I have to meet his brother, Victor,' Richie repeats.

He hands Dee her glass and takes his shot.

'I have to meet him because of a thing that happened,' he goes on. 'I slagged off his son who presents this lousy game-show and then the guy topped himself. So this Victor says he must meet me, like there's a connection. Like, Paul Bartley reads the paper, and says fuck it, I'll top myself? Me,

I reckon this guy Victor just needs to let off steam. Johnny Oregon is looking after it. It's a pain in the hole.'

Dee goes quiet, inhaling her whiskey, barely sipping it. She takes the mobile phone from Richie's top pocket and dials. In Drumbolus, Simon Bartley is opening the front door of Midlands Community Radio when the call comes.

'Dee Bellingham.'

'How are you, Dee?'

'A bit shell-shocked. I've just been informed that you have a brother with a grudge against Richie Earls.'

'I . . . ah . . . have a brother, but . . . I don't follow the rest of it Dee.'

'You have a brother whose son committed suicide. Paul Bartley?'

'Very sad . . .'

'It seems that Richie Earls criticised him in the paper and it seems . . .'

'I . . . am . . . stunned, Dee. You hear? This is . . . devastating. I am . . . speechless.'

'It's a real pity.'

'The truth is, Dee, that I do have a brother. But I honestly and sincerely did not know he took umbrage. Nobody told me he took umbrage. Nobody told me. Oh, Christ. I am absolutely flabbergasted by this. Absolutely shattered, Dee. You must believe me.'

'It still leaves our side with a headache.'

'I promise you, Dee, on my word of honour, this is news to me. Victor and I are . . . at loggerheads. But I will most certainly find out what is at the bottom of this. Will you give me twenty-four hours? Will you please give me that?'

'I've just got back to Kinsale. You're pencilled in for tomorrow. But you're not to come without phoning in advance with something positive. We can't meet until I am satisfied that this is kosher.'

'Absolutely.'

Dee stops it there, with no goodbyes. At Simon's end, an executive decision is taken on the spot, none of your cute hoor hemming and hawing, no strokes, enough of all that. He is back to Dee in seconds.

'I'll be totally straight with you, Dee. Cards all face up on the table. My brother has . . . eh . . . has been in prison. It was a few years ago. Do you recall reading about that . . . tragedy?'

'I've never heard of the man.'

'Right, Dee. Of course not. It was a case of manslaughter. His wife, you know.'

'You think he wants to add Richie Earls to his portfolio?'

'I believe that he's still dangerous if you don't keep the lid on him. But I also believe that we are well able to keep the lid on him. Absolutely.'

'I think you're an honest man. But . . .'

'Just give me the twenty-four hours and please accept my heartfelt apologies. Ciao.'

Richie Earls is looking out over the lake.

'Musical differences?' he offers.

Dee, thoughtful, comes to him and takes him by the hand and leads him to the sofa.

'What do you know about Victor?' she says in a sympathetic tone.

'Just that he's an old showband head. Had a bit more cop-on than the rest of them but never delivered.'

'Bit of a reputation?'

'Bit of a fuck-up. A bread-head.'

'And anything else at all?'

'And he's looking for me because I slagged his son. I've never met the bloke or anything.'

'Right.'

'Looks like I'm never going to meet him now, eh?'

'Good. You didn't know he's been in jail for killing his wife?'

Richie lets out a whoop and starts to snigger. 'Fuck me pink.'

'Obviously you didn't know that,' Dee presses, 'or you wouldn't dream of meeting him. Right?'

'Good fuck.'

'Manslaughter.'

'Fuck me pink.'

'Simon tells me he'll deal with it. You think we need any of this?'

Richie needs a drink and a smoke.

'He killed the wife, eh?' he says. 'The fucker. The stupid fucker.'

Richie takes a swig of whiskey from the bottle.

'Johnny Oregon is supposed to keep me posted on all that mad shite,' he says.

'I'll need to have words with Johnny about this,' Dee says.

Richie lights a cigar.

'Jesus,' he coughs. 'There's you worried about the taxi-man looking in, and there's me thinking of having a few beers with the mad axeman from Drumbolus.'

'It's my fault really for not being totally focussed,' Dee says. 'You were just being sweet, meeting this poor guy who's lost his son. Or so you think. That takes balls.'

'Thanks.'

Dee plays with the rattlesnake bracelet on Richie's right wrist, a gift from Jerry Lee Lewis while The Killer was chilling in Dublin.

'I don't understand what you do,' she whispers. 'I don't understand how you get up in front of eighty thousand people and give it loads. But you must understand that you're the talent, and that's what you do brilliantly. And I do everything else. Everything. The talent just doesn't go around meeting unhappy people. Consider this a wake-up call.'

'You're the boss.'

Dee is back in the zone now, tall in the saddle.

'We'll see what Simon brings to the table tomorrow,' she says. 'Simon sounds all right, actually. Like he's got his life sorted. I'm not being paranoid. I won't blow out the gig right now just because the promoter's brother is a nutter. We'll take the ballpark view.'

'I'll give Johnny a buzz.'

'Johnny wasn't on the case. It's disappointing.'

'I'll check if that tree arrived.'

Richie gets no reply from Muscle Shoals, so he leaves a message for Johnny. He can't meet Victor in person for security reasons, and that's final, and by the way, did a big tree arrive? Nothing about the dogs being castrated. He's starting to cope.

Chapter 11

Drumbolus, County Westmeath

The call from Kinsale hits Simon Bartley like the whack of a baseball bat. He takes the first instalment standing inside the door, and then races up the stairs to his office for round two. For some daft reason, the use of a desk seems crucial at the time. But he makes the right call, phoning Dee back with the full SP about Victor. This thought is consoling him, poleaxed as he is from the force of the blow. When hardy came to hardy, he made the call. Cards on the table, face up. It's the only way to deal with a serious player like Dee Bellingham. The old days of the nod and the wink are gone. He did well to remember this, even as he took the lash. It would stand to him that he did not stall or stonewall on the Victor question.

But his insides are still spinning from the shock that Victor, Mr Forrest Fucking Gump, can bugger up everything without even trying. He is in shock, he thinks, opening the heavy door of the tiny studio, taking a sordid Midlands Community mug from the presenter's table. In shock, he reckons, boiling the kettle for a cup of instant coffee, shook enough to drink it out of the dirty cup in this day and age.

Simon sits back in one of his small toys, an executive swivel chair ill-matched with a tumbledown desk. He attempts to kick away a pile of desk debris, but the clutter won't disappear quickly enough, so he brings his heels down violently, collapsing the desk like a Kung Fu master discovering some crazy new move.

The scattering of paper, the wreckage he has wrought, brings a despairing moan out of Simon, a close-your-eyes-and-think-of-Victor moan. Somehow, this mess seems like the brother's doing as well. Like Victor is out there, fluttering his wings.

Simon finds that he is comforted by the moaning, and so he keeps up this pitiful sound, ignoring the kettle, closing his eyes and really letting go with a moan so baleful, it gives Nulty coming up the stairs the uneasy impression that he is about to encounter some horrendous porno romp.

'Maybe I'm not ready for this, Simon,' he says.

Simon ends his moaning with a sigh. He doesn't mind being discovered in distress. Appearances seem like small potatoes to him at this moment.

'I'll come back later,' Nulty ventures.

Simon says nothing at first, but stares at the ceiling, gathering his thoughts.

'Could I make one request from the bottom of my heart?' he says in a voice weary and sincere. 'Just one request, that on this day there be no talk about my brother, Victor, or anything to do with him, in any shape or form. Could I ask you that from the bottom of my heart?'

Nulty, here to be told about this massive project, picks through the debris.

'Did you have a woman in here, Simon?'

Simon fingers the waistcoat of his three-piece bespoke black suit, as though his superb tailoring is sufficient answer to any question about wild sex.

'You're mocking me, Nulty, you're mocking me. But I can live with that.'

Nulty picks up a plastic bucket seat and sits down slowly.

'Just one small thing I really need to know, Simon. He hasn't . . . your brother hasn't been in here by any chance?'

'Christ, no. Just bear with me, Nulty, bear with me, and we'll tackle it later.'

'You always say that the hardest job of the day should be tackled first.'

'Right. That's what I always say.'

'So?'

'Maybe this is too hard.'

Simon leans back in the chair until he eyeballs the sign on the wall behind him. 'Who The Hell Is Tom Waits?'

'You know what this means?' he says, ripping the sign off the wall and tossing it to Nulty, sitting in the chair which used to have the desk in front of it.

'Shite records all day,' Nulty says, toying with a small box of multi-coloured paper clips that has taken his fancy. 'We know all that, Simon.'

Simon seems to be daydreaming, disconnected. 'We have to get out of here,' he mutters.

Nulty slips the box of paper-clips into his inside breast pocket.

'In fairness, Simon, radio is finished. It's for langers. Jocks with shiny tour jackets. A crowd of langers . . .'

Simon interrupts. 'Cards on the table, face up. This is not the project I want to bring to you.'

Nulty is pleased that his heist of the paper-clips goes unnoticed as he sits in the middle of a small room with an observant person in it.

'Langers,' he says.

Simon is up on his feet, stretching.

'This project I have in mind has nothing to do with radio.

101

It's nothing to do with lost dog radio, or classic hits radio. You will never want to work in radio again if you get a taste of this. I'll tell you about it in the car. I really have to get out of here. Come on. This is massive.'

Nulty takes the front passenger seat of the big silver car.

'If you didn't have a bird in there, Simon . . .'

'This is lovely music,' says Simon, switching on Lyric FM.

It is Saturday afternoon in Drumbolus but except for some movement inside Grogan's store, Drumbolus is quiet. At least half of the old houses, about twenty of them, seem derelict. There's nothing stirring around either of the two pubs, Malone's and Elliot's. On a dull autumn afternoon, it is profoundly peaceful to Nulty, almost spookily quiet.

At this moment, Nulty thinks that the locals don't know how lucky they are, living in the midlands in a one-horse town. This is officially Main Street but Nulty calls it the Old Walled City. He can turn against it too. You can go mad just as quickly from the quiet as from the noise. If you stand in the middle of Drumbolus and think of all that's going on in New York, you feel lonesome enough to hang yourself.

And if you were in New York yakking away on a mobile, you'd feel lonesome enough to hang yourself too. So it makes no difference really, where you live.

Only when you steer right at the top of Main Street do you appreciate the vision of Simon. Houses are going up on land owned by him, forty houses under construction but bought and paid for by desperate people who are willing to commute the seventy miles to Dublin. Work has started on a branch of Supervalu, part of a small shopping complex which Simon hopes to fill with a hairdresser's, a dry cleaners, a chemist, whatever the growing commuter population of Drumbolus will require up to and including a motor showroom, and eventually a restaurant that is frequently mentioned in *The Irish Times* as a candidate for a Michelin star.

Lyric FM fills the big car with the weirdly gorgeous sound of Andreas Scholl the counter-tenor singing Handel's 'Such Haughty Beauties!' Simon drives out past Nulty's bungalow-shack which is daily becoming less remote than he would like it, past the Drumbolus Golf and Country Club where the clubhouse is really coming on and there's maybe two dozen quality motors in the car-park, then left down a by-road about three hundred yards shy of the motorway.

'We're going to Drumbolus House,' Simon says. 'It's mine now.'

Nulty looks across at Simon and Simon is smiling. 'It's mine to do whatever I want with it,' he says, taking a deliberate step back down the evolutionary ladder by blaring his horn at the empty fields. A mile across the flat boggy land stands Drumbolus House, visible to them now, a grey granite pile of the early nineteenth century which was thought locally to be owned by some German industrialist, and before him a long line of lords, the Clonmellons. They were fair to middling as Brits went, so Drumbolus House escaped the IRA torchings which were so often the first fruits of freedom. The Clonmellons were better than they needed to be. But when the first Lord Clonmellon looked out from one of his eighteen fine bedrooms at the bleak landscape from which this glory had risen, he could not have foreseen that a local type would ever keep a Clonmellon from his rest, let alone buy it all up, the big house and the stables and the noted gardens with their columns topped by statues excavated at Ostia, and shipped to the Irish midlands for fun.

'Two point eight million,' says Simon. 'And that's probably a fraction of what it'll cost to restore. Am I mad?'

103

Nulty is feeling giddy against his better instincts.

'You know what I've always thought about this place?' He can see the top half of it from his kitchen, nearly two miles away. 'You know that thing about location, location, and location? Well, I could never figure out how they could build a magnificent house like this in a total fucking hole like Drumbolus. I mean, Drumbolus is fine by me, but I'm not Lord Muck looking to build my pleasure dome.'

'So I'm mad?' says Simon.

'You're different,' Nulty says. 'Have you moved in?'

'Nah, you don't understand,' says Simon. 'It could take years to renovate it. I'm happy where I am.'

Simon lives on the other side of Drumbolus in a bungalow not much bigger than Nulty's. Nulty can't figure out if this is hopelessly cheap or a touch of true class. Simon loosens his tie, as though he is overheating with the buzz.

'They weren't the worst,' he says. 'The Clonmellons.'

They see the big house head on, driving past the gate lodge and up a gravel avenue that leads straight to the front entrance. On either side the tightly mown lawns and the well-groomed cedar trees show the benefit of heavy gardening.

'The German let it go a bit inside. He ran out of cash,' Simon explains.

Simon parks outside the front door. The two of them are quiet for a time, taking in the granite façade, three storeys with twenty-one windows, a wing to the right and to the left of the main block, each a mansion in miniature.

'It must have been hard for the fuckers to give up all this,' Nulty says, the old socialism beginning to gnaw.

'What do you think I should do with it?' says Simon.

'You're asking me?'

'Just for pig-iron.'

'I know nothing about houses, Simon.'

'For pig-iron?'

'Well . . . for pig-iron . . . I suppose you should live in it, Simon.'

'There's really not much of it fit to live in. Times are hard in Germany. Come on, I'll show you.'

Simon leads the way towards his all-time great acquisition.

'That's Wicklow granite,' he says solemnly, looking up at the façade. 'It's actually mellow Wicklow granite,' he adds. 'Mellow.'

He opens the glass-panelled front door and ushers Nulty into a powder-blue hallway with an elegant white staircase to the left that invites the eye all the way round to the landing high above them.

'It would have cost four mill in good nick. It's a bit fusty.'

Nulty stands before a large painting in an ornate gold frame, one of two renderings of mournful-looking women in long eighteenth-century dresses on either side of the hall fireplace.

'Lovely,' he says.

Simon laughs. 'You can't help gawking, can you?'

Nulty is looking up at the high ceiling like a tourist in New York.

'Lovely ceiling,' he says. 'Fashioned by local craftsmen for tuppence.'

Simon opens a door off the hall.

'Very old-fashioned, the pictures,' he says.

Nulty trails after him into a huge room with an almost obscenely relaxing feel to it.

'The German lived here mainly,' Simon whispers, as if the German's spirit is still in the room. 'He did it up nice.'

The colours are cream, gold, beige, fawn, every soothing shade and tone thereof, from carpet to ceiling, the gamut of soft hues from the off-white lampshade all the way through

105

to the rich brown coffee-table, making a mood so tranquil it could becalm all of life's pain. There's a crystal chandelier with pale yellow candles.

'Lovely work,' Simon says. 'Italian.'

Nulty sinks into the nearest couch, one of three settees facing the marble fireplace, with a coffee-table just within reach of the longest legs, laden with coffee-table books.

'We can never go back to Drumbolus now,' he says.

Simon slumps into the next couch, powerless to resist its luxurious invitation. Nulty studies the walls cluttered with near-replicas of the unhappy women in the hall, and landscapes from the same sturdy school of art.

'I must apologise for the formal attire,' Simon says, breaking the peace. 'I got the suit made up specially. It's like the bumpkin who gets dolled up for his trip to the big house. I wonder . . .' Simon pauses. 'I wonder if we'll ever get used to having a few bob?'

'I have no money.'

Simon gets in quick, to stop the drift towards socialism.

'Not yet,' he says.

'Tell me, so.'

'You make the mistake, Nulty, of thinking that because I have a few bob I don't want anyone else to have a few bob. In fact I'm the real socialist. I think everyone should have a big car. Even the Hare Krishnas.'

Simon's feet don't quite reach the table so he stands up with his back to the fireplace.

'All right, so,' he continues. 'Cards on the table, face up, so. I am presently in negotiations with a certain Dee Bellingham with a view to staging a massive rock concert at Drumbolus House next summer.'

'Dee Bellingham . . . Richie Earls,' Nulty says. They are fresh in his mind from *VIP* magazine, a photo-spread of the exotic couple at the lodge in Kinsale.

'Correct,' says Simon. 'Now listen to me. I want you to help me to make it happen. I want you to run this for me. You know rock 'n' roll and I don't. I know it sounds corny and you'll probably shoot me down for it, but . . . cards on the table, face up . . . you're the brightest and the best around here. I believe in Irish people. I believe that young Irish people can do anything if they're let, and they can do a world-class job. That's my contribution.'

Simon sits back down. His proposition stays in the air for some restless moments. Nulty re-arranges himself so that he is lying full length on the sofa, a beige cushion under his head as he stares at the fine detail of the ceiling and the chandelier.

'At present,' he says finally. 'You are not in negotiations presently, you are in negotiations at present.'

Simon for a moment looks beyond Nulty and into space.

'You hear a lot of that kind of thing now,' Nulty says. 'Instead of gaining access to the Internet, people access it. Instead of politicians making progress in talks, they progress the talks. It's all wrong.'

Simon walks over to the window with slow and rigid movements. He can see the column with the statue excavated at Ostia. Then he bursts out laughing.

'Nice one, Nulty. Nice one. But you're not getting out of it that easy.'

Nulty keeps staring at the ceiling. 'Dee Bellingham . . .' he says. 'I have a thing about Dee Bellingham.'

'Like, she's a member of the upper classes?'

'I mean, I have a thing about Dee Bellingham, in a good way.'

'Fine-looking woman.'

'When I came here, Simon, I made a promise to myself that I would do nothing but low-responsibility jobs.'

'Well you were a fucking eejit then.'

On the drive back to Drumbolus, Nulty outlines his principled objections to open-air rock concerts, with their eerie echoes of feudalism. He spends the evening in Malone's drinking rum-and-blacks, thinking about Dee Bellingham.

Chapter 12

Rathmines

Victor Bartley is having a shave in the bathroom which he shares with three students and a couple of actors, when the pay-phone rings in the hall downstairs. His flat is the nearest to the phone, so he takes messages for the others. It's a chore he doesn't mind. Gets him out of the room. The students will all be down home on this Sunday morning, he reckons, and the actors will be resting, ho-ho. So he tips downstairs to answer the call, his face half-covered with lather.

'Hello?'

'Nulty.'

He is delighted by this, as he hardly ever gets a call for himself.

'Hello, Nulty,' he says, 'phoning me on my day off.'

'How are you, Victor?'

'At this moment I'm calm. Calm enough. I suppose it hasn't sunk in yet.'

'I can't say I knew him well or anything. Paul, I mean.'

'You'd have liked him.'

'I enjoyed our chat after the funeral,' Nulty says. 'I just wanted to say that.'

'Good company . . .'

'You must look after yourself.'

'It takes very little now to keep me going,' Victor says.

'What are you trying to do to Simon, Victor?'

'What am I trying to do to Simon?'

'He couldn't even talk about it. He brought me out to Drumbolus House yesterday, which he's bought incidentally, which he has bought for two point something million, and he's talking about massive rock concerts, the works. But he couldn't bear to talk about the hassle you were giving him.'

'I knew he'd buy the big house some day.'

'He said he'd tell me all about you later on, but we got distracted.'

'As a matter of fact, Nulty, I haven't spoken with Simon since my operation. I have tried to speak to him since, many times, but he refuses to talk to me. I have left messages on his machine, but he has not returned one call since the plate went in. People are odd like that.'

'I didn't know about the operation,' Nulty says.

'Just a little bit of metal nailed to the skull.'

'Jesus.'

'Not so much nailed as screwed.'

'Fuck.'

'I know it's not easy for people.'

'About Paul . . . We'd want to help you with anything, Victor.'

'It's a very nice thing you're telling me.'

'We'll keep in touch, Victor, like we said.'

'Listen,' Victor says, 'I'll be down in Drumbolus, like I said. I'll make it my business now.'

'See you in about ten years then.'

'Over a pint in Malone's . . .'

'Best drinks.'

'Best drinks.'

Victor tips back up the stairs with a new sense of purpose. It'll wear off again soon, he knows, but the call has definitely given him a jab of energy, a rush.

He is on the sixth day of a Contour blade that he began the morning of the funeral, and he drags it quickly down his lathered neck, ejecting it into the bin at the tail-end of its natural blade life. To use it any more would be miserable, but not unknown in this time of want. A new blade tomorrow.

Fuck it, he has Simon's used tenners and he would be calling in a few more of them from the new master of Drumbolus House. Live a little, Victor, live a little. Go mad and use a new blade every day.

Now, how can he hold this mood that he is in at this precise moment? Could he freeze it? Best drinks, he said. Best drinks. That was a nice poem too, that Nulty gave him at the funeral. Victor knew a few poets in the glory days. Contrary bastards, but some of their shite sticks.

He doesn't trust September. Never did, since back-to-school days, since it meant the bands lashing together shite records for the Christmas market, and him paying tax. And he always gets a dirty cold in September, which has probably just been postponed this year until the shock of Paul wears off. He's wearing his Crombie with nothing underneath, buttoned up to the waist, bare-chested like Oliver Reed pissed to his pin-stripes on *The Late Late Show*, the night he wrestled Susan George to the studio floor.

Victor remembers it well because he was drinking with Ollie Reed that day, around the time that Ollie discarded his shirt in Madigan's, and went on drinking with just the good jacket over his proudly bared chest, the beer stoking his desperate horn for poor Susan George. Victor was at the centre of things back then, introduced to visiting stars as a serious man in the business. And Ollie back then was one of the biggest stars in Europe.

But Ollie's gone now. Don't look back, Victor, don't look back, he tells himself, buttoning the Crombie to keep away the cold, not quite the Noël Coward look, but safe enough on these silent Sunday mornings, when he likes to pretend that the whole house is his. Could he hold that good feeling about Nulty, that lightness, could he freeze that too? Maybe he needs a woman. Maybe he needs that and nothing else.

September always gets him down. Whatever good fettle he stores away gets wasted soon into September, when the dying light brings this blackness upon him. When it came to the death of his wife Sheila, his own Chappaquiddick, the one part of it that stood to reason was the fact that it happened on the day of the All-Ireland Final, the last Sunday in September. The hurling final was last week, if he is not mistaken. The first Sunday in September. He missed it all, he doesn't follow that stuff any more, even in a good year.

He opens the curtains for the first time in a long time, as though he is undressing a wound. The sky is a brilliant blue, the trees at the end of the garden are pure Vermont, but nature doesn't do it for Victor. Scenery, none of that stuff does it for him like a darkened lounge at noon, the tang of lemons, the bitter waft of beer, that first hiss of porter through the tap.

The daylight is doing him no harm today. There's not enough of it coming through the back window to make a big difference, no sudden illumination like Newgrange. He switches on the telly with the sound down, re-running the conversation with Nulty in his head. The old butterflies. Victor reaches over to the kitchen counter and switches on the transistor.

It's *The Sunday Show* with Andy O'Mahony, and reviewing the papers is the rock journalist George Byrne. Victor always gets a laugh out of George when he runs into him on the town. A good jeer at the showbands, and then they're off. Gaelic football is bogball to George, the hurling is stick-fighting. He'll only tolerate country people if they're embarrassed about it. Knows his rock 'n' roll music, likes his beer.

Is Nulty a bit mad? Victor figures that he might have the mad gene alright. But then a man might need to be a bit mad to see the good in Victor Bartley.

Greta? Is she a bit touched? She didn't flinch about the plate. With Greta, he is over the hard part.

Enough, the thought of a woman far out of his bracket is starting to unsettle him and anyway, a little revelation is dawning on him. George on the radio is having a go at last Sunday's stick-fighting exhibition, and Victor starts counting back the dates from the first Sunday in September, the fourth he is sure, to the previous Wednesday when Paul went missing. There's no doubt about it. Paul died on the thirty-first of August. It just felt like September. The curse of September then, dead September, is out. It's just one of those tricks that Paul used to talk about, tricks that we use to fool ourselves, superstitions that keep us sick, to give it the full RD Laing.

Victor has a tremendous urge to tell someone about this, to tell Johnny and Greta. An old familiar thrill buzzes through his gut, thinking of slow pints all day Sunday in the uncrowded pubs of Dublin, supping beer at a married man's pace in the International, in Mulligan's and the Palace, and then the switch to Baggot Street, to Nesbitt's and O'Donoghues and Toner's, and up to the Horseshoe Bar, at a married man's pace.

If you're going to give controlled drinking a chance, this

is where to start, not in a deluxe madhouse like The Jester, too soon, far too soon after burying Paul. And he will kick off with brunch down in some Rathmines tavern, the full fry in its most fashionable form, with all the fixin's and a read of the Sunday papers. He will treat himself to a civilised day of eating and quaffing, and then tomorrow he will attack the supermarket, to make this place vaguely fit for a professional.

A man could let himself go very easily. You can only cope with death, you can only go *mano a mano* with the likes of Richie Earls if you're living right. Victor can hear Paul saying this, begging him not to let everything slide, to keep the faith. He can see Paul, too, on the television, and it startles him as though he himself has suddenly appeared on the box without warning. It's Paul on the television and it's *Goin' Nuts!*

He guesses quickly that RTÉ has taken to repeating shows at strange times of the morning and night, and that this is *Goin' Nuts!* getting its very last outing. The professional in him clocks that one just before the panic sets in. Now it's like he has built up a morning's supply of good intentions, but this is thrown at him to test him. He can't bear to turn the sound up, but the silent version is no picnic either. And he can't switch it off, because he just can't. Victor grips the arms of the chair. A jolt of panic shoots through him, puncturing the bit of serenity he has squirrelled away since Nulty called. It is happening and he knows it is happening, this rare morning of peace wiped out by what has appeared in front of him. Is this what he has to look forward to for the rest of his existence? The odd hour of relief and then the breakdown?

He watches Paul working his ass off, jollying up these stiff fuckers, and his plans for a leisurely day suddenly look like a sick joke sent to taunt him. The show is torture. It's the lowest type of game-show, the type that doesn't have the money thrown at it to look right. Victor is sitting through it because he feels that confronting it is his only hope. Didn't Paul always warn him never to let these things fester? Paul was a hero to do this show, knowing what he did. Most of the guys who do this stuff are brain-damaged, and better off for it.

Paul looks like he is announcing an ad-break, but they don't bother with ads on the Sunday repeat because no sane punter would be watching this shit at this time. Only the immediate family at home or in institutions. So it begins again, round two, Paul in his daft jacket with deck-chair stripes, moving through the studio audience, meeting next week's contestants who are in to get the vibes, who are probably shattered now that there is no next week, and they'll never get to Manhattan.

Victor reaches for the plate like it could keep his brains from spilling out, massaging his temples faster and faster until it makes him dizzy, and Paul is still there working the room but there's nothing to him any more except these false rays of sickly light from the TV, no man there any more who will call around looking for an opinion after the show, no gay man who will make little suggestions about this horrible room and match up your misfortune to his psychobabble.

It's going to go off again, this explosion in the heart of Victor Bartley that makes him weep as he watches Paul losing the battle, and makes him fall to the floor weeping, flattened by this sudden bombardment of grief that makes him beat his head off the floor, and again, and again, and again, to feel some other pain but the one that is ripping him apart, and that he knows in the bitter depths of his being is not all about Paul, just like it wasn't all about Paul the last time, because it is about waste, the waste, the fucking waste of it all. Paul's life was wasted on this rubbish. He will never get to do what his heart desired. He is trapped for ever in this poxy show like something only half-human, some plastic creature blasted with radiation.

But it's over now for Paul. It is not over yet for Victor Bartley, who has wasted, wasted his one life and wasted a few others along the way with his bad calls and his bad timing and his bad influence. He crawls a couple of yards to the kitchen and rips out the cutlery drawer. It's not stopping like the last time, there is no relief, it will not go away. Knives and forks and spoons spill on to the floor. They came with the flat. But there is nothing with a proper edge to it, it's like the cutlery is just a toy set.

Another tremor takes hold of Victor, stretching him face down on the kitchen lino in a black fit, no stopping it this time for sure, no more the sensation of relief, no more the gay philosopher on his way round right now to put it into words. No way that a man can live and know the full extent of this waste. The bottle of Chilean wine is empty on the kitchen sink.

A huge delirious child with one convulsion rolling over to the next, Victor heaves himself off the floor and grabs the neck of the empty bottle in his right hand. He falls back down on the lino, and sits contemplating the label of the bottle, as though it contains vital instructions. He is not all wept out yet, the tremors are getting weaker, but he's going to put a stop to it anyway.

The bottle will not break off the edge of the fridge. Six or seven strong wallops, and Victor goes for the kitchen sink instead, smashing the bottle with the first swipe. He unbuttons the Crombie with his left hand and walks naked to the shower, brandishing the jagged weapon in his right. He pulls back the shower curtain and turns on the water.

'That'll heat up now,' Paul said, the last time he was here.

Holding the neck of the bottle tightly, Victor fixes the

temperature to very hot with his free hand, and steps into the jet of scalding water. He stabs the jagged glass into his left arm and rakes it down to the wrist, slashing at his pulse with full force. The hot water gushing over the slash wounds fascinates him for a moment, but he keeps going, chopping viciously at the veins, ankle deep in his own blood with one last proud thought to take with him as he goes down, down on his knees with the life spilling out of him, that he is going about this in a professional manner.

Chapter 13

Muscle Shoals, Kilbrittan Hill, South Dublin

Johnny Oregon and Greta are in the bath and Johnny is letting her shampoo his magnificent head of red hair, because he is in love. He doesn't even know her second name, but the way they understand each other, she'll tell him if she thinks it's important. Sunday morning begins the way Saturday night ended, with a colossal fuck in the vast bedroom facing the sea, Johnny's Vixen Pit as it has come to be known as by its true owner, Richie Earls. The bathroom is just off the Vixen Pit, and again he is impressed by Greta's acceptance of the natural order, how she doesn't press him to have a go in the jacuzzi in Richie's master bathroom, or even in Richie's own four-poster. She knows things, this chick.

In the big, deep, old-fashioned bath she shampoos his gingery mane with the thoroughness he would bring to the task himself, especially on the road way back, when a rare day off for the crew would see Johnny the tour manager throwing aside his gear-humping rags and getting heavily dolled up in white silk shirt and freshly pressed jeans and a pair of two-hundred-dollar Texas boots, then a big splash of the overall smell of Brut and it's off with a certain swagger to get a lot of beers in and then to suss out some coin-operated beaver. She knows, she knows these things that road crews do, she knows that Johnny would call it coin-operated beaver because Greta is the rocker's soul sister, a member of the catering crew.

She's been feeding her excellent steaming broth to the movie crowd for the past year, but she catered for bands before that, and now that she has connected with top man Johnny, before too long she may find herself ladling goulash for the gods. But this is not a career thing, no way. They both know that. She dunks Johnny's soapy head under the water, once, twice, three times to wash away all the suds, and then a vigorous squeeze of the soaking tresses that proceeds to a massage of Johnny's shoulders, the younger partner restoring the energies of her admirable mate, fifty years young and fifty fucks coming up so thrillingly soon in their relationship.

'It's all I've ever been any good for, is lovin',' Johnny says, impersonating the hick Jon Voight in *Midnight Cowboy*.

He turns around to face Greta and to reciprocate with a dunk of the Ian Hunter corkscrews, a kind of official rock 'n' roll baptism of this thing they have going that began with just the third-leg boogie, and which is now up to the point where Johnny is proud of this lady, proud that she actually knows what backstage passes hang from, that the string-thing you fix to the laminate and pop around your neck is called a lanyard.

'You're some lady,' Johnny says, 'to know about lanyards.'

'This guy I knew in Wales who made them. He was retired from the Motorhead crew.'

'Lovely geezers.'

'I'll give you his number.'

'Oh, cheers, Greta. It's important, you know, to have decent lanyards made out of proper stuff. '

'This guy does them really nice. His name's Click.'

'People would laugh at this, but I've knocked out a lot of passes on my old laminate-maker, and it's a very responsible position to be in. It's like you're playing God, deciding who's a VIP and who's a VVIP and who gets near the talent. Richie is chopping the list all the time.'

'Click made me a lanyard for something else. I have this dagger and he made the cord to hang it around my neck.'

'I'm jealous.'

Greta plunges under the water once more and rises quickly.

'Don't forget you're ringing Victor first thing,' she says, 'to tell him Richie cannot speak to him.'

Johnny massages Greta's wet shoulders, imagining a dagger hanging around her neck, the Huntress.

'It's cool to have someone reminding me of things for a change,' he says.

He reaches out for a towel to dry his hands and picks up the mobile from the floor beside the bath. Victor's number is engaged.

'He's entitled to know about this. Will we drive over?' he says.

Johnny had just entered Greta from behind on the big leather couch in the Big Boys' Room when Richie's message came through on the machine, nixing an eyeball with Victor under any circumstances, and wondering if a big tree had arrived.

'Poor Victor,' Greta says, getting out of the bath. 'He'll go crazy.'

'He's entitled to go crazy,' Johnny mutters, admiring his young lady's perfect body, giving himself a few points for an almost equally cute-looking ass and an overall condition that would not shame a man of twenty-five. He gets out of the bath still muttering. 'More than he knows, he's entitled to go crazy.'

Muttering important things is a habit of Johnny's from way back, things that you want people to know but you don't necessarily expect them to do anything about, like when some member of the road crew OD'd and was breathing his last up in the hospital, and the band members had to be told, without making some big announcement that put them in an embarrassing position where they felt obliged to visit. So you mooch around muttering the essentials and it's cool.

'There's something else, isn't there?' Greta says.

Kinsale, West Cork

Simon Bartley orders a grapefruit juice at the bar of The Neptune. It is five minutes after noon opening on Sunday, so he has less than half-an-hour to be right for his meeting with Dee Bellingham and Richie Earls. Twenty-four hours on, he is no closer to delivering what he promised, some definite word on the Victor question. How he would have loved to cruise down to Kinsale with the sounds of Lyric FM, then a saunter around the grand old town itself, a whiff of the sea breeze, a spot of window-shopping at the auctioneer's, full of well-being for the meeting. He searches for some serenity in the seafood menu, but his eyes glaze over and he declines to order, taking his grapefruit juice to the window table, turned right off by the lobsters skulking in the tank.

Twenty minutes now to explain to Dee Bellingham that he made no progress at all on eradicating the Victor problem. It won't wash. That was the old way of doing business, excuses, excuses, and useless ones to boot. He is now in every way the perfect example of the reinvigorated Irish entrepreneur, except for the one tiny detail that whenever his brother enters the frame, even enters the conversation, he bottles it.

'Cards on the table, face up, I bottled it.'

With ten minutes to go to the off, he can hear himself saying this to Dee Bellingham. But he can't hear any reply that doesn't go something like 'Cheerio, and safe home.'

He had the phone in his hand last night, but he couldn't bring himself to dial the number, and say to Victor, look, sorry for your trouble, we should stay in touch more, never mind the money, we'll sort it all out, head, and by the way, why in the name of Jaysus are you harassing Richie Earls and ruining my fantastic plans, you mad bastard?'

Outside Mitchelstown, on the last leg of the trip to Cork, he got one more urge to make the call and to hell with it, but the car-phone only reminded him in some weird way of Victor racing off the edge of the pier, and the last terror-stricken moments of poor Sheila.

He sees Richie Earls and Dee Bellingham crossing the road on their way to join him and he is trembling, his hands are actually shaking as he rattles the ice around in his glass of grapefruit juice. He stands up and signals to them as they come in. These guys won't take any shit. They will want the facts and he must give them the facts.

Richie goes straight to the bar, pushing his Ray-Bans up on his forehead, no beret today, the stubble manicured.

Simon gives the paw to Dee.

'Simon Bartley,' he says. 'Delighted.'

'I'm sorry about yesterday on the phone,' she says, giving his hand a firm shake, and adding a peck on the cheek. 'I was so strung out after a long flight from France.'

Simon senses a soft line. 'I took what you said on board,' he says. 'I'm getting there.'

Richie grabs Dee around the neck in a playful arm-lock. He places two straight whiskies on the table.

122

'I'd shake hands with you, squire,' he says to Simon, 'except you are the devil.'

And then he laughs, offering his hand to Simon, all affability as though they had read about Simon's anxiety in the Sunday paper and they were all aware of the need to be kind.

'I took some people around Drumbolus House yesterday,' says Simon, 'and the thing dragged on and on the way things do. These people are very important for the project so I couldn't just run them. You know the way.'

'From our end, it's really, really, exciting,' Dee says. 'I've filled Richie in on it, and he's so up for it.'

Richie picks something from his teeth and examines it intensely. He holds it out for the inspection of the others. Dee breaks up laughing and Simon joins in because he doesn't know what else to do. Richie is holding a pubic hair.

'I know what you're thinking,' says Richie, holding the short black hair in the palm of his hand like an insect he has just captured. 'Well, you're right.'

And he creases with laughter, handing the hair gingerly to Dee, who gives a little yell and tucks it into the top pocket of her denim shirt, while Simon giggles away, his nerves swallowed up in the general hilarity.

These guys, he thinks, are mucking around with him. They are having a good jeer for themselves at the bog monster. And then he gets a hint of something else, an intuition born out of being sober in the company of exuberant drunks for the whole of the showband era. These guys . . . these guys are on drugs.

'Here's my guy,' Richie shouts, as the young barman to whom he tipped the fifty quid comes to wipe the table.

'You must meet Dee, my old lady,' he says to the barman. 'Dee got in yesterday and gave this man a hard time . . . but I sorted her out.'

123

'I'll survive. Could we have the same again please?' Simon says.

Richie grabs the barman by the elbow. 'She's got something for you. Haven't you Dee?'

'Have I?'

'A lock of your hair,' Richie says to Dee.

Dee takes out the hair and gives it a bit of a twirl, then hands it to the barman.

'At least,' she says, 'at least I hope it's mine.'

The barman takes the hair from her, and looks at it in the palm of his hand.

'Thanks,' he says, 'thanks very much, Mr Earls.'

'The young lad doesn't appreciate it,' says Simon. 'I'll take it,' he says, playing ball with the big guys. 'I'll take it as a souvenir of Kinsale.'

Simon takes the hair from the barman, who is remaining calm and cheerful throughout, as only a Kinsale barman can when faced with the lewd antics of the glitterati.

Simon is rocking and rolling with these guys.

'Now can I have the same again?' He lays the hair delicately down on the table, opens his wallet, and slides the barman a twenty-pound note. 'And keep the change.'

Richie splutters a mouthful of whiskey.

'This kid is getting rich out of me. Aren't you, kid?'

'You're embarrassing him,' Dee scolds.

'It's all right,' the barman says, taking Simon's twenty-pound note. 'Two Irish whiskies and a grapefruit juice then. And no lobster for Mr Earls.'

He slips away to the bar.

'He's so sweet,' Dee says.

'They have them well-trained down here,' Simon says, sliding Dee Bellingham's pubic hair carefully into his wallet.

Richie and Dee start another fit of laughing. Dee holds her hands up in helpless apology to Simon.

'You're being really cool about this,' she says. 'We've been partying.'

'I'd like to join you,' Simon says. 'But I'm driving.'

Richie goes to the bar to collect the drinks, and to get another round in.

Dee leans her head towards Simon and speaks quietly to him. 'Richie is really freaked out about your brother,' she says. 'We had a few toots to take the edge off it, you know?'

'I know.'

'You guessed.'

'Suffice it to say, I've got your pubic hair in my wallet.'

'Right . . . sorted. We really like this project and we don't want it fucked up.'

Richie returns with an armful of drinks.

'How's Victor?' he says.

'Are we doing business?' Simon says, feeling himself growing in stature now, making himself big, unfazed by any old madness they are throwing at him, and determined to press home his moral advantage.

'We were hoping to take you back to the lodge,' Dee says. 'And do business there.'

'Now,' says Richie. 'I need to know now, if Victor is after my arse.'

'He needs to know now,' Simon says.

Richie throws back a whiskey.

'Then we can go home and party,' he says.

Simon leans towards the coked-up pair.

'I'll be totally straight with you. I've driven all the way down here this morning feeling very blue about Victor. Nervous that I haven't been able to thrash this out with him, because frankly, I'm afraid of drawing him on me. And now that I'm down here, and the two of ye are a bit . . . relaxed, I see more clearly that it was you, Richie, that drew Victor on us in the first place. It was you, and not me.'

Richie folds his arms and leans back.

'Big swinging mickey, Simon.'

'The point is, my friends, if we pool our resources on this, we can eradicate it. But I stress the word "pool".'

Richie chews on an imaginary stick of gum. Dee nods her head slowly, taking it all in.

'I am fantastically sorry,' she says. 'You are a million per cent correct and this will not be a problem for us and please, you're an honest man and, Christ, I haven't met one of them lately and do me a really big favour and consider it a deal.'

She holds her hand out to Simon, and they shake. Richie doesn't budge.

'Do we kill him?' he says.

Dee and Simon laugh.

Dee raises her whiskey to Richie. 'The talent.'

Drumbolus, County Westmeath

Nulty is having a Sunday lunch of rum-and-black to celebrate his phone call to Victor. Simon might think it a bit naughty of Nulty to be making unauthorised calls to Victor, but Simon doesn't own him. Well, he does, but Nulty is still chuffed about it, about taking the initiative just to say something like sorry for your trouble, just to let some other human know how he feels. Maybe this big new job as a rock promoter is making him touchy-feely, or it might just be the thought of Dee Bellingham. It might just be that.

The barman sticks his head around the door and beckons Nulty to come with him straight away.

'Not good,' he says. 'Cannon.'

They jump into Nulty's Fiesta and head out to the Drumbolus Golf and Country Club.

'Cannon,' Nulty says. 'This is bad isn't it? '

126

The ambulance is parked, but idle. A few clusters of golfers stand around the car-park, looking solemnly over to the building site where a couple of guards and ambulance-men are going through the procedures, chatting about the dead man amid the collapsed scaffolding.

'Double time on Sunday,' Nulty says.

Rathmines

'There was something else wasn't there?'

Greta sussed it getting out of the bath, just by Johnny's muttering. In the Daimler on the way to Rathmines, Johnny Oregon gives Greta the something else, the facts about Richie Earls killing Paul Bartley, including the part about Johnny and her being hard at it in the security den, and his unspoken suspicion at the time that things were going pear-shaped up at the master's house.

Greta just takes it all in like a top boffin in the forensics department of rock 'n' roll, noting the fact that it is all on videotape as an unusual feature of this case, and asking a supplementary question about Richie Earls's total estimated intake of cocaine.

'White speakers?'

'White speakers big time,' Johnny says, turning the Daimler into Leinster Road, again utterly impressed by Greta's suss of the practice whereby the on-stage speakers would be painted white to camouflage the lines of marching powder so neatly laid out by Johnny for the artiste.

They skip up the steps to Victor's front door hand-in-hand. There are no names in the slots beside the buzzers. Johnny rings the third bell down, and squints through the letter-box. He sees a young man in a dressing-gown coming down the stairs.

'Cheers, mate, we're looking for Mr Victor Bartley,' Johnny says.

'First on the right.'

'You must be the young actor he mentioned.'

'Right.'

'Hope you get a part soon, mate.'

The actor scurries back up the stairs. Johnny knocks on Victor's door. He can hear the sound of running water inside. He knocks again loudly. The water just keeps on running. Some primeval roadie's instinct is starting to throb, telling him perhaps the oldest story known to rock 'n' roll man, that on the other side of the door there is a man in bad shape.

Johnny looks at Greta and she nods in silent agreement. He tries the door handle and it gives an encouraging rattle. He breaks open the door with one strong shoulder and they're in.

Greta slams off the shower and Johnny pulls Victor out of the pool of red water.

'Talk to him,' he shouts, grabbing a towel to stop the bleeding.

Johnny goes to work. Greta cradles Victor's head. She thinks that he gives her the faintest smile.

'Tell me a story, Victor. Tell me about the man who ate the money, Victor . . .'

Chapter 14

West Cork

Simon Bartley is savouring a new pleasure, the loveliness of West Cork. He drives Dee Bellingham and Richie Earls wherever the fancy takes them, enjoying the buzz of partnership with these guys, thinking that this must be how they spend Sunday afternoons in heaven, stopping for drinks in Robert's Cove, in Crosshaven, and up near the Old Head of Kinsale, feeling famous. He might strike some as the chauffeur on the mineral water, but to the punters in pubs making heroic efforts to look unimpressed by the entry of Richie Earls plus two, he has the inside track.

When the news headlines on Lyric FM tell him about the death of a building worker in Drumbolus, he feels so distant from all that, it takes him a few moments to focus on the fact that it must be one of his workers, on his building site. He pulls into a lay-by opposite a pub near the Old Head.

'Only one man could be doing overtime on Sunday morning,' he says.

He feels a flash of annoyance that he can't get away from Drumbolus for one weekend without them somehow hassling him from afar. But it's a challenge too, on his first day as a bona fide member of the super league. He

129

imagines that later he will feel a bit sorry about Cannon, the big eejit.

Richie is waking up from a snooze in the back seat. Dee in the passenger seat sees the implications of Cannon's death straight away, and is impressed by Simon's calm. She also wonders if it is just the drink and the Charlie, or if she detects a slight lisp developing in Simon's speech.

'Insured?' she says.

'Nothing on paper. He wanted cash for everything.'

'Trouble?'

'I might have to square the widow. Agree a lump.'

'Fucking cowboys,' Richie says, awake now behind his Ray-Bans.

Simon switches off the radio.

'The trouble might be that it's not good for our image. There's always some clown looking to object to a pop concert. You don't want encouraging them.'

'Our lawyers have the experience now,' Dee says. 'On your part, it just needs diplomacy. Make all the locals feel part of it. You've got nearly nine months to get them excited about it.'

Richie interrupts. 'Stroke the bastards. Give them all soft jobs. Planning permission my hole.'

Simon starts up the engine and then switches it off again.

'Victor will be at the funeral,' he says quietly. 'No way will he not be at the funeral.'

'Good,' Richie says. 'Let's meet the fucker and tell him what he wants to hear and get on with it.'

Dee shakes her head, but Simon is starting to envisage a positive scenario from fragments that have been teasing him all afternoon.

'I think Richie might have something here,' Simon says. 'I see something like this: we meet him, the three of us, together, next week at Drumbolus House . . .'

There is no immediate reply from Dee or Richie. They are thinking about it.

'Any security we need . . .' Simon adds.

'So I do the grovelling bit,' Richie says. 'What do you do Simon?'

'I give him money that he says he's owed, but he isn't really. And I say sorry for avoiding him like the plague.'

'He'll want money from us too,' says Richie. 'Victor's a bread-head.'

Dee is holding back. 'And what guarantees have we got that he'll go away then?'

'Victor,' Simon begins, looking at the sun bidding a grand farewell to West Cork, 'Victor is like the IRA. He'll never say that the war is over. You just be grateful that the guns are silent.'

'I support the IRA,' Richie says. 'I am a republican.'

'We support the peace process,' Dee says.

'This is just blackmail,' Richie says. 'It's fucking blackmail.' He opens the window and sticks his head out, shouting, 'I hate all of you fucking mad bastards. Why are there so many of you mad fucking bastards out there? Give me a fucking break, all right, you bunch of cunts?'

Then in a normal voice, back in the car. 'If it gets him off our case . . .'

'If we make the right noises,' says Simon, 'you'll probably never hear from him again.'

'Hang on,' Dee says, as they cruise willy-nilly towards Kinsale. 'We have Johnny briefed differently.'

She gets Johnny Oregon on the mobile straight away. 'I won't hold you, Johnny darling. I just want to know if you've spoken to Victor Bartley.'

'I haven't spoken to him yet,' Johnny says.

'Great. Fantastic. Change of plan, do nothing till you hear from me.'

End of call.

'Ciao,' Simon adds.

These guys, he thinks, these guys get things done.

Muscle Shoals, Kilbrittan Hill, South Dublin

Johnny Oregon puts the phone down on the bar of the Big Boys' Room, and splashes a few fingers of Jack Daniels into a glass for Greta.

'That was Dee,' he says, 'heading me off at the pass.'

'You had a big thing with Dee once?' Greta says.

'Please,' Johnny says, joining her on the leather sofa. 'My head.'

They are chilling out in a big way after a super rescue job on Victor, hauling him back from the brink and then bombing out to Kilbrittan Hill with Greta sweet-talking him in the back seat of the Daimler, and then some top emergency treatment by Dr Gary Featherstone, the first fully-qualified rock 'n' roll doctor in the Republic of Ireland. Dr Gary is just gone, leaving many unique remedies to be fed to Victor, who sleeps in the room across the hall. Johnny and Greta are feeling deeply exhausted but equally relieved that they made the right moves, passing at least two fine hospitals along the way to get to Muscle Shoals and the excellent Dr Gary, thus keeping Victor out of the system that might see no alternative but to hand him over to the men in the white coats for this latest tour de force.

Johnny bows to no medic in an emergency of this type. In his time he has answered more cries for help than the Samaritans.

'It's not cool for Victor to be here,' he says, giving a masterclass in rockers' etiquette. 'But it's even less cool for Richie to be wasting geezers who come to the door.'

He stretches out full on the sofa, his red mane resting on Greta's breast, feeling a lot closer to fifty than he felt this morning in the bath.

'Tell me a bit about you and Dee,' she says. 'She was your old lady?'

'It was the touring did for us. It's a big, big problem in this business. You've seen what happens when the wives and girlfriends arrive for a couple of days. Total chaos.'

'So how does she figure it will be different with Richie Earls?'

'Richie's different. He's a very complicated individual. He relies on Dee a lot, and I guess she gets off on that. And it's a sort of a class thing as well.'

'Like, he's the big star?'

'Nah . . . well, yeah, in the sense that he's a big star but he's just a little working-class guy really. And Dee's, like, posh. And she can never get away from it, and she never really lets him get away from it.'

'You have this all worked out.'

'Naturally. I've thought a lot about it.'

'You loved Dee?'

'I worshipped the woman.'

'But you screwed around?'

'You've seen the way it is. She'd join up with the tour and she'd be, like, all cool and my-old-man-got-pissed-with-Dylan-Thomas-down-Soho, but deep, deep down she'd be like of those sniffer dogs I told you about, the one that went crazy sniffing six months of drugs and drink and fuck-knows-what off Lazzer McGeegan's trousers. Behind it all, she'd be like one of those.'

'And she can control Richie? With his mad dogs?'

Johnny sits up and wipes the fatigue from his eyes. He goes to each of the three long, tall windows in turn to pull the drapes against the sea below and the lights of the bay.

He switches on a lamp in each corner, the soft light fondling the acres of leather, and he tucks away a few pool balls on the blue baize table. He takes *Richie Earls Unplugged* from the video collection and slips the tape into the machine. He sits beside Greta and holds her hand, weird though it might look in the light of what they are about to see, like some hick couple on a first date waiting for the hardcore to start.

Greta sees it through in silence, her firm grip of Johnny's hand a sign of her intense concentration.

'I'd like to see it again,' she says. 'Put it on again, please.'

Johnny runs the tape again on the huge television screen. Greta leans forward towards it, like she wants a closer look. Then her head drops to her knees and she wraps her arms tightly about her middle like she has been kicked in the gut.

From across the hall, Victor Bartley sees the sobbing figure of Greta and the back of Johnny Oregon as he consoles her. He sees the tape all the way through on the big screen for a second time, sees the killing of his son, and slips back to his room because this is his best instinct through the haze of Dr Gary's best. He lies back down on his bed. He is utterly at peace.

Kinsale, West Cork

The lodge is under observation as Richie Earls surfs the channels on the small television in the galley. Titus and Phil from the Raw Power security firm are parked at the top of the lane in a Range Rover.

They gave Simon a scare when they stopped him on what is still a public highway. For one second, when the torch shone in his eyes, Simon saw terrorists. Titus and Phil being black somehow cancelled that thought in Simon's head. He

134

is back in Drumbolus now, sitting up with the widow Cannon.

And Dee is done for the day in Kinsale, her last act a woozy ascent of the steel ladder, staying with the architect's theme by resembling a sailor returning unsteadily to his bunk.

Richie stops at a sports highlights programme on RTÉ. Dundalk, his home town soccer team, are playing Athlone Town. He is not really interested in the match, but it reminds him of his childhood, his youth, when he followed Dundalk avidly, never missing a home game at Oriel Park. Highlights of Irish football were a special event then, but none of it seems to matter now. Once he would look forward to this stuff all week. Dundalk still play in the same colours, white shirts and black shorts, but what intrigues Richie Earls is how Oriel Park is barely recognisable to him. It's not anything they've done to it by way of renovation, it just looks like so small, and there are hardly any people at the match. How was it that when he was young, he thought this place was brilliant? The game on television takes him back, but he can't see himself there any more, he just can't relate this strange little ground to the stadium of which he was once proud, no less proud than he was of his glorious record collection. Except he was so right about the records and unbelievably wrong about Oriel, looking at its modest little stand now, which he once regarded as huge.

No wonder he started talking like he was from some-where else. How, how, how the fuck did he get from where he was then to where he is now? It is blackening his already charred brain to think of this, to locate some missing link that would explain how a chap who was once happy with a permanent spot at Oriel Park could be so unhappy as he hunkers down in his Kinsale lodge with platinum albums in the tank and two goons up the road and one exotic lady on the top deck.

And then he thinks that he might lose all this, that very soon he will sit down with Victor Bartley. He wants to go back and start again, somehow, not just to rub out his crime, but to return to the exact point at which the guy who loved Oriel Park and that sweet Southern Soul became the man whose luck raised him above it all, and to hold it right there, and to make the change without ditching all the innocence in his soul. A Dundalk player is talking after the match. He has a broad Dundalk accent.

Just like me, thinks Richie Earls. Just like me.

Chapter 15

Muscle Shoals, Kilbrittan Hill, South Dublin

Victor Bartley wakes up with a feeling of such total inner tranquillity, he wonders for a while if he is dead. His left arm is bandaged from the wrist to the elbow, but then it took a fair slashing. It stings like a bitch, the more he drifts out of sleep. The bedroom surprises him with its old-fashioned look, like it has been this way since the nineteenth century. He always imagined that someone like Richie would have the interior designers in to scrap all these heavy old furnishings and fittings, and convert it into a Japanese sushi bar or something, jazz it up like the room where Johnny and Greta were watching the big screen.

He knows where he is and what he's done and what he's seen. He knows. This is the thing that is making him so mellow. He knows. He knows what happened to Paul. And he knows what he is going to do about it. And no doubt Dr Gary's little brown bottles there on the bedside locker are rocking him gently too, sweetening the knowledge.

He is wearing a black silk dressing gown with a dragon's head motif on the back in blazing orange, though he has no recollection of putting it on. He shuffles over to draw the heavy green drapes. It's a big old dreary green room and nothing more, like it's set aside for Richie's granny. Or broken-down showband heads who can't take it any more.

The morning is so clear he imagines he can see Wales across the water, but his eye is drawn down to the back garden leading away to the sea, where Richie's dogs chased Paul into the high tide. There they are now, dozing on the lawn below, the evil fuckers. He saw the effect it had on Greta, but it didn't upset him like that. It made him glad, glad to be still alive, and to know the truth. Paul isn't coming back anyway, but he has left this beautiful present behind him, the truth, liberating Victor from the hell of not knowing. Granting him the power, the power to do almost anything he pleases to avenge this atrocity, and the absolute inner conviction to do it right. A man needs a cause.

Johnny Oregon wheels in a trolley laden top and bottom with breakfast things, a full buffet stretching from a bowl of Weetabix through to yoghurts and jugs of orange juice, grapefruit juice, tomato juice, silver pots of tea and coffee and hot milk, a rack of toast with butter and jam and marmalade, and plates of the old classics, the sausages, rashers, eggs fried or scrambled, and mushrooms.

'We thought you needed a change,' he says.

He takes a freshly-rolled joint from behind his ear, and lights it up. He takes a quick suck on it and hands it to Victor.

Victor laughs. 'I'm better already Johnny.'

He takes three, four, five, six, seven deep blasts on the thick spliff and hands it back to Johnny with his good hand.

'Irish or continental? Tea or coffee?'

Johnny leaves the joint lit in an ashtray. The smoke with its whiff of some sublime promise drifts over the trolley, bringing a sense of occasion to the breakfast.

Victor laughs. 'I'll have bacon and eggs, my friend. Bacon and eggs, tea and toast.'

138

'Excellent, mate.'

Victor sits down on the edge of the bed, and Johnny gives him a warm plate from the trolley. Victor refuses a tray, preferring to hold the plate in his lap.

'And I'd like the truth as well, Johnny, if you don't mind . . . but I suppose you can't have everything.'

'Fucking hell, mate, you're up for it today.'

'Just the facts, Johnny.'

'The full SP or just generally?'

'Generally.'

'You nearly checked out. Greta played a blinder. Fried or scrambled?'

'Scrambled, thanks.'

'Tea?'

'Three sugars.'

'That's very bad for you, mate. Bad for your teeth to begin with.'

Victor takes the mug of sugary tea from Johnny. He takes it in his left hand, to show that he can. Johnny scoops a big portion of scrambled eggs on to the plate, and adds three rashers, picked up with a tongs, the full room service.

'You're a good man, Johnny.'

'How's the arm?'

'Medium.'

Victor puts the mug down on the floor and eats briskly, concentrating first on the scrambled eggs.

'Dr Gary left you a load of painkillers and pick-me-ups,' Johnny says. 'That man is a fucking genius. They struck him off because he knew too much.'

'And Greta is a good woman, Johnny. You're both very lucky.'

'You're the lucky one, mate. Strong as an ox.'

Victor heaps some scrambled egg on top of a slice of bacon. 'I get very down, Johnny.'

'I've pulled a few out of the fire, mate.'

'Lazzer McGeegan?'

'I've got a bit of bad news for you, Vic. Well, it's some good news and some bad news.'

'The bad.'

'Dee Bellingham just phoned me about a friend of yours called Cannon. I'm sorry, but he's checked out. Accident on a building site.'

Victor closes his eyes and takes a deep breath. He remains completely still for about a minute, holding his breath, both hands gripping the plate of bacon and eggs in his lap. He opens his eyes and cuts away a mouthful of rasher.

'I loved that guy,' he says.

'It's a fucking scandal,' Johnny says.

'Don't worry about it, pal.'

'No justice, mate.'

'Don't worry about that.'

'The good news is you've got a result out of Richie.'

Victor puts the plate aside and gets up slowly off the bed. He goes to the window, still holding the fork with a piece of rasher on it. He massages his temples gently.

'Your brother Simon will see you too,' Johnny says. 'They're doing business.'

'He'll see me too, will he?'

'They figure you'll be down in Drumbolus for the funeral. You can meet up at Drumbolus House.'

'They're doing business? Simon and Richie are doing business?'

'It's Ireland. Everyone knows everyone.'

'They don't know me,' Victor says, his forehead touching the windowpane.

Johnny joins Victor at the window. The dogs are stretched below, three living sculptures.

'What are they called?' Victor asks.

Johnny looks him straight in the eye. 'Emerson, Lake and Palmer.'

'My favourites.'

'More breakfast, Vic?'

'What happened, Johnny? Why will Richie see me now?'

'I think they reckon they can handle you all together.'

'I might have a little surprise for them, Johnny.'

Victor unfastens the catch of the sash window with his right hand. He pulls it up from the bottom and opens it.

Johnny grabs him in a lightning reflex and pins him against the wall.

'Jesus, Johnny, I'm mad but I'm not that fucking mad,' Victor shouts.

Johnny relaxes his grip on the silk pyjamas.

'Couldn't risk it, mate.'

'You don't think I'd throw myself on top of Emerson, Lake and Palmer, do you chum?'

'Sorry, mate, I'm wired.'

Victor sits back down on the bed, distracted for a while by Johnny's T-shirt seen through the smoke, featuring the full itinerary for The Sensational Alex Harvey Band's World Tour 1975. The stinging in his arm brings him out of it around the four-night stint at the Hammersmith Odeon.

'I will surprise them in Drumbolus, Johnny, by being as sweet as pie,' Victor explains. 'I will remind them that there is still a code of honour in this business, which says that one professional doesn't slag the fuck out of another professional in some poxy paper. And that's all I will do.'

'That's the way to do it, mate.'

'And one other thing. A lump sum for Mrs Cannon.'

'There's a right way of doing these things.'

'That's all I wanted all the time, Johnny. The right thing.'

'Go for it.'

'And I'll take all Simon owes me. I'll take a cheque.'

141

Johnny picks Victor's mug off the floor and puts it back on the trolley.

'We'll drive you down, mate. But if anyone asks, we didn't all start from here . . . if anyone asks . . . like, say, Dee.'

Victor gets up and gives Johnny a hug, like they do in Johnny's end of the business.

'No worries, Johnny. I wouldn't want me wandering around my mansion either.'

Victor opens the window and shouts down. 'Emerson! Lake! Palmer!'

He throws his rasher out, and it lands close to the dogs, but they do not stir.

'I gave them something to chill them out,' Johnny says, 'like these sniffer dogs that went for Lazzer McGeegan down in Spain. The pigs were all over us looking for gear, big pig production, the dogs and all. And they line us up beside the tour bus, all bug-eyed and half of us carrying, and the pigs think it's Christmas. But old Lazzer saved the day. His trousers were all manky with six months' worth of drink and drugs and spunk and cat's vomit and fuck-knows-what, and the dogs went doo-lally.'

Victor lets a whoop out of him. His face changes from ghastly pale to crimson. He motions helplessly to Johnny through the convulsions. Johnny goes on, matter-of-fact.

'Lazzer's trousers fucked the dogs up completely. They were rolling on their backs and howling something rotten. They let us go out of embarrassment.'

Victor is breathless with laughter. Johnny has to support him as he leans against the window, each effort to speak beaten back by another wave of hilarity. Johnny fears that the laughing is almost too intense, that Victor may be about to go off again. He figures that Dr Gary might have something for this in one of the bottles. But then it seems to be subsiding of its own accord. Victor is eventually able to speak.

'You should write a book, Johnny.'

'It's all hush-hush, mate. Code of honour.'

'You told me.'

'You're my mate.'

'You told Greta.'

'She's family.'

'They don't own you, chum. Richie Earls and Dee Bellingham and the lot of them. They don't own Johnny Oregon.'

Johnny shuts the sash window with a ther-clump.

'How do you know I told Greta?' he asks.

Victor is unable to answer. He doesn't want Johnny to know that he was eavesdropping last night, watching Johnny and Greta watching the video, even if it was under the influence of Dr Gary's remedies. He doesn't want Johnny to think ill of him if he can possibly help it. Johnny will think ill of him soon enough, like all the others.

Victor points dumbly to the plate in his head as another fit of hysterics takes hold. Then he falls back on the bed kicking his heels in the air, deranged with mirth.

Johnny figures Victor was just rambling about Greta. Rabbiting away on Dr Gary's fine elixirs and seven gulps of ganja before breakfast. But he looks at Victor rolling around on the bed like a crazy dog, and it gives him the shits.

Chapter 16

Drumbolus, County Westmeath

Simon Bartley and Nulty sit in the big silver car outside Nulty's bungalow all morning, deliberately not going to play golf, listening to classical music on Lyric FM as a mark of respect to Cannon.

'Poor Cannon,' Simon says. 'I feel responsible.'

'We are all prostitutes,' Nulty says.

'Victor's coming down,' Simon says. 'We got word to him.'

'Good,' Nulty says.

Simon clears his throat guiltily.

'Did I . . . did I tell you that Victor is going after Richie Earls over that thing Richie said in the paper?'

'No, Simon. You didn't.'

'I was going to tell you . . . .'

Nulty gives Simon a give-us-a-break look.

'I was going to tell you when we went out to Drumbolus House. I really was now, Nulty. Cards on the table, face up.'

'But you didn't.'

'I suppose I was still in shock . . . I really thought Victor was out of the loop on this one.'

Out of the loop. It's another line of corporate bollocks

144

that Simon has picked up. But Nulty tends to believe that Simon really would be in shock over this.

'Is there anything else I should know about Victor, while we're here?' Nulty says. 'You didn't tell me he killed his wife in case I'd be a bit prejudiced, you just forgot to tell me he's after our man Richie Earls . . .'

Simon offers his hand to Nulty, the first businesslike handshake between the two men that Nulty can recall.

'I won't leave you out of the loop again,' Simon says.

They shake on it.

'And Victor is coming down tomorrow?' Nulty says, feeling vaguely corrupted.

'Face the music,' Simon says. 'It's the only way.'

'You're taking it well,' Nulty says.

'It's all happening tomorrow,' Simon says. 'Richie Earls and Dee Bellingham will be around too.'

'Like, Victor wants compo or something?' Nulty says.

'Satisfaction,' says Simon.

'I'll look forward to that.'

Kilbrittan, South Dublin

Johnny Oregon picks up the softball and throws it back full force to Victor Bartley. On the beach the two men wear overcoats against the stiff breeze driving the incoming tide, Johnny in an ankle-length brown leather job, Victor in knee-length fur belonging to Richie, but then rejected by him as a vegetarian sympathiser. The fresh air is more medicine for Victor, and it is meant to restore the sprits of Johnny Oregon, who left Victor at breakfast that morning, and came back to the kitchen to discover a note from Greta beside the toaster:

Bye bye, Johnny. I think it is not so heavy in the film

business. Thank you for your time. Greta.

Johnny walks towards Victor with the softball, preferring to stroll along the beach. He is not proud of the fact that he dashed upstairs straight away on reading Greta's note, to check if *Richie Earls Unplugged* was still there. Only after a paranoid running of the tape to be sure to be sure did he give himself to grieving for his lost love.

Victor takes the softball from him, like it's just too much for him to carry right now.

'We've all been there, pal,' he says.

The two men look up towards Muscle Shoals and admire their positioning of the tree, a full-size copper beech. Victor directed the operation while Johnny dug a hole for it, the delivery man hanging out until the job was done, a bit of a professional Dubliner helping Johnny with the humping and heaving to prolong his visit to the top of the world. It's a perfect fit. From where they stand, you can see just about nothing of the back garden now. They have it to themselves, the sea to the right, Kilbrittan Hill to the left with its fine houses which seem to have been born on the slopes and brought up there to full maturity, just the odd small castle looking like it's trying a tiny bit too hard.

They walk along the stony strand in leather and fur, perhaps two debauched emperors from the heroic age of rock, taking a break from some vastly perverse activity in one of the mansions above.

'Do you know what a lanyard is?' Johnny asks.

'I don't, no, Johnny,' Victor says.

'Have a guess.'

'Lanyard?'

'Lanyard.'

'Like a knacker's yard, maybe? A place for cutting up animals?'

'It's the string-thing that you hang a backstage pass from.

146

An old sea-faring term. And fuck me if Greta didn't know it.'

'It's me, Johnny. She left because of me.'

'It's me, mate. It's Johnny Oregon. What goes around comes around.'

'It's me, Johnny. There's a few little things about me that put people off.'

'It's all the coin-operated beaver, mate. That's what it is. It's all the chicks I blew out coming back at me. All the wang dang sweet poontang.'

'Have I told you about my wife Sheila?'

'Come on, mate. I'll show you the studio.'

Kinsale, West Cork

Richie Earls brings the fish 'n' chips out of Dino's, with a slice of lemon and tartare sauce, because it's Kinsale. Dee Bellingham is across the road, standing against the Harley, arms folded, wearing Ray-Bans.

'You look like the cop in *Psycho*,' Richie says. 'The fella standing across from the petrol station.'

He unwraps the fish 'n' chips and lays them out on the hot leather seat of the Harley. A young couple in the queue at Dino's recognise Richie and look away again, grinning.

'I saw that re-make of *Psycho*,' he says. 'The colour version. Exactly the same as the original. Fucking loved it.'

Richie stabs a plastic fork into some chips. 'My favourite movie,' he says. 'There's your one making her break for freedom, and what's waiting for her at the end of the road? Norman Fucking Bates, that's what. That'll teach you, girl.'

'I'm so disappointed about Johnny,' Dee says.

She picks up a forkful of battered cod and feeds it to Richie. The couple in the queue have evidently spread the

147

word, and now a dozen people in Dino's are grinning, displaying that giddy self-consciousness which the unknown feel in the vicinity of the known. Dee goes around the other side of the Harley and turns her back on them. She and Richie sit side by side on the bike looking across the harbour, the fish 'n' chips on the seat between them.

'I'm so, so, disappointed,' she says. 'Got a call when you were in Dino's. The guy delivered the tree. Said he got help from two men. One was Johnny and the other was called Victor.'

Richie squeezes the lemon hard. The juice dribbles over the chips. He thinks better of taking a chip because he fears his hand might start trembling.

'Fuck . . . me . . . pink,' he says.

Dee keeps talking in a cool, flat tone.

'Two things. First up, he doesn't share with us that this guy killed his wife. Then he takes him up to Muscle Shoals. Like, hello?'

Richie focuses on a long row of holiday apartments across the harbour, known locally as the Toblerone. He tries to get his head around the latest, but it just sickens him. He knows this sickness, this tension that usually hits him just before a gig, too much to take, it seems, too much fear pounding away at his gut too long.

'I'll quiz him about it,' he says. 'Up the bogs. Tomorrow.'

Dee feeds him a chip. 'I think Johnny will be happier with another artiste.'

'Do what?' Richie asks.

'Say goodbye,' Dee says.

'What if he's up to something? If you just sack him . . .'

'What could be up to?'

'I'll do it so,' Richie says. 'I'll take him up the bogs.'

'Just say goodbye.' Dee is insistent now.

'Like, after the funeral?'

'Whenever . . .' she says.

'We're mates for a long time. Can you sack mates?'

'Johnny and me were lovers.'

'It's just you keep saying that the talent should do nothing except . . . talent.'

'I really wouldn't give this to the artiste any other time.'

Richie puts his arm around Dee's shoulder, partly to steady himself.

'We'll have to get a boat,' he says. 'Just for down here.'

Chapter 17

Muscle Shoals, Kilbrittan Hill, South Dublin

Victor wants a chopper. He wants a chopper because he wants a new suit, and it's ten in the morning and they won't get down the country on time if he has to go to Dún Laoghaire and get the suit and then come back to Muscle Shoals and put the suit on and drive through the traffic of Dublin and down to Drumbolus.

Johnny pours him another cup of java, sitting beside him on the bed, another heavy breakfast down the hatch, the patient's spirits and general self-esteem apparently rocketing. They'll have a go later at a fresh dressing for the arm, and all the thoughts of Greta it will bring. Johnny Oregon has plotted trickier itineraries in his day, getting Lynyrd Skynyrd across Europe all in one piece a stand-out.

'It's an evening bash, mate. Kick-off five-thirty.'

'I expect we'll be there for the removal, Johnny. I expect we'll make the prayers all right. But it's a tight fit with Richie and Dee and Simon. Is it three, three-thirty?'

'We went through it last night with a fine comb Vic. Three o'clock rock.'

'It's the butterflies, Johnny. Know what I mean?'

'You speeding mate?'

150

'No.'

'The chopper is Dee's call.'

'So call her up there, Johnny me boy.'

'Slight problem, Vic. You're not supposed to be up here in the first place.'

'No problem, John. Say we're just using the pad to take off.'

'You need to take the medicine now.'

Destination: Drumbolus

Richie Earls is explaining the Roman Catholic burial rituals to Dee Bellingham, how the removal is not the actual funeral, which takes place the following morning.

'I've been at them, natch, without paying attention,' she says. 'Always out of it.'

Titus the driver stops the BMW at the crossroads of Horse and Jockey. Phil in the passenger seat takes a small mirror from his inside pocket and lays out two thick lines of the best cocaine on it. He hands it gingerly back to Dee, who hoovers the two lines up with a twenty-pound note. She hands the mirror back to Phil.

'Later,' Richie says. 'She has me on a diet.'

Titus swings the BMW left and towards the midlands. The car-phone rings. Phil picks it up and mumbles something and gives it back to Dee.

'Johnny Oregon,' he says.

'Late and breaking, Dee,' Johnny says. 'Our man fancies the big bird.'

'Bloody hell.'

'He wants us to whistle up a chopper.'

'Can we justify that, Johnny? Can we justify it? I don't think so.'

151

Victor is standing with his back to the window of the green bedroom, arms folded, smiling and giving Johnny the high sign while Johnny paces the floor. Johnny can discern the vibes down the line, he can hear Dee getting heavy in her beautifully bred way, jerked around by some sad asshole promoting himself to the chopper bracket, mixing it with the top people.

'It's the logistics, Dee,' Johnny says. 'The traffic.'

Victor winks at him and starts pacing too, following the Oregon trail.

Johnny keeps talking. 'We might as well go the full fifteen with this geezer. He's been through shit.'

Dee has gone as far as she can possibly go. 'Where are you Johnny?'

'Rathmines, Dee. Picking up the client.'

'Don't know about that, Johnny.'

'Logistics, Dee.'

'We can't justify this.'

'I'll be sincere about this, Dee. I don't think you should underestimate this geezer.'

'It's bad practice, Johnny. I don't have to tell you that.'

'Ask Richie about it, Dee. Ask him.'

'I already asked Richie to do something.'

'Please, Dee. Run it by Richie.'

'Where are you, Johnny?'

'Is Richie there with you?'

'Tell me where you are.'

'With respect, Dee . . .'

'This is goodbye, Johnny.'

'I'm a man who can't be sacked, Dee. I'm a friend of the vibe. You know this ain't your nine-to-five.'

Victor is getting the drift of the proceedings. He takes the phone from Johnny and is speaking before Johnny can react.

'Victor Bartley,' he says softly. 'I suppose we won't be meeting today then.'

'We won't be meeting you, Mr Bartley. You ask too much. We can't justify it.'

'I really do need to speak to Richie,' says Victor, his tone remaining mellow.

'We've done everything to accommodate you, Mr Bartley. We're going ahead with our plans for the gig and we'd like to see you there.'

Richie is barely able to speak, anyway, because he is getting the drift of the proceedings too, and he is panicked out of his gourd, helpless in the back of the car, his right leg pumping up and down in a nervous reflex, suddenly bursting for a piss.

Victor continues in his dark chocolate voice.

'Dee? I'd like to tell you a little story about an old man in County Monaghan . . .'

Dee takes the phone away from her ear. She can hear the little voice on her lap telling the story about the old-style republican who ate the money. She breaks into Victor's yarn.

'Put me back to Johnny,' she says.

'No,' Victor says. 'Fuck off.'

Dee Bellingham puts down the car-phone. Titus stops the car and Richie gets out for a long, relieving piss at the side of the road, impervious to all the horn-blowing recognition from passing cars. They are back in Kinsale in two hours, flat out.

Muscle Shoals, Kilbrittan Hill, South Dublin

Victor in his mellow zone doesn't notice Johnny slipping out of the room. He finishes with Dee, and in a haze of triumph

he goes looking for Johnny. Across the hall in the Big Boys'
Room, the television is on. Victor sees that it's the video of
Paul's murder, just as he hears the front door closing down
below.

He races down the stairs, the black silk dressing gown
with the dragon's head motif flapping behind him,
otherwise naked. He slides the latch and pulls open the
heavy front door and runs in front of the Daimler, barring
Johnny's way out the gate. Beaten, Johnny rolls down the
electronic window. He looks his age now, all of fifty, a fit
and muscular fifty, a fifty with a fine red mane and a lady-
killing white silk shirt, a fifty with two-hundred-dollar
Texas boots and a powerful waft of Brut, but fifty all the
same in this present abyss of the spirit.

'It's the hardest thing in rock 'n' roll, mate,' he says.
'Getting out before they blow you out.'

Victor feels suddenly exposed. He closes the dressing-
gown over his pale blubbery gut, and ties the cord tightly.
The slashed arm stings something rotten under yesterday's
dressing. He grabs Johnny by the neck and kisses him
passionately on the lips.

'Fuck Greta,' he says. 'And fuck Richie Earls.'

'I'm shitting it, Vic. You hear?'

'I knew about the tape, Johnny. Do you hear me? I knew
about it the first night you brought me here.'

'Oh mama . . . oh mama . . .'

'It's all right.'

'Just shoot me, mate. Just shoot my ass.'

'You did as much for me as any man could, Johnny.
You're a sound oul' fucker.'

'I'm shitting it, Vic. I think we're gonna see some ugly.'

'We are, Johnny.'

Emerson, Lake and Palmer are barking out the back.

'Get in,' Johnny shouts.

Johnny jumps the Daimler out the gate and down the narrow little roads towards Dún Laoghaire.

'We're going to see some ugly,' Johnny says.

He takes up most of the pavement outside Barr's men's shop in Dún Laoghaire, blocking off the door so Victor can hop out of the Daimler in his dressing gown and get quickly in.

Victor selects a plain black suit and a plain white shirt and a pink silk tie. He takes a black tie for the funeral. Johnny waves his American Express plastic, before anyone asks. A bit of tailoring to the trousers and it's ready to wear out the door.

'We're going down the country,' Victor explains.

Chapter 18

Monkstown, South Dublin

They are about thirty seconds into their journey when Johnny Oregon stops the Daimler outside Goggins of Monkstown.

'Quick half?' he says.

'I'll have a half with you,' Victor says.

They shut the maroon doors with a superior thunk, and amble into the suburban lounge, slack after the lunchtime crowd. Victor feels dressed to the teeth in the black suit and the crisp white shirt and the pink silk tie.

'Half of Guinness,' says Johnny to the barman.

'Pint,' Victor says.

'Pint for me, actually, mate,' says Johnny. 'Sorry, mate.'

They stroll on down to the back of the lounge, empty of its usual assortment of southsiders on the beer, a venue with some resonance for Victor. It was here that he spent one endless summer's day drinking with the painter John Ryan and a sports commentator from RTÉ and some local fellow with a cravat. They had a row about Sinatra, Victor recalls. John Ryan hated Sinatra, called him a thug. All gone now.

'We have time for a drink,' Johnny says, throwing himself wearily down on the back seat of the lounge.

*

Four hours later they're thinking of ordering sandwiches.

'That's the thing about shock,' Victor says.

The shock of rejection by Greta and then by Dee is going hard on Johnny, but what is sticking him to the spot in Goggins is the plan of action that Victor is laying out over many pints of Guinness, a strategy which is driving both men to drink with a mounting fervour, even as Cannon is being lowered into the ground.

'To Cannon,' says Victor, hearing a church bell striking four.

'Cannon,' Johnny says.

'I loved the man,' Victor says, lowering a third of his pint, sucking it out of the glass.

'Anyway, it wouldn't be right to go up against Simon now,' Johnny says, repeating some of Victor's reasoning.

'Not with the ammo we'll have in a week's time.'

'I know Mrs Cannon. I know the people. They'll think no less of me,' Victor says.

'You're thinking so straight, mate.'

'Strike it while it's hot. Hit the road to Kinsale tonight.'

'If it was me, I'd want to chop Richie's rocks off.'

'Maybe I'll do that too, Johnny.'

'Professional time. The fucking tape. Do we pick it up on the way?'

'I guess so.'

'At times it might seem like I'm holding you back, Victor. I'm a very careful man.'

'We need the fucking tape, pal.'

'You're just thinking so straight.'

'Maybe too straight?'

'Maybe too straight. Maybe you're in shock as well.'

'But you'll give me the benefit?'

'I'm with you, mate. The thing about your plan of action,

it beats bringing Richie down to the bunker and shoving a red hot poker up his arsehole. They've got a bunker down there you know. A nuclear bunker.'

'You're not serious.'

'Lovely set-up. It's like this underground penthouse apartment, all stocked up with food and drink and drugs. It's, like, if Sellafield goes up, Richie and Dee and their famous mates will be the only survivors. Them and the government.'

'You mean, they've got, like, the Library in Lillies still happening when all other living things are kaput?'

'That's what success is all about. The little extras.'

'It might be tempting, Johnny, to think in terms of shoving a red hot poker up the man's arsehole after all down there in the bunker when you think of what these cunts have done to me and my family.'

'I hear you.'

'But it would be less than professional.'

'Chinese? There's a top place.'

'I'll have a Chinese with you, Johnny. And then we'll drop by Muscle Shoals to collect the tape. And then we'll barrel down to Kinsale to straighten out the boy Richie. It's like I've got things to do now, Johnny, after twenty years a-rotting. A man needs a cause.'

'Chinese, so.'

The two men rise, bursting with Guinness. Victor loosens the belt on his new suit trousers as they breeze out to the front door of Goggins, all business.

In the Chinese they are quieter, savouring the potential of their situation. Going to the police will always be the last option for such men. Not with what they've got. They've got an international superstar so tightly by the balls, if they choose they can make him go on television and call Nelson Mandela a war criminal. They can make him donate a million pounds to a defence fund for paedophile priests. They can make him join the army. But they have something else in mind that seems to have more class, more meaning, more righteousness, provided they hold their nerve and use their terrible power wisely, and provided their hearts have the courage to stand up to Dee Bellingham when she comes back at them with all she's got.

Victor is having no food, just some wine to keep his spirits high. He raises a glass of house red.

'Cannon,' he says. 'He ran the race, he finished the course. He fought the good fight, he kept the faith. And now he has gone to his house, justified.'

'Nice one,' Johnny says, addressing a plate of kung po chicken.

'And you, Johnny. You saved my life.'

'Uh-huh.'

'Have I ever told you about my wife Sheila?'

Johnny springs out of his seat and disappears into the gents with the mountain-goat agility of his kind. Only this time he is not bolting across the stage at the Reading Festival to hand Jimmy Page a replacement axe. He is giving up the day's takings in the cubicle, kneeling, hugging the bowl tightly, splattering all the sickness in his gut against the porcelain in one, two, three, four, five, six pump-action pukes, until the tears roll down his cheeks.

Victor can hear the pitiful gawking sounds. He sees that the Chinese waiter is worried.

'No problemo,' he says. 'Food is beautiful.'

Johnny has not touched his kung po chicken.

'No problemo,' Victor says, lashing a few forkfuls of the meal into himself and giving the waiter a big thumbs-up.

Johnny returns, pale and glassy-eyed.

'Technicolour yawn,' he says, dabbing his eyes with a napkin.

'All up?' Victor says.

'Fucking state of me.'

'You should try this controlled drinking, my friend.'

'It's not the booze, Vic. It's the grief.'

'Give me the keys, Johnny.'

'I'm all right.'

'Please, Johnny. The keys.'

'You mean . . .?'

'I want to drive that big fucker all through the night.'

'Nine pints is it, mate? Ten pints? And a glass of vino?'

'I'm up for it, Johnny. I need this baby.'

'It takes some handling.'

'I'll be careful, Johnny. I'll be as careful as . . . I'll tell you how careful I'll be. Right? I'll be as careful . . . as careful as a fellow who's had the snip, but still uses johnnies.'

'How's the arm?'

'Better.'

'You need to swing by Rathmines?'

'Why the fuck would I need to do that, Johnny?'

'Just to check in, I guess. Clean up the blood and the broken glass and so forth.'

'And pick up my mail? No, no, no, Johnny, I sincerely hope that I will never be swinging by Rathmines again so long as I may live. You're forgetting I'm one of the top people now, almost. What'll we do tonight, us top people? I know, we'll fuck off down to West Cork just because we can. Because the horn is on us.'

Johnny pays for the meal with his plastic, adding a tip of £100 for the disturbance in the toilet.

'We'll be recommending this place to our friends,' Victor says.

He eases himself with exaggerated care into the Daimler, and switches on the ignition. He flexes his fingers like a safe-cracker. The dashboard is a gorgeous blend of some lovely old wood and some futuristic playthings.

'I'll do the sounds,' Johnny says.

'Remember this moment,' Victor says, revving her up gently. 'Remember I was happy here, for a moment, on this soft white leather seat. And that this moment was delivered to me through the agony of my son. Because he has gone to his house, unjustified.'

'Mahalia Jackson,' Johnny says, selecting a tape. 'It's gotta be Mahalia.'

'Unjustified,' Victor says as the deep gospel music plays them away and up through Dún Laoghaire and on towards Kilbrittan Hill. 'He has gone to his house unjustified.'

'I love the road at night,' Johnny says.

'Love it,' Victor says.

'In and out. I'll just pick up the tape and get out of there. Unless we want a flask of something. Soup maybe?'

'A flask of soup?' Victor asks.

'No trouble,' Johnny says.

'Settle the stomach?'

'I've got this set of flasks. Picked 'em up in Madrid. A set of four flasks. Spent some time with The Who. The guys loved them.'

'The Who drank soup out of flasks?' Victor says.

'Loved it. I had a flight case made up specially.'

'You had a flight case made up to carry flasks of soup?'

'You get the cases made in the exact shape of the object. It's standard.'

Victor checks if Johnny is winding him up, but Johnny looks sincere.

'They locked me up for years you know', Victor says.

Kilbrittan Hill, South Dublin

Victor slows down on the approach to Kilbrittan Hill, extra careful out of some vague sense that he is being watched from the mansions behind the high walls. Johnny's gospel tape has Curtis Mayfield now, singing 'People get ready, there's a train a-coming.'

'Funny thing, Johnny,' Victor says. 'The Irish can't do that religious stuff without making fucking eejits out themselves. Did you see poor Sinéad O'Connor?'

'Eh?'

'You're quiet, Johnny.'

'The booze isn't my first love, you know.'

'Nice drop of soup now, coming up.'

'Bollocks. Fucking bollocks. Keep driving. Step on it.'

Johnny sees Muscle Shoals before Victor does, and sees that the floodlights are on at the front.

'Keep driving,' he shouts.

Victor cruises past the front gates. They are shut. 'We left them open, didn't we?' he says.

Johnny picks up the car-phone, pauses to compose himself, and dials. He listens for a few seconds and puts the phone back down.

'Dee,' he says.

'What did she say?'

'She said . . . hello.'

'Are you sure?'

'Keep driving.'

'She's up there.'

'Fucking chopper.'

'Fucking tape.'

'Pull up here.'

Victor eases the Daimler to a stop down beside the beach. They can make out the back of Muscle Shoals from here, way up near the top of the hill. They can't see much, except that the floodlights are on.

'I really must be losing it,' Johnny says.

'Steady, chum.'

'Of course she'd be up there. She'd make it her business. Fucking hell, there's a couple of loonies loose in the gaffe. Fucking right she'll get the chopper up and sort it out. Fucking right.'

'It's been a mad day, Johnny. An exciting day. Let's not get too down in ourselves.'

'We need that tape, Vic.'

'We've got it, Johnny.' And he taps the plate. 'In here.'

'It's just sitting there in the fucking machine, ready to roll. *Richie Earls Unplugged*.'

'Well, there you are. I mean, does she sit around looking at Richie's poxy videos?'

'It's a bad break, Vic. Straight away it's a bad break.'

Victor doesn't deny it, but he is still warming to this strange sensation of being the nurse instead of the patient, pulling Johnny Oregon through this crisis of faith. He feels the old butterflies, but he somehow doesn't feel another collapse coming on, maybe because he's sitting at the wheel of a beautiful big car and not in his mean little armchair, maybe because he can smell a bit of success for the first time in twenty-five years.

'You think Richie's up there as well?' he says.

'I can try him in Kinsale.'

Johnny dials the lodge. He listens for a moment and then puts the phone down.

'He's there,' Johnny says.

'What did he say?'

'He said . . . hello.'

Victor lets out a sudden bark of laughter.

'It's actually better this way,' he says. 'It's actually better.'

163

'How?'

'It's better if we get Richie on his own, right?'

'OK.'

'So, if we can get Richie on his own tonight, Dee knows a lot less. And that's fine by me.'

'The fucking tape, Victor. The fucking tape?'

'Maybe she'll look at it, maybe she won't.'

'I need a smoke.'

Victor revs up the Daimler again.

'The gear is up there too,' says Johnny. 'Fuck it.'

The Staple Singers are harmonising softly, immaculately. Victor turns up the volume, as though the serenity of Papa Staples can banish the dark side of any deal.

'It's actually better this way,' he says.

It is eight o'clock as he starts the Daimler along the coast road. He aims to be in Kinsale by midnight.

Drumbolus, County Westmeath

The lounge of Malone's is full and getting noisy with the funeral crowd. Nulty takes his half-time break from spinning the discs, playing mostly country tonight, George Jones, George and Tammy, some tearjerkers for the day that is in it.

Up at the bar, collecting his rum-and-black, he gets out a 'Sorry for your trouble' to one of Cannon's brothers. Nulty tells the brother that he drank many times with the man inside the box, and was close to him. Yes, he was close to Cannon.

Simon walks in through the bar, fills up a glass of whiskey from the optic and signals to Nulty to join him upstairs. Nulty takes his rum-and-black and follows Simon up to the former premises of Midland Community, the floor still strewn with paper, the table collapsed.

'Listen to this,' Simon says. He switches on the answering machine.

It is the voice of Victor. 'Simon, I'd like you to tender my apologies to Mrs Cannon. I just could not be there today, but my thoughts were with you all, and I trust you will reach a fair settlement. As you know, we had an appointment today, but that too was not to be. Simon . . . I'd like you to know that I hold you responsible in no way for this. I'd also like you to know that your willingness to meet me in the first place is a great boon to me, and that our troubles are now over. You owe me nothing. I hope that we can work together in the future. Thank you for your time.'

Simon's hands are trembling as he holds his whiskey up to the light.

'I've never had a drink of whiskey before, would you believe that?' Simon says.

'Go on,' Nulty says.

Simon drinks it in one go.

'No effect at all,' he says. 'I'm too happy.'

Nulty offers him his rum-and-black but he waves it away. Simon echoes Victor on the message. 'You owe me nothing.'

'When?' Nulty says.

'Just in,' says Simon. 'Ten bells.'

'He sounds. . . up.'

'Tomorrow, Nulty. Tomorrow we set up shop in Drumbolus House.'

'Anything from the others?'

'We'll raise Richie and Dee tomorrow, no worries. They'll get up here, no worries, Richie and Dee. They'll take one look at our set-up in Drumbolus House and then they'll know we're for real. Tomorrow, Nulty, we get massive.'

Nulty has a nagging suspicion that Victor sounded a bit

165

too 'up', but he goes with Simon's take on it. He leaves Simon upstairs, listening back to Victor's message. At the bottom of the wooden stairs he stops. Then he goes back upstairs. Simon pauses the machine.

'Just a thing,' Nulty says. 'About funerals. When I was about eighteen my auntie died. And the night before the funeral, me and this other bloke hit up with these two French girls. Backpackers, you know. And my one was wearing this black nail varnish. So she painted my nails black as well. And then I wake up with her the following day and I'm late for the funeral and I have to rush. Hung over and all. So I shake hands with my uncle Bill outside the church in Bishopstown and say, "Sorry for your trouble, Uncle Bill," and I've still got the fucking black nail varnish on.'

Simon closes his eyes, and winces.

'Uncle Bill doesn't know if I'm taking the piss or what, but I scarper back to find the French one gone for the boat. Left me her address in Brittany and a bottle of black nail varnish. I went off and joined the Hare Krishnas.'

Nulty swallows the last of his rum-and-black, and grins.

'She was mad about me, boy.'

Destination: Kinsale

'Now,' Victor says calmly. 'Call him now.'

They are leaving Cashel at the start of the second leg to Kinsale. Johnny Oregon turns down the high lonesome sound of Gram Parsons's 'Hickory Wind', picks up the carphone, and dials Richie Earls.

'Yeah?'

'Johnny here.'

'Johnny.'

'How are you, mate?'

'Fucking awful, Johnny.'

'I see you're on the Rich List again mate. Worth thirty million.'

'Bollocks. We've gotta meet, Johnny.'

'What's that, Richie?'

'We've gotta meet, Johnny. Get this shit sorted.'

'Dee gave me a lot of verbals, mate. A lot of verbals.'

'Dee's away.'

'You want to see me? I want to see you.'

' You want to see me?'

'I'm trying to get out of. . . where is it?. . . Tipperary.'

'You're on the road?'

'Great minds *et cetera*.'

'We can still sort this out. Just you and me, Johnny. Dee's away.'

'What about Charles Fort?'

'What about here?'

'Nah, mate. Charles Fort.'

'I'm kinda dug in here . . .'

'Richie . . . help me out here.'

'Are you carrying?'

'I've got a little something.'

Kinsale, West Cork

Richie Earls is grateful for the call. It feels like a spot of luck after a day when it was all getting away from him, Dee on a solo run, shafting Johnny like he was some stable-hand. She is some operator, some player on the big stage, but in Richie's bones, he feels there is a daft native angle to this Victor Bartley balls-up that Dee doesn't really get, but that he gets, and that Johnny gets. They can still bury this under a heap of bullshit, while Dee figures what she can justify and what she can't justify.

He shins down the pole to the ground floor of the lodge. He needs a drink and a smoke after a long lie-down, in which he thinks he got some sleep. He's never completely sure, these days. When this is finished, once and for all, he plans to get his body-clock back in gear. And his bladder. And his desire to hump, free from this desperate fatigue. It never stopped him before, fatigue. But this was the wrong type, the wasting type, not like when you're flaked out after a gig, still buzzing.

In the galley, Richie Earls fills a tall glass with Hennessy brandy, and lights up a Marlboro, like he still needs this latest addiction to keep all the others company. He can get it up once a day for Dee since she came back from Antibes, but mostly for the wrong reasons, like habit, like to keep her off his case. He can still surrender, and phone her right now up in Muscle Shoals to tell her he has killed a man, because if you love your old lady, this is the sort of thing she should know. But how much better, ah how much better it will be if he can square this shit with no-one any the wiser, if he can square it tonight, even, with the one and only Johnny, how much more balls does that take than some sad bastard confession scene, how much more balls?

You see, Dee will get the benefits anyway. How many was it again that her crowd murdered to get their horny Anglo-Irish asses up there in the first place? Was it hundreds? Was it thousands? He'd be a better man for this, with heavier balls, and Dee would feel his power, and he would feel her power back, and neither would quite know where it all came from, this wild thing, this careless love, except that it was forbidden to the plebs and the punters and the also-rans. It could even improve his voice, give it that blue note.

What sad bastard confession? Richie is pulling on his Cuban heels, with this strange question in his head. What confession? For a moment, he feels like a different person to the one who killed Paul Bartley, like he has to force himself to remember the thing now, because it won't come to him unbidden. He stomps his heels on the wooden floor. He is starting to suspect that he could deny this, deny everything, and mean it. In his own Dundalk accent too, like it was in the beginning. It could be that the Charlie has just eaten away his conscience. It could also be that a couple of days off the stuff and he is able to see more clearly that it was a different man who did that thing up in Muscle Shoals, and that the real Richie Earls is not a bad man, just a man who fucked up big, and who saw the terrors and felt the agonies that await a top man when it looks like it's all going to get away from him.

Tonight, tonight it can still be fixed, thank fuck. He takes a bomber jacket that he got in New Orleans, to go with Jerry Lee's rattlesnake bracelet for a double dose of Louisiana luck. He is really looking forward to seeing Johnny again, face to face, and to getting this shit shovelled away, whatever it takes, if it takes a full-page apology to Victor Bartley in *The Irish Times* for his poor judgement of *Goin' Nuts!* so be it. And then, he thinks, he'll go for two weeks to Cuba.

Richie Earls stops the Harley at the end of the lane and knocks on the window of the Land Rover. Titus is alone, reading the colour supplement estimates of Richie's wealth. He's ahead of Chris de Burgh and behind Enya.

'It could be all gone tomorrow,' he tells Titus.

'Sorry sir. You read any shit. . .'

'I'll tell you a secret, Titus. I love that sort of shit.'

'I love it too, man.'

Richie steers the Harley out of the lane. He puts on his

helmet ostentatiously for Titus, who should really be following him. But Richie bungs the boys an extra grand to cancel Dee's instructions, and leave him alone on the bike.

He boots it up to seventy until he reaches the outskirts of Kinsale, and slows it right down for the left turn that takes him away from the town along the harbour and up through Summer Cove and further up the steep hill to Charles Fort, the ruin desolate in the cold and the darkness under a quarter moon. He dismounts the Harley in the car-park outside the front gate of the fort, abandoned to its ghosts after nightfall. He leaves the bike standing there and walks over to the wall to look across at the lights of Kinsale, and the silhouettes of the boats in the harbour, making his soul sigh. Behind him, at the other end of the car-park, a pair of headlights switches on and off, like an old smuggler's signal. He turns around, and out of the darkness he sees Johnny Oregon walking, smiling, regal in his full-length coat.

They embrace, with the squeak of fine leather.

'Thanks for making the effort, mate,' Johnny says.

'Ah, it does a fella good, Johnny, to get the finger out of his arsehole.'

They turn to the sea, as if some passing night-walker might eavesdrop.

'We had a bit of blow here once, you and me,' Johnny says. 'And some reasoning.'

'And some reasoning.'

'The gear is up in Muscle Shoals. I know I said I had a little something, but. . .'

'One of these, then.'

'You're back on the fags, mate.'

'You must give me that book again.'

'Give me one of them, mate.'

'Ah, Johnny . . .'

170

'It's been a fuck of a day, mate.'

Johnny takes a Marlboro and Richie pulls a Zippo out of his bomber jacket to light it. It was a thing he picked up from Johnny, being quick on the draw to light another person's cigarette.

'I'll be all right tomorrow, mate,' Johnny says, sucking on the Marlboro. 'It's like I've got one of them twenty-four hour bugs.'

'I've got one of them bugs. Three weeks now.'

'It's time for healing.'

'That's right.'

'And sometimes the healing can feel worse than what ails ye.'

'The way I reason it now, Johnny, the only problem here is Dee. But she doesn't have to know. Does she?'

'Know what?' Johnny asks.

'She doesn't have to know if I meet Bartley and bury this shit.'

'Sometimes you can't bury everything, mate.'

'We need you back, Johnny.'

'Dee doesn't need nobody,' Johnny says.

'Well I need you, Johnny.'

'That's sweet of you, mate.'

'And Dee needs me,' Richie says.

'That's cool.'

'At the end of the day, she still needs Richie Earls to make sweet music.'

'The less Dee knows about it. . . it's better that way.'

'Right.'

'She really does need you, doesn't she?' Johnny says.

'So Victor wanted a fucking chopper. What else does he want? Flying lessons?'

'Respect, Richie, respect.'

'You mean money?'

171

'It's not about money,' Johnny says.

'But he'd still like some, the hoor.'

'Yeah, I guess.'

'Where?' Richie asks.

'Right here.'

'When?'

'Tonight.'

'Like, now?

'Basically, yeah.'

'I've got nothing on me now, Johnny. I mean I can talk to the geezer. . .'

'Talk won't do it, my man.'

'How much, then?' Richie asks. 'Name it.'

'Money won't do it either, mate.'

'I'm not on your wavelength here, Johnny.'

'Talk won't do it any more. And money won't do it any more. It's all different now. There's a tape. . .'

'A tape. . .'

'A video tape. . .'

'He wants a video tape. . .?'

'There is a video tape of you running Paul Bartley into the water. Well, the dogs. And you.'

Richie Earls feels the fear rushing through him, the fear seizing his whole body in one awful attack, drilling his guts, pulping his bones. Johnny touches his elbow and turns him away from the calm sea, away from the lights of Kinsale to face the figure of Victor Bartley walking towards him, ambling across the car-park in his new pin-striped suit and crisp white shirt and pink silk tie.

Johnny keeps a grip on Richie's elbow. He seems unsteady, like all the strength has left him. In his right hand he still has the Marlboro going. He lets it drop to the ground as Victor gets up close and offers him his hand to shake. He puts his hand in Victor's, and Victor squeezes the poor shivering paw of the stricken Richie Earls.

'Victor Bartley,' he says.

'Don't try to speak, Richie,' Johnny says. 'Just listen to the man.'

Victor releases Richie's hand. It flops back limply by his side.

Victor smiles at him. Richie stares back, and tries a pathetic grin.

'I expect Johnny has filled you in on the relevant details,' Victor says softly.

Richie makes a noise back to confirm. 'Unnnnnnh.'

'Cigarette him, Johnny.'

Johnny reaches into the top pocket of Richie's jacket for the packet of Marlboro and the Zippo. He lights a cigarette and places it between Richie's lips. Richie takes one drag off the cigarette and throws it down. Victor stamps it out. Richie makes that noise again.

'Unnnnnnh.'

'Now, Richie,' Victor says. 'We have a new situation here. A new situation, you might say, going into the new millennium.'

Richie nods his head slowly.

'Emerson, Lake and Palmer, what?'

'I'm. . . I'm. . .'

'Say again, Richie?'

'I'm getting them. . . done away with.'

'Oh I hate that, Richie. Three lovely big dogs. . .'

'Unnnnnnh.'

'But if it has to be done. . .'

'Anything. . .'

'Anything you can do, I can do better? Anything what?'

'Anything you want. . . from me.'

'I'm not enjoying this, Richie.'

'Sorry.'

173

'I'm not enjoying this. Say again, Richie?'

Johnny squeezes Richie's elbow, to steady him.

'Sorry. . . sorry. . . I'm sorry. . .' Richie moans.

Victor claps his hands. Richie is too dizzy with fear to figure if Victor is mocking him. Victor stops clapping.

'Well, that in itself,' he says. 'That in itself is something. But you haven't heard my proposal yet.'

'Unnnnnh. . . the cops?'

'Fuck them, Richie. Fuck them boys. They were very cold to me when I was grieving for my son. Very unfeeling.'

'Oh no . . .'

'Oh yes. Very unfeeling.'

'But. . . but they don't know?'

'You could call this a citizen's arrest.'

'Ohhhh. . . Dee? Does Dee know?'

'We're getting our voice back?'

'Does she know?'

'Don't worry about Dee. Worry about me for a minute.'

'Sorry, sorry, sorry, sorry.'

'No cops, no Dee. This is about justice, Richie. And not about retribution. Well. . . maybe a bit of retribution too.'

'Anything. . . anything. . .'

'I'll give you one thing. You're not running away. You're not making any excuses.'

'No, no, no. . .'

'That may count in your favour.'

'No excuses. . . no excuses. . .'

'We can confirm the details of what happened another time. I'll need to know everything. Exactly.'

'No excuses . . .'

'What do you think is going to happen now, Richie?'

'What?'

'Well, what do you think you can do for me?'

'My money. . .'

'You don't think that money can compensate me for my son?'

'No way, no way. . .'

'I know that's not what you're saying. But we'll have to do better than that. Won't we?'

'Houses. Houses. I've got five houses. Beautiful houses. Just take them as a. . . as something.'

'We're not talking the same language here, Richie.'

'Oh, God. Oh, God, I see.'

Victor gives a delighted little chuckle.

'You want my woman?' Richie whispers.

Victor throws his head back, laughing. 'What if I do?'

Richie rises to a whimpering little giggle. 'That's kinda. . . hard. . .'

'I don't want your woman, pal. I don't want your woman. . .'

'Of course not.'

Victor folds his arms and bows his head. He massages his temples with the thumb and forefinger of his right hand. Victor speaks, still massaging his temples.

'Richie, think not of what you can do for me. Instead, think of what I can do for you.'

Richie stares at him dumbly. Victor takes his hand away from his face and gives Richie a big smile.

'The question is not, what can Richie Earls do for Victor Bartley? The question is, what can Victor Bartley do for Richie Earls?'

Richie shakes his head. He doesn't get it. Victor puts it another way.

'You see, Richie, you can offer me money. You can offer me fine houses. You can even offer me fine women at that. And fine wine. And I could do with all of that. All of it. But, you know, you're the one in serious shit here. Richie Earls needs Victor Bartley now. You hear me? Richie Earls needs

Victor Bartley now.'

'Anything. . .'

'Just one thing will do.'

'Whatever. . .'

'I can't offer you money, or fine houses, or fine wine, or beautiful women. I offer only good management.'

'Unnnnnnh. . . Unnnnnnh.'

'We're losing you again, Richie.'

'Unnnnnh. . . Unnnnnnh. . .'

'Gentlemen's agreement, of course,' Victor adds.

Victor offers Richie his hand. Richie looks with awe at the big hand stretching towards him. Victor spits on his palm and offers it again.

'Ten per cent sound fair to you?' he says.

Richie stays silent, stunned.

'I'd say sleep on it, but, you know. . .' Victor presses.

Richie puts his hand in Victor's, and they shake.

'Welcome back to the business, mate,' Johnny says.

He steps between Victor and Richie, directing them gently towards the Daimler.

'Johnny will be with us, of course,' Victor says. 'Johnny will do . . . whatever Johnny does.'

Richie is dazed. He gestures to the Harley.

'It's better if you come with us,' Victor says. 'I don't like my artistes to ride motorbikes.'

Chapter 19

Muscle Shoals, Kilbrittan Hill, South Dublin

'I am going to the Shelbourne to get fantastically drunk,' Dee Bellingham says.

She says this to Greta, climbing the stairs to the Big Boys' Room at Muscle Shoals. Apart from hello and come in, it's the first thing she says to Greta. She looks like she's just up after a hard night, with her untidy hair and a tartan dressing-gown that reminds Greta of something you'd see on an old man in hospital.

'I am going to get absolutely pissed in the Horseshoe Bar and then... then I'm going to fuck goats in fucking Tasmania,' Dee continues.

Greta follows her into the big room, and repeats what she said at the door.

'I am looking for Johnny Oregon.'

'You're German or something.'

'Dutch.'

'I'm Dee Bellingham, by the way.'

'Greta.'

'Anything to the Conynghams? You look like...'

'Just Greta.'

'And you're his lover?'

'Yes.'

'Darling, he's not around here, but we'll find him for you.'

Dee directs Greta to sit on the vast leather couch. She goes behind the bar.

'Do you drink Bloody Marys in Holland, or do you just smoke?'

'I like Bloody Marys,' says Greta.

'Seriously, I'm looking for a boozing partner today. I have been dumped.'

Dee pours two bottles of tomato juice into glasses, and throws large measures of vodka and chunks of ice in after them.

'These are not real Bloody Mary's,' she says. 'Bloke in the Shelbourne makes the best. Sure you're not a Conyngham?'

'I work on catering.'

Dee hands the drink to Greta and sits about a yard away from her on the couch.

'You can hang out here if you like,' Dee says. 'It seems to be open to the public.'

Greta, avoiding her eyes, focuses on the initials 'FDR' in gold lettering on the breast pocket of Dee's dressing-gown.

'Roosevelt stayed with my father once, and left this behind him,' Dee says. 'It's a horrible old heirloom. A bit like me really.'

'You are a gorgeous chick,' Greta says.

It is the mouth that Greta finds especially gorgeous. The better parts of Dee's nature seem to live in the softness of her mouth. Men would probably favour those brown eyes, full of high-born yearning, but Greta reckons Dee can turn that on and off like a tap. It is around the mouth that you sense her vulnerability, and understand how, even when she is talking in that curt way of the blue-blooded wastrel, she sounds somehow charming. This is why Johnny worshipped the woman, Greta thinks. This frightening need in her, buried under all that class.

'Greta, right?' Dee says. 'You'll find Johnny down in Kinsale with Richie. And you'll find both of them with a Mr Bartley.'

'Victor. . .'

'You know this person?'

'Johnny introduced me.'

'He did it over the phone, you know. Richie ended our partnership over the phone. Five years.'

'I don't know what's going on here. I'm sorry.'

'Coke. It's the bastard coke. There's no other sane reason why Richie would turn me over for some ghastly lunatic ballroom manager. Coke, my girl, the old marching powder. What the bloody hell is wrong with plain old hooch?'

Dee returns to the bar for more vodka. Greta doesn't fancy one right now. There, on top of the video machine, is the cover of *Richie Earls Unplugged*, where Johnny left it when he played it to her. Greta has to suppress a strong urge to wail with pain.

'Richie sounded so bloody wretched,' Dee says, returning with a fresh drink. 'Do you mind me banging on like this?'

Greta shakes her head.

'Come on, Greta, let's go to the Shelbourne and get arseholed. I can tell you things about Johnny. We were lovers, you know.'

'I have to go now, to find him.'

'You're very sweet.'

'This is all very mad.'

'It's rock 'n' roll,' Dee says. 'It's fun, but it drives people insane. Good people.'

Greta, as cool as she can manage it, reaches for the empty video case.

179

'This is Richie's best,' she says. 'I would love to have this.'
'You're a fan?'
'Something in his voice, you know.'
'Then you must have it,' Dee says.

Dee sets down her drink and rummages through a pile of videos scattered about the huge screen. Greta in her meticulous way recalls that Johnny left the tape in the machine after he played it to her. She gambles on it still being there. While Dee searches the pile, Greta kneels and ejects the video from the machine. Instantly she sees by the label that it is the security video, the horror show.

'This is the one,' Greta says quietly.

Dee hands her the empty case. Greta looks into those big sympathetic eyes and snaps the video case shut.

'You must have another drink,' Dee says.

Greta laughs with relief.

'More Bloody Mary,' she says. 'I'll make it.'

Greta skips to the bar and mixes up a couple of serious Bloody Marys, salt, pepper, Tabasco, Worcestershire sauce.

Dee sits back and watches her closely, like she is trying to memorise the recipe.

'Richie lost it once before,' Dee says. 'Went off on this S and M kick. Carried around this big bag with him all the time, wouldn't let the roadies touch it, kept it next to him on the tour bus and all, full of whips and chains and nipple-clamps and whatever. He'd say to me, the doctor will see you now. Coke, I need hardly add.'

'Maybe it will go, this coke madness.'

'I said to him this morning,' Dee says, 'business is business, and if you want this daft new management deal, then go for it. Let the lawyers thrash it out. But in the meantime, can we work out the love thing?'

Dee takes a sip of Greta's cocktail.

'Delicious,' she says. 'So Richie tells me that Johnny's

180

back on board like it should be and I'm a stuck-up cunt and he hates me. I don't think he's coming back from there.'

'Johnny . . . Johnny thinks a lot of you.'

'Likewise. I adore the man. So, like an absolute cow, I go and sack him.'

'I think I am mad to be with these people.'

'It can be exciting.'

'I need to be with Johnny, I guess.'

'And I'm some bitter old hag who'll be sitting up here waiting for a beautiful career to go horribly, horribly wrong.'

Greta slips *Richie Earls Unplugged* inside her leather jacket and moves towards the door. It is all she can do to stop herself running out the door with her prize.

'You'll stay here?' she says.

'I'd like to pull up all these awful carpets that Richie likes. I like an oak floor underneath me.'

'That's exciting,' Greta says.

'You're absolutely positive you won't go with me to the Shelbourne to get wasted? I'll phone Ronnie Wood. . .'

'I'm sort of wasted already,' Greta says.

'When it starts to go pear-shaped, call me. I mean it.'

'We can maybe go to the Shelbourne.'

'I mean it,' Dee says.

'You're sure it will go pear-shaped,' Greta says.

'Seriously,' Dee says. 'Would you trade me in for Victor Bartley?'

Dee walks out to the gates with Greta, past the security den where Greta got it together with Johnny. Greta is starting to feel thrilled with herself for heisting the tape, apparently unwatched by Dee. She is looking forward to Johnny's reaction when she gives it to him tonight. She will phone him on her way down to the DART, to say she still wants him. She knows it will be cool.

But she is wrong. Dee has played the tape many times. It was almost her first discovery when she returned to Muscle Shoals last night. She knew it as she listened to Richie's ravings from West Cork.

She could have reacted in obvious ways, unworthy of her. A straight confrontation might purge some of her fury at Richie, but that way lay nothing but a bloodbath. Sure, the tape was in her possession, but she didn't want to get hung up on that. There could be more tapes. What matters is what is known, and by how many.

And by that criterion, this is already beyond the control even of Dee Bellingham. For one despairing minute, she thought she'd just go down to the police in Dalkey and shop everyone for offences ranging from possession of drugs to blackmail to murder. But that, too, was unworthy of her. That was just middle class.

She waves Greta a warm goodbye at the gate. When you operate at Dee Bellingham's level, knowing something that the other side doesn't know is not just a good idea. Knowing something that the other side doesn't know is the meaning of life.

Greta notices that, on the stony gravel, Dee is barefoot.

Chapter 20

Kinsale, West Cork

Richie Earls wakes up out of a bad dream. Victor Bartley is sitting on the edge of the bed. Consciousness rushes in to Richie like floodwater. He usually takes a moment after waking up to try and remember his dream, but Victor sitting there jabs him awake.

'Still here?' Richie says quietly.

'Still here.'

Richie slumps back on the pillow, staring at the stars through the glass panelling in the roof. He is naked, though he can't remember taking off his clothes, or climbing up here to the top deck of the lodge.

Victor picks up the duvet from beside the bed, and covers him with it.

'Johnny's gone to collect Greta off the train,' he says. 'Full house tonight.'

Richie keeps staring at the stars as the infinite sadness of his situation engulfs him, the way that they shafted him up at Charles Fort, and sat up drinking with him all night, all bastard night to realise that there's no way around this, that he is that guy who made it, and blew it. That guy he swore could never be him, he is that guy, he. . . is. . . that. . . guy.

And Victor did this crazy dance to 'Iko Iko', Johnny cranking up the Dr John records to the max, stomping, all caught up in this lowdown voodoo.

And the phone call to Dee, mother of God, there's that coming back to him too, the kind of call you need to be banjoed to make, this morning it must have been, and then Johnny gives him some shit to make him sleep, and now here's his new manager sitting on the edge of the bed unbuttoning his white shirt and loosening his pink tie, and slipping off his shoes.

'Mother of God,' Richie whispers.

'Very good idea that,' Victor says, pointing up to the solar-heating panels. 'But it gets a bit close, these nights.'

Richie runs his eye quickly over the man who now manages his affairs, this battered old beast of Irish entertainment, this gargoyle of the showband business, who doubtless has bad, bad stuff in mind for Richie Earls.

'Mother of God,' he says again.

It is ten feet to the edge of the top deck and then another fifteen feet of a drop to the ground floor, easy for Richie to take a run at it and break his neck and end his ruined life.

'I've been sitting here with you for some time,' Victor says. 'Watching you.'

Richie sits up to face Victor. There is a baleful expression in Victor's eyes. The energy and optimism of last night seem to be wilting.

'Do me now,' Richie says. 'Fuck me over the edge.'

Victor sighs, and smiles.

'I was thinking that I sat like this a long time ago, with Paul. Poor lad was being beaten up in school. Wouldn't stir out of the bed. Wouldn't eat. Wouldn't even talk to my wife Sheila. So I went up to try and reason with him and you know what?'

'What?'

'He came to. He said. . . and this is true now. . . he felt that I would look after him.'

'Oh no. . .'

'He came to. . .'

'Fuck me over the edge, Victor. Just. . .'

Victor whips the duvet from Richie.

'Get up,' Victor says.

Richie slides off the bed.

'Now walk over to the edge,' Victor says. 'Go on, walk to the edge.'

'I . . . I need some clothes.'

'Just imagine you're a swimmer, and you're going to jump off the diving board. You don't need clothes.'

Richie walks slowly to the edge of the top deck.

'Now turn around,' Victor says. 'Turn around and face me. Right out on the edge there, like you're going to dive backwards.'

With Victor directing him, Richie backs up slowly until his heels are touching the edge. Then Victor gives a signal to halt.

'Now, I'm telling you about a nice thing that happened to me and Paul, and all you can do is think about yourself. "Fuck me over the edge, Victor, fuck me over the edge, Victor." Put your hands behind your back there.'

Richie puts his hands behind his back. He is aware of the need to stay absolutely still, or else fall backwards. Then Victor walks over to him and stands no more than two feet away, close enough to topple him over with the slightest effort.

'If we are to work together, you must stop this shit,' Victor says.

Richie grunts in agreement, afraid that any words might be the wrong ones, unsure about what shit exactly he must stop.

'I am giving you a chance,' Victor goes on. 'And you're not even listening to me. I am offering you my best shot, my experience, my contacts, my professionalism, you hear me? And all you can say is "Fuck me over the edge, Victor. Fuck me over the edge, Victor," just so you won't have to look at me any more and think of what you've done to me and my family.'

Richie scrunches up his toes to steady himself, fearful that the force of Victor's ranting will blow him over. Victor lowers the volume, to admonish himself.

'But there I am, you see, with the old self-pity. I've got it too, my friend. I've got it bad. I spend most of my life in sorrow, thinking, Where did all my time go, where did it all go? And why the fuck did I not know when life was beautiful? On a summer evening when I was seventeen, in this seaside place, I heard a jukebox for the first time, playing "Save The Last Dance For Me". It was beautiful, and I knew it was beautiful, but I couldn't feel that ecstasy. Not the way I feel it now, the way it enchants me. The way it torments me. Now that it's gone.'

Richie swallows hard. 'I don't want to go over the edge, Victor. Please.'

Victor takes a step back, and then another. Richie moves away from the edge, his body limp with relief. Victor goes back to the bed, and puts his shoes on. He seems weary now, rubbing his temples.

'At last, the man stops bullshitting me,' he says. 'At last the man is sincere with me.'

'Can I put on some clothes?' Victor grabs Richie's jeans and throws them to him.

'Thanks,' Richie says, pulling on his jeans.

Victor walks slowly to the edge and looks down. It's a man's room below, the old sofa against the wall, the big television, a few rugs of no distinction.

186

'Make no mistake, Richie. Every day I want to batter you. Every day I want to burst you. But Paul left me a couple of things. He left me the bit of psychobabble and he left me you, you little bastard. And I'm going to look after you.'

'Right,' Richie says.

Victor reaches out and grabs the pole firmly. He has been practising this, climbing up the ladder and shinning down the pole like a child on his first day at Butlins. He lands perfectly and looks back up at Richie.

'I hope our relationship will settle down into a normal one between manager and client,' he says.

Drumbolus, County Westmeath

Nulty is set up in the powder-blue staircase hall of Drumbolus House, his back to the fireplace, one sombre painted lady of the eighteenth century on either side, his elbows resting on a marble-topped table with carved mahogany legs on which he surmises the Act of Union was signed. The phones are working, a day late, but working now, and he is about to make his first business call. He will ring up *Hot Press* magazine to tell them that a big one is going off at Drumbolus House next midsummer, and off the record, while they're at it, do they know anyone who knows how to put on an open-air festival?

Simon comes out of the Cream Room, where in half-an-hour Richie Earls will sign his name to the contract.

'They're on their way,' he says to Nulty. 'Richie and someone called Johnny. His lawyer, maybe. We're going to do business.'

Simon sticks with his bespoke tailoring for today. He enjoys the sensation of getting dressed up to visit his own house. He is still savouring his freedom from Victor. The words on the answering machine resonate for him like a victorious Churchill speech on the wireless. 'You owe me nothing.' It's over, and life can begin again.

'You know, I don't even like Richie Earls's stuff,' Nulty says. 'I think he sold out.'

Simon laughs, like he's remembering an old joke.

'I don't like his stuff either,' he says. 'I never liked it.'

Nulty is sure that Simon is developing a slight lisp.

Destination: Drumbolus

Leaving Mullingar at the wheel of the Daimler, Johnny Oregon turns up Bob Seger full whack, Bob Seger and the Silver Bullet Band, lovely geezers all. Lovely geezers are all around again for Johnny, the Main Man above is a lovely geezer who sent him back his lady with a super bonus of the baddest rock 'n' roll video on earth.

Greta rides alongside him now, for keeps he is sure, their vibe all the stronger because she gave herself some space to be sure, to be sure. Not since Dee herself has a lady done it for him this way. He is not a million per cent convinced that the same Dee let that video go in all innocence, but at this precise moment, fuck it.

Victor and Richie occupy the back seat. All is quiet between them for most of the journey up. Johnny figures they are due some time out to mull over the change in their respective circumstances. And, hell, as a management deal, it's no more crazy than the Colonel and the King.

The sign says eight miles to Drumbolus, maybe eight kilometres. You get the last of the bad roads here in the midlands.

Victor holds his hand up, a signal to Johnny to turn down Bob Seger.

'Over there,' he says, 'is where I played handball.'

There is indeed a handball alley on the right, overgrown, like the mean fields are claiming it back.

'You'd wonder how a thing like that falls apart,' says Victor. 'Erosion, maybe.'

They pass little boxes of bungalows, neglected, discoloured. Victor waves out at a limping old man opening his front gate. The old man stands back from the Daimler cruising by, and then hobbles off down the road.

'Remember, you can see him but he can't see you,' says Johnny.

Victor is tickled by the smoked windows. It gives him a buzz, the thought of riding though Drumbolus like a top person, and the triumph that is to come at Drumbolus House.

Would he prefer if the locals could see him perched in the back seat of the Daimler? No, it's better that they find out later and say to themselves, 'So that was him. . . the bollocks.'

'This is some fucking hole,' Richie says.

They reach the Old Walled City.

'It's *my* fucking hole,' says Victor.

They are through the village and past Simon's built-up precinct in about thirty seconds, Victor waving at people who don't wave back. He looks intently at Malone's, like there is a prize for spotting some small alteration. He is longing to be there later, longing to be supping to a big future, and longing to be seen to be supping.

Victor directs Johnny down the by-road off the by-road that leads to Drumbolus House.

'I can't sing in the middle of a bastard bog,' Richie says.

'No worries,' Victor says. 'The way I remember it, when we came out here as young fellas, there's a natural amphitheatre out the far side.'

'Like Slane,' Johnny says. 'A natural amphitheatre.'

They are halfway up the avenue to the big house when Victor asks Johnny to stop.

'One more time,' he says. 'You get out first, Johnny, you and Greta. Then you, Richie, you give the paw to Simon, and for Jaysus' sake look friendly about it. And then at last, Victor Bartley steps out to meet his long-lost brother. I wish we had it on video.'

Drumbolus House, County Westmeath

The Daimler draws up outside the front door and Johnny blows the horn. Simon is at the door in seconds. He stand with his arms folded, smiling.

Johnny gets out and salutes him.

'Johnny Oregon, mate,' he says. 'Nice one.'

Greta gets out the door nearest to Simon.

'This is Greta, my good lady,' Johnny says, shaking hands with Simon.

'Greta,' says Simon, giving Greta a peck on the check. Richie gets out the back door at the other side, and offers a watery smile.

'The one and only,' Johnny says.

Richie gives Simon a quick thumbs-up.

'Good to see you again, Richie,' Simon says.

Nulty appears behind Simon.

'This is Nulty,' Simon says. 'My depitee.'

Nulty gives a little wave.

'Nice one,' Johnny says. 'We've got another party to the proceedings.'

'Right,' says Simon.

Johnny looks to Richie for the next word, but Richie's head is bowed.

'It's actually Richie's new manager,' Johnny says.

'New manager?' Simon says.

'Don't worry about it, mate. The gig is still rock solid.'

Johnny opens the near door of the Daimler. Victor is sitting there, smiling like a bold boy. Simon looks to the other faces for assistance.

'This is. . . Victor,' he says.

Victor climbs out of the Daimler. Simon takes a quick step backwards, and looks to Nulty for an explanation, like there is some macabre joke going on here that he doesn't get. Nulty shakes his head.

'I look forward to working with you,' Victor says. And he bows. 'Lord Drumbolus.'

'Dee . . .' Simon stutters to Richie, 'Dee is your manager.'

'I sacked her,' says Richie.

'But Victor . . .' Simon can say no more.

'You think I can bring something to the party?' Victor says.

'I thought. . . you left a message. . .' Simon moans.

'Right. We're quits.'

'This is a new vibe,' Johnny says.

'You are managing Richie Earls?' Simon says.

'I am managing Richie Earls,' Victor says. 'And if you don't bring us in out of here I'm pulling the gig.'

Simon laughs weakly, and leads the party into the Cream Room. He opts for the couch to the left of the fireplace, and Victor takes the couch directly opposite him, a scene vaguely resembling the set-up when world leaders chat for the cameras. There is a copy of the contract on the coffee-table between them.

Johnny and Greta fall into the sofa, touching and squeezing and stroking. Most couples would think this rude, but Johnny and Greta have the knack of canoodling while rock 'n' roll business is being done without in any way harming the atmospherics. You either have it or you don't have it, this ability to please their rocking majesties just by your way of being in the world, your presence at high negotiations a sign of your loyalty, and how cool it is that the top guy can command such loyalty.

The top guy elects to stay on his feet, aloof, prowling on the outskirts of the meeting, all fucked up because somehow, astonishingly, he contrived to lose Johnny's loyalty, though admittedly it took a spot of killing and a pig-ugly sacking and maybe even musical differences. And it took Victor, sitting there now at the top table murmuring about a dream come true.

Nulty pours brandy from a decanter into six balloon glasses, and leaves them on the coffee-table for anyone who wants them. He takes one himself, and hands a glass to Victor.

'Nice to see you again, Nulty,' Victor says. 'I kept my promise.'

'Looking well, Victor,' Nulty says. He laughs nervously, not knowing quite how he should be reacting to Simon's mortification, except to stand there looking giddy and sipping strong drink that doesn't agree with him.

'What promise?' Simon enquires.

'I promised Nulty that I'd be down,' Victor says.

'But. . . not like this,' Nulty says.

'It's nothing really, Simon,' Victor says. 'Just a chat we had at the funeral.'

'I'm just. . . stunned,' says Simon.

This is unmistakeably honest, and it gets them away from the topic of funerals.

'Don't think I don't know that Simon. Don't think I don't understand,' Victor says. 'You're expecting to do business with Her Royal Highness Madame Dee Bellingham, and muggins here shows up instead. Ah, the look on your face. Priceless.'

Victor takes a sip of brandy, chuckling to himself at the all-round pricelessness of it.

Johnny takes a glass and hands it back to Richie.

'This is mad,' says Simon, looking at Richie for some assistance.

Richie sniffs his brandy, and continues to prowl.

'It's a dream come true,' Victor says. 'I know what they mean now, when they say it's a dream come true.'

'I suppose, congratulations . . .' Simon says.

'All this . . .,' says Victor, looking up at the ceiling in awe. 'All this. . .'

'It's beautiful,' says Simon.

'Remember we came out here when we were young fellas,' Victor says, 'progging apples?'

'I do.'

'Mattie used to run us. Remember oul' Mattie, Simon?'

'He's still alive.'

'He was old then.'

'You were getting me in trouble from day one, Victor.'

'And then the German bought it,' Victor says.

'Nice man. Had to give it up in the end.'

'It's very relaxing here.' Victor is impressed. 'Lovely big armchairs.'

'He found it hard getting up the stairs in the end. The German.'

'He let it go a bit?'

'Victor, are we on *Candid Camera*?'

Victor sighs. He scratches his left arm, itchy with the healing process.

'I'm looking at property myself of course,' he says. 'But this is. . .'

'And you're representing Richie, like, all over the world?'

'It was Paul that brought us together, believe it or not. Richie said some harsh words about Paul which I took to be

193

unprofessional. Harsh words indeed. So we had a meeting about it, a very, very good meeting as it turned out, and we found there was more keeping us together than driving us apart. That's what we found.'

Simon looks to Richie for clarification.

'I forgot something,' Richie says. 'I forgot to say, Victor, about Sellafield.'

'What about it, Richie?'

'Well, Victor, I want Simon here to make a donation to my campaign against Sellafield.'

'Very good, very good,' Victor says. 'Why?'

'Because it's there,' Richie says. 'Because it's there.'

'I have a better idea,' Victor says. 'Let's start small. Since we're talking about how Paul brought us two together, how about it, Simon, if we take the few shillings you sent up to me by motorcycle messenger, and put it towards a headstone for Paul?'

'Of course,' Simon says.

'You couldn't make it to the funeral,' Victor says. 'But then, I couldn't make it to Cannon's funeral. What's that they say? Shit happens.'

Richie turns away. Victor keeps talking.

'Out of bad things, good things can come,' he says. 'I had the pleasure of meeting Nulty here when Simon couldn't make it. And I met Johnny again, after many years. And his good lady Greta of course. And last but not least, I met Mr Richie Earls. And we are very much an item.'

Simon addresses Richie again.

'So, Richie Earls ends up dealing with a couple of old showband heads,' he says.

Richie makes no response.

'To tell the truth, I see no great difference between me and Dee Bellingham,' says Victor, 'except that I am lacking in the total hypocrisy of her and the whole rock crowd. And

without blowing my own horn here, Victor Bartley knows
his music, and loves his music. All sorts, and top drawer
stuff too. Top drawer. Not the kind of shite that Dee
Bellingham was putting in front of my man here, just for
filthy lucre. Richie Earls is a quality vocalist, and he will do
only quality material from now on. Isn't that right, Richie?'

'Will you sign the deal now, Victor, so we can get down
to the fucking pub?' Richie says. Then he swallows his
brandy and hands the glass back to Nulty with a grimace of
approval.

'You read my mind,' Victor says. 'Now, on the subject of
price, I'd like to confer with the artiste for one minute if I
may.'

'I'll do it for a million,' says Richie. 'End of story.'

'Ah, humour me,' Victor says. 'Till I get the hang of it,
humour me. Step out into the hall with me, Richie, and we'll
make up a few mad riders for this unfortunate man. Jelly
beans, or something, to be provided for the artiste, in forty-
seven different colours. Come on.'

Victor ushers Richie out the door in a welter of
bonhomie, and when they are outside in the powder-blue
staircase hall, he takes *Richie Earls Unplugged* out of his
inside breast pocket.

'You see this?' he says, holding the video under Richie's
nose. 'If you don't take that fucking puss off you,
immediately, I will ram this up your arsehole. Do you hear
me?'

'Yeah,' Richie says, sullen.

'Take that puss off you,' Victor says.

'What the fuck do you expect? What the fuck?'

'OK. . . OK . . . You know what? I respect that, as a
professional. I respect that you're pissed off about your
career, and where you think it's going. You're headstrong.
And that's how the artiste should be. The artiste should

195

know his own mind. But let me tell you, kid, your career is going only one way. It's going places you wouldn't believe, with Victor Bartley. You know what I'm going to have you doing?'

Richie shakes his head.

'I'm going to have you doing the stuff you did when you were good.'

Richie laughs. Victor grabs him by the lapels.

'Listen to me, you little bastard. I'm going to make you respect Victor Bartley. I'm going to make you see that Victor Bartley knows this business. I can make you good again and sell twice as many records. I can.'

'You mean. . .'

'Southern Soul. Isn't that the stuff you like? Am I right. . .?'

'Well, yeah.'

'Numbers like "Do Right Woman, Do Right Man" and "The Dark End of the Street" I looked it up. I know about these things. Am I getting warm?'

'Twenty people bought my records back then. Fuck's sake.'

'How do you feel about "Gypsy Woman" by Don Williams?'

'What do I feel about it?'

'Would you do it?'

'I don't know. . .'

'You'll do it.'

'It's country-and-western.'

'It's good, though.'

'It's not bad.'

'I'd like you to do it.'

'I could give it a go. End of career, but I could give it a go.'

'Try it later, in the pub.'

'In the pub. Right.'

'You don't want trying it either with this tape up your arsehole.'

Victor pushes Richie back towards the Cream Room. Richie enters the room laughing.

'Musical differences,' he says.

Victor puts an arm around Richie's shoulder. 'Music is my life,' he says.

Simon takes out a Parker pen. 'A million you say?'

'A nice round million,' Victor says. 'Seeing as we know you.'

Simon hesitates for a moment, and then hands the pen to Victor.

'You'll be dealing mostly with Nulty here,' he says. 'I haven't a clue how to do business with you, Victor. I never did.'

'I know you got a terrible fright, Simon,' Victor says. 'But this is one of the happiest days of my life.'

They sign the papers quickly.

'Jesus Christ Almighty,' Simon mutters. 'Come on. We'll walk the land.'

Drumbolus, County Westmeath

The Daimler stops outside the house of Cannon in the Old Walled City. When Johnny switches off the headlights, it's like there's a power cut on the main street of Drumbolus.

There is something to be done before Victor can have his night in Malone's. He must call on Mrs Cannon, and pay his dues. Nulty and Richie and Greta, well-walked and well-watered after their tour of Drumbolus House and grounds, get out of the car and go on to Malone's, leaving Victor and Johnny to call on the widow, whose first name Victor can't recall.

'Don't even try it mate,' Johnny says. 'No guessing.'

'I'm ninety per cent sure it's something like Shirley,' says Victor. 'Or maybe Sylvia,' he adds.

'No name is better than the wrong name,' Johnny says.

Victor is stalling too, at the thought of women weeping. This is the image that fills his head, Shirley or Sylvia or whoever is on the other side of that door, weeping. On a day like today, when he's winning and winning big, Victor feels entitled to some respite. He figures he is probably entitled to a painless ride for the rest of his days, if you add it all up.

But he must do right by Cannon too, or he won't feel right, he won't feel free. Cannon always had time for Victor Bartley, all through the dark days, Cannon being enough of a musician himself to know that Victor had a point about the showband scene going nowhere, that it wasn't just pure vanity on Victor's part. Although to tell the truth, there was vanity in it, and Victor knows there still is vanity in his high-class musical tastes. Victor tells himself that maybe, just maybe, that bit of pure vanity is exactly what Cannon was missing, what they were all missing back then in Ireland of the eight hundred showbands, just that ounce of vanity or plain confidence that would have enabled them to write their own stuff, just a couple of songs that might have lasted, just one song.

They are starting to die off now, mourning one another with the songs of other men, songs that are playing in Victor's head as he tries to get it up to press the flesh of Cannon's widow, songs like 'Eve of Destruction', 'Young Girl' by Gary Puckett and the Union Gap, and 'Galveston', the songs of other men who didn't refuse the challenge. Victor is not the better of this, this final wrench before he is free, and the pain leaves him for all time. With one last brutal kick, the music in his head reminds him of what a freak he must have seemed back then, like some experiment that went wrong and landed him with the mind of a sophisticate in the body of a bogman, with only kind souls like Cannon who seemed to understand.

Cannon was kind to Paul too, let it be said. And now the two of them are gone, within days of each other, and there's nothing Victor with all his new-found clout can do about it, except to recall that gypsy woman, to cling to some Don Williams song that was better than it needed to be. What he can do is look after himself. Did Paul not say that you have to be selfish if you want to get well? Victor takes an envelope from his inside pocket and hands it to Johnny.

'This is brutal Johnny,' he says. 'I can't do it.'

'No problem,' Johnny says.

'It's like I'm refusing at the last fence,' Victor says.

'Cheque?'

'Twenty grand.'

'Generous.'

'I want you to say that it's. . . it's nothing.'

'Don't worry about it, mate.'

'There'll be women weeping in there. I can't do that any more.'

'Don't worry about it.'

Johnny gets out of the Daimler and comes around to Victor's side to open the door for him. It's as if Victor has made some irrevocable step into the big-time, delegating such a sensitive duty to Johnny, refusing to let this guaranteed downer spoil his enjoyment of a million-pound deal well done.

Victor dallies at the door of Malone's, watching Johnny Oregon disappearing into Cannon's house, his thoughts with Johnny of course, drifting towards an evening of controlled but quality drinking, a little intoxicated already by the waft of beer from the lounge.

He takes a deep breath. 'Home,' he says.

*

'The thing that has always stood in my way,' says Victor, 'is that I know the difference between a good record and a bad record. No-one who knows the difference between a good record and a bad record ever got anywhere in this country.'

He is sharing his wisdom with Nulty in Malone's, over a continuous but controlled succession of rum-and-blacks and snipes of red wine.

'I can prove it,' says Victor. 'You, Nulty, are a man who knows the difference between a good record and a bad record. Have you ever got anywhere? Not until now, you haven't. And not through the usual channels.'

Nulty is listening carefully, feeling that Victor is not wrong on these matters, but afraid at all times that Victor will break off from his monologue and throw some sort of fit.

'I knew the difference, even though I did nothing about it for years. In fact, I did the opposite, and put a lot of shite out there. But I knew the difference, and I still know the difference, and now my hour has come. Hasn't it, Richie?'

Richie Earls nods in absent-minded agreement, which Victor sees as some improvement from the afternoon's surliness. He won't be persuaded to get up and sing 'Gypsy Woman' in Malone's after all, but he has taken that puss off him as requested, and this is something.

Victor could probably push it, and force Richie to perform the song to the jaw-dropping and everlasting awe of the locals, but most of all he wants no unpleasantness here in Malone's, flush from his million-pound deal, a top man again fending off the clumsy attentions of about a dozen of Simon's regulars with suitable grace.

'I mean, tribute must be paid,' says Victor. 'Tribute must be paid to the good. Tell me, Nulty, do you know who John Raitt is?'

'No,' Nulty says.

'Well, John Raitt is Bonnie Raitt's father. You know Bonnie Raitt?'

'Sure,' Nulty says.

'John Raitt was a big Broadway star, very handsome man, appeared in the first production of *Oklahoma!* Not your cup of tea I know or even my cup of tea, but good, good stuff, you know?'

'Don't know the man,' Nulty says.

'Here is a man who has done good, good stuff, and very, very, very few people know about it any more. He's still alive, you know. Like oul' Mattie. He's still out there maybe wondering if it was worth his while. Tribute must be paid. These things must be known, and it all must be added up. Because otherwise, no-one knows a fucking thing. Tribute must be paid, but it is not paid, because the world is run by men who don't know the difference and don't care. It's not run by me, and it's not run by you, Nulty.'

'The tide is turning, Victor,' Nulty says.

'We can do good, my friend. If Richie here takes my advice, he'll have a set of songs ready for next summer that will put every other fucker to the sword. I mean, seven Grammies for Mr Carlos Santana? Was it seven or eight or nine he got? There's nothing left out there, pal. The business is sucking on its own prick.'

It is clear to Nulty that Richie Earls is not exactly ablaze with enthusiasm for the new regime. Victor is outlining other parts of his strategy, ideas about Richie being himself, telling it like it is, and cutting the crap, which receive an equally tepid reaction from the star. Nulty can see the merit in Victor's diatribe, as it confirms his own views about Richie Earls. Basically, that he's a whore, but a very talented whore, and therefore the saddest type. In each half-assed Joe Cocker-style stomp, each Simply Red-type power ballad, you can imagine what might have been, way down beneath that plastic soul surface.

Nulty is feeling queasy, though, about his own purpose here, and Simon's instructions for the evening, to check the vibes between Richie Earls and Victor Bartley. He has some information from the afternoon that he is not authorised to share with Victor.

When they finish walking the land and marvelling at the natural amphitheatre, Simon goes off and calls Dee Bellingham. She is hysterical, and she tells him she doesn't feel safe around these people any more, and could she please, please pop down to Drumbolus maybe next week just to chill?

Victor's eyes are dancing now, as he grabs Nulty by the arm.

'Will I tell Richie here about the taxman?' he says.

Nulty is lost for a moment, and then he remembers the story that Victor told in the airport hotel.

'I think you should,' Nulty says.

Chapter 21

Drumbolus House, County Westmeath

Dee Bellingham gets the chopper down to Westmeath the next afternoon. The ugliness is getting to her, stuff she doesn't want to know about, bad feelings that were there from the start. She can't just hang around Muscle Shoals drinking Bloody Marys or she might never stop. She fancies a spell in the country. She fancies staying in the loop. Drumbolus House has a bit of history for her, but she can handle it.

Her performance for Simon on the phone seems a bit boisterous now, but necessarily so. He's only ever seen her cool. People need to know that Dee Bellingham has been hurt by this, that she bleeds like anyone else.

It is a cloudless afternoon. She can see the city below her, becoming the countryside, but not like it used to be. The cranes and the diggers are at it in rural Ireland too, the motorways are turning all Ireland into one huge Dublin.

Straight up, she feels as disconnected from Paul Bartley and his grisly fate as she would be from some farmer in the fields of County Meath below. Sorry that it would happen to anyone, but nothing special. This is where she is different from the Irish, she reckons, who tend to grieve big for people that they barely know, famous people who have to snuff it before all this love comes down. Some might say she's a hard bitch, but she feels what she feels, and she doesn't pretend to feel what she doesn't feel, and she's staying that way.

Dee Bellingham doesn't go hanging people either for their moments of madness. She's hip enough to her Aleister Crowley to know the difference between a monumental cock-up and the mark of Evil. So she is appalled by Richie's foolishness, but her instinct is to get cracking and manage the problem and sort it out, rather than tut-tutting to no purpose. The high moral ground is for arseholes. And you get nothing done there. You get too excited to make good decisions, like letting that Dutch chick walk away with the tape, making the other side relax a tad, making them vulnerable.

The events in themselves are just events, and no serious person would be too judgemental. What is really bugging her, what is strafing her, is the hatred in Richie's voice on the phone, hatred for her and for all like her, hatred that was far beyond any anger he might feel for her handling of the Victor Bartley problem, a vein of pure contempt that he had always had for her, and that he couldn't help unleashing when it looked like the end for them.

What was he on? He must be suffering down there in Kinsale. But in his grief he couldn't find it in himself to send some signal to her, something in his voice that said he needed her. He was too screwed up to suss that, to realise that he would never get out of this shit without her, no way, never. She can hear instead the pent-up loathing, she can hear it now, as Titus guides the chopper towards Westmeath, she can hear all the pretence disappearing, all that shit about the Anglo-Irish being no mean people, all that cancelled in the final spasm.

What was he on? Christ, she has loved Irish men and she

probably still loves Richie if she tries hard enough. She even supports Sinn Féin and the Peace Process, knowing as she knows now that nothing can kill this hatred, nothing. That on the last day they'll shove it in your face, no matter what you've been through together. This hatred alone can make her cry all night into her Bloody Mary. The way the Irish turn into beasts. Only this can make her doubt that she has the gumption to soldier on.

But Yeats was right. They are no mean people, the Bellinghams and the few aristos who are left. And Dee Bellingham will demonstrate that she can still cut the mustard, that you can burn her house, steal her car, drink her liquor from an old fruit jar, but you can't just treat her like some fuck-off, in any circumstances.

The chopper touches down unannounced on the front lawn of Drumbolus House. Nulty comes out to see Dee waving to the pilot as he takes off again.

'Dee Bellingham,' she says.

She pumps Nulty's hand with surprising jolliness for a woman who told Simon yesterday she was up the walls. She carries a backpack, like she is a hitchhiker who happened to get picked up by a helicopter. Dee surveys the front of the old mansion.

'This is wonderful,' she says. 'I spent some time here, as a little girl.'

Nulty remembers that he is a man.

'I'll take the backpack,' he says.

'I'll make it to the door,' she says. 'It's just some old rubbish.'

'I'll call Simon,' he says.

Dee drops her load in the hall and Nulty goes to his Act of Union desk to ring Simon. She is wearing an old blue Aran jumper and jeans, like she needs to dress down to give everyone else a chance.

Nulty picks up the receiver.

'He's at the golf club,' he says. 'Just down the road.'

'Let him play his golf for goodness' sake,' Dee says. 'It's awfully rude of me to barge in like this. Let him play his golf.'

Nulty puts down the receiver. 'Simon thought. . . next week?'

'Oh God, I was so wasted yesterday. I thought I left it vague.'

'I meant to get some coffee organised for here,' Nulty says. 'We've got brandy.'

'That's sweet of you. Thank you.'

Nulty opens the door of the Cream Room for Dee.

'My mother knew the Clonmellons,' Dee says.

'Simon is. . . eh. . . doing the place up.'

'I said to Simon not to go to any trouble, I'd love to curl up in an old sleeping bag. Maybe hit the road and spend some time in Doolin. I so need to get around Ireland again.'

The decanter is still on the table from yesterday's signing ceremony. Nulty takes two fresh balloon glasses from the cabinet. He pours two glasses and hands one to Dee. Dee takes the glass from him and smiles.

'You're an absolute angel,' she says.

'This is it, really,' he says, 'this room and the hall.'

Any bigshot can intimidate Nulty at first, like it's their world and he just lives in it. But there's something else again going on with this one, something else again.

'God, I remember this room,' she says. 'You know, it's the brandy that's bringing it back. My mother and Philippa Clonmellon sat in here drinking the hard stuff and my brother and I would run in and out getting this wonderful smell of booze.'

'I'm Nulty, by the way,' he says.

'Cheers, Nulty.'

206

'Just Nulty.'

'You're an absolute angel, Nulty. I mean that.'

'It got a bit mad here yesterday. Victor and all.'

'Would you believe, I feel free of the whole bloody racket? I woke up this morning and I thought, hello, no calls to make, no faxes to send, no record company arseholes to keep sweet, no lunch to do, no security to check out. . . You know, the first daft thing they did was to sack the bodyguards? I mean, Titus was a mate.'

'Daft.'

'But the real reason I feel free of it is the old nosening. I just can't be around coke-heads any more. Next please!'

'Simon's not the better of it.'

'Simon's a nice man. How's he coping?'

'He's left me in charge.'

'He had a dream. I hope it works out for him.'

'He'll smash a golf ball around for a few weeks.'

'I know he's got issues around his brother.'

'He was looking forward to working with you.'

'I've become a big fan of Simon's you know. He's got a thing called integrity.'

Nulty laughs. 'Right,' he says.

Dee doesn't join his laughter.

'I think it's so exciting to have the Simon Bartleys on board,' she says. 'I remember when a lot of Irish promoters wouldn't touch rock 'n' roll. The devils' music, you know. Then U2 and the Cranberries and Richie Earls and it's, like, hello, the Irish are coming, and they're coming with a thing called integrity.'

'You know them well,' Nulty says.

'You'll be wonderful, Nulty. I mean that.'

'It's about confidence, I guess. A hard thing to come by.'

'You've got it,' she says. 'You've got the courage of your convictions. You old communist, you.'

Dee has clocked the tiny hammer-and-sickle badge which Nulty attached to his jacket one mad night in the Phoenix bar in Cork six years ago.

'I forgot about this,' he says.

'You're a communist?'

'A socialist, anyway,' Nulty says.

'Likewise.'

'You're a socialist?'

'Absolutely,' Dee says.

'I'm kind of. . . retired.'

'Absolute nonsense, Nulty. You've got this marvellous opportunity now, to do things decently. That's what socialism is all about, doing things decently and standing on your principles, and I know it's not fashionable, but Richie and I have always insisted that there's a world outside of rock 'n' roll, and rock 'n' roll must speak to that world or it's just. . . garbage.'

'I suppose I'm out of practice.' Nulty wants to say that what he is trying to organise, a full-blown open-air mega-gig, is like some ugly throwback to feudalism, with all these categories of people branded according to their importance, from the golden people who will make it to the inside of Drumbolus House, to the liggers who are only important enough to drink champagne in the grounds, and all the way down to the scum with no laminates of any description who comprise most of the paying punters, and who, by the most sublime illusion of the age, are inclined to view this as the natural pecking order, and even the liberating spirit of rock 'n' roll incarnate.

Nulty wants to say, socialism my arse. He wants to tell her that these gigs are cast-iron proof that you can actually fool all the people, all the time. But more than this, he wants to please Dee Bellingham.

'You'll be stonkingly good,' she says. 'And don't for a

minute think I'm going to raise a finger to help you.'

Nulty is thinking that this woman is a magician. Simon has been giving him pep-talks that don't register at all with him, whereas Dee Bellingham can waltz in and stroke him with a compliment and make him feel like a god.

'I won't let you down,' he says.

'Simon and you . . . you're not . . .?'

'Jesus, no.'

'I'm quite old-fashioned about these things,' Dee says. 'If a man like Simon isn't married, I tend to assume. . .'

'He just likes his independence, I guess.'

'It's a wonderful way to be,' Dee says.

'Free as a bird.'

'I'd like to get back there.'

'Me and Simon, we're just two lonely people. Really.'

Dee puts her brandy down and walks over to the window. Looking out at the gardens she folds her arms, and Nulty is touched to see that there is a hole in the elbow of her Aran jumper. She's bringing out his compassion too.

'I suppose it's just typical of someone like me to say something like that,' she says. 'Something flamboyant. Is that what you think?'

'Maybe just a bit,' he says.

'It's a bitch, you know? I came here before when everything fell apart,' she says. 'My mother was leaving my father and she brought us down here. It got horrible. We spent about six months moving from one bloody castle to the next bloody country house, because the only people we knew were the gentry, as Richie calls us. I love Richie deeply but he could never see people like me as people. Not completely. There was always something about us that he loathed. And there we were, just a bunch of fuck-ups. Flamboyant fuck-ups.'

Nulty brings Dee her brandy.

'No thanks,' she says. 'On top of it all I've become a functioning alcoholic.'

Nulty thinks he would know if someone was milking his compassion with bullshit or with the real thing. As they stand there at the window he figures he can say something sincere, like he sees people like her as people, like he understands. Except he can't do it, because he just can't.

'Let's go to the pub, then,' he says.

Dee laughs.

'I mean, it's getting dark in here,' says Nulty.

'That's an excellent reason for going to the pub,' Dee says. 'I must remember that one.'

'Actually, I play records down there. I can set it up tonight.'

'No, I want you to talk to me tonight.'

'If you don't want to drink. . .' he says.

'I do want to drink. I'd like to have a drink with you.'

They leave the room in darkness, all those soft tones suddenly turned to gloom. Walking quickly down the avenue of Drumbolus House, Dee returns to her Simon riff.

'I feel so sorry for him,' she says. 'I reckon his heart is broken.'

'Simon's heart is fine.'

'Believe me, Nulty. You broke his heart the first time he clapped eyes on you. I'm right about this. I'm always right about these things.'

'I can't see it.'

'Do you notice anything in the way he looks at you?'

'The guy just likes his independence.'

Do you know how pretty you are? she thinks. But she doesn't say it.

They pause for a moment and then march on. Nulty is enjoying the badinage now; it is Dee who is watching what she says in case she says too much or says it all wrong. It is

Dee who is wondering if this exquisite creature has landed in her life just to mock her, to open her up for another knifing.

'Let's get down to the pub and get him on the mobile and ask him straight out,' she says. 'Ask him if he wants to . . .'

'To what?'

'To fuck you, I suppose.'

'A bit flamboyant there,' he says.

'Sorry.'

'He's my landlord, for Jaysus' sake. Your landlord can't very well fuck you, can he?'

'They can do anything now, Nulty.'

Dee imagines that at this taunt he lunges and she wriggles free, running down the white line of the road with Nulty in pursuit. She reckons she could keep ahead of him all the way into the village, but she prefers to be caught by him, like in a movie, and wrestled to the ground by him, like in a movie, and she is desperate to tell him how beautiful he is, but she can't do it. They are face to face, she underneath him, both breathless, and she can't say that when she was talking about Simon, she was talking about herself.

On this woebegone stretch of road, the moment passes, and she keeps her secret. This is what she imagines. But Nulty does not react in that way. Something went wrong with his life, robbing him of spontaneity.

They walk on, the Old Walled City coming into view like a line of three-legged old dogs waiting patiently to be put to sleep, past a sign advertising Malone's.

'Best drinks,' says Dee, quoting the sign.

She imagines that later, when the drink is flowing, she will tell Nulty. She will tell him that of course Simon is not after him. She was talking about herself.

'I was talking about myself,' she imagines she will say. But she can't say it now and she will not say it later.

A red Mercedes convertible lights up the way, forcing them into single file. The guy driving looks about twenty years old, the girl in the passenger seat the same. They look straight ahead, inscrutable. It is Friday night.

Chapter 22

Kinsale, West Cork

Even if there was no professional dimension to it, or nothing emotional going on, the sheer amount of physical movement which Victor Bartley has done in the last fortnight is all new to him, a big deal for a man who didn't move much out of his little armchair in front of the telly since *Live Aid*. He lies on the sofa this Saturday morning, his temporary bed on the ground floor of the lodge, calculating that the funeral was less than two weeks ago, and in that time he has been out to The Jester and back, out again in that direction, only unconscious this time, then down here to Kinsale, with a brief stop for re-fuelling in Monkstown, and up to Drumbolus, a journey which he had been planning in his mind's eye for years, never daring to imagine that it could be such a success. That *he* could be such a success again. And back down to Kinsale last night after an evening of controlled drinking in Malone's.

Yes, he's keeping a lid on that aspect, like Paul would want him to. And the journey back down last night is something he will remember fondly all his days, Greta playing great sounds, Greta the lady who saved his life, the genuine rock chick who whipped the video from under the nose of Dee Bellingham. And Johnny driving, driving through the night the way that Victor loves it, and him perched on the back seat with Simon's million-pound contract in his breast pocket, and his new client Richie Earls snoozing there beside him.

'Tired but happy,' he says to himself. 'Tired but happy.'

He still has a special treat set aside, a promise to himself that he is about to keep this morning, a secret delight to savour. His body may be nearing exhaustion, he will need a little time to get himself right for the big-time again, but there is exhilaration in it too, and there will be time, there will be luxuries now that he thought would never be his, after blowing so many shots at the title, after all that terrible waste. This is a sweet morning for what he is about to do.

Richie is asleep on the top deck. Johnny and Greta snuck off early this morning for a few days in Antibes. Johnny will have the tape with him, he'll be over there in the South of France, because apart from being the South of France, most likely it doesn't have Dee Bellingham in it.

It feels like the right time now. Neatly folded next to Simon's contract in his breast pocket is a cutting from Thursday's *Irish Times*. The jacket is on a hanger at the other end of the sofa, near enough for Victor to reach without getting up out of bed. It is a cutting from the property supplement. Victor knows it nearly off by heart at this stage, but he scans it again for pleasure, like a football fan who can't help looking at the league table again and again, to confirm that his team have risen to the top:

This impressive two-storey house on Kilbrittan Hill stands on two acres of ground that include an orchard and a coach-house, which could be converted into a separate dwelling. It is surrounded by beautifully-kept gardens that enjoy a magnificent view of the Bay. Inside, this is a fine period house with five bedrooms and gracious reception rooms. The double drawing room to the left of the hall is a good space for entertaining and it has a Bossi fireplace. On the other side of the hallway is a large, formal dining-room and beyond that is a conservatory. At the back is the kitchen, opening into a breakfast room, where there is a staircase leading up to a family room.

Upstairs, all the bedrooms are spacious doubles with big sash windows taking in views of the garden or the sea. The main bedroom has a large en suite bathroom.

The garden backs on to a laneway leading down to the DART station.

There are photos of the house and the view, and the guide price is three million pounds.

Victor is interested. He can't quite make out if he is interested in actually living in the house, up there on the Hill with all the greats, or if he is just immensely chuffed that he can afford it now. When Richie comes down from his slumbers, Victor hopes to hammer out the business end of it. But it's fair to assume that when your client is picking up a million for a day's work, you can look at houses like this, and seriously think of warming your arse in front of the Bossi fireplace on the long nights after Samhain.

Two weeks now since he buried Paul, less than two weeks, more like ten days. And Cannon gone too, in sympathy it seems. And Victor's looking at property.

He reads the cutting again, without guilt. So something good has come out of something terrible. Is this not what Paul wanted for him, did he not devote himself to getting the old boy started again, and wouldn't Victor have to be one miserable shite to do a Matt Talbot on it, mortifying himself?

Victor thinks he'll have that cup of tea now. He drags himself off the sofa chuckling. He recalls this screenwriter telling him once that in screenwriting, you never, ever, ever

215

have someone say that they'll have that cup of tea now. Not if you can help it. And there was some other line this guy hated, what was it now?

Victor puts the cutting aside and pulls on a pair of Calvin Klein boxer shorts that Johnny appears to have left out for him, like a jockey's valet. He steps into his pin-striped trousers and buttons his white shirt, and shuffles over to the galley, preoccupied by these stray lines from long ago.

He makes a pot of tea thinking about his favourite Matt Talbot story, how Matt loved tea, and how he would come home from a hard day's work in the docks every day and make himself a big pot of tea, and then mortify himself by letting it go cold.

Victor needs to remember the other line that the screenwriter never used. It seems very important now, to be able to remember something like that, from the fat years. They were in the Marine Hotel in Dún Laoghaire, he remembers, drinking pints all day, and the screenwriter, a top Hollywood guy, was telling Victor the tricks of the trade. It seems so important now to remember this line, to remember the laughter, to draw on that good feeling, to recall that Victor Bartley was happy and successful once, and he will be happy and successful again, maybe more mature now for his terrible experiences, his mind as agile as the day he shot the breeze with a top screenwriter, before they put him away and put a plate in his head.

Victor sits at the table sipping his tea, trying to remember. There's an invitation card on the table, sticking out of its envelope. Johnny seems to have opened the mail, and left this one out so that Richie would get it. Richie or his new manager, perhaps?

It's a plain invitation, but the event is not plain. It's a barn dance at Baltrudder House in Wicklow, to celebrate the fiftieth birthday of the film producer Martin Mann.

The old butterflies. Victor is excited just to be holding this card in his hand. In the ten years since Mann moved to Wicklow, his home has been the first sight of Ireland for numerous A-list celebrities, a safe house for the rich and talented passing through, pausing for an Irish idyll and maybe even a night of the *craic* with The Chieftains.

In Victor's mind, off the top of his head, he can see U2 and the Corrs and Van the Man and Brian Kennedy and Ronan Keating and Ron Wood, of course, and maybe even Jagger and John Hurt and a rake of supermodels, Naomi herself for Jaysus' sake, and maybe David Bowie and Iman and Liam Neeson and your one Richardson and John Boorman and Damon Hill and Eddie Irvine and Chris Evans, who loves it here, and you can't rule out the likes of Jack Nicholson, and Julia Roberts might be knocking around, and Salman Rushdie.

And Richie Earls. And Victor Bartley. Can he see himself there? Well, somewhere on the edge of that mirage, he's beginning to see himself maybe chatting with the caterers.

'Richie, you fucker, get down here!' he shouts.

After about three minutes of moaning and sighing and coughing, Richie shins down the pole. To Victor he looks dog rough but still somehow bristling with a raw energy, the restless demon within that makes this bad-humoured bollocks a star.

Victor pours Richie a mug of tea and slides the invitation in front of him. Victor flashes that bold boy smile that Richie is starting to dread. Richie manages a weak grin.

'No way,' he says.

'Could I hear your objections?'

'Couldn't be arsed. This is Dee's crowd.'

'We're going.'

'Please. . .'

'It's the barn dance bit that caught my eye.'

217

'Please, please. . .'

'Sounds like they'll have a country band. Sounds like a certain Richie Earls might get up and do an impromptu rendition of a certain Don Williams number.'

'Oh shit. . .'

'Run it by a discerning audience.'

'Look, what is this "Gypsy Woman" shit? The record company will just tell us to shove it. End of story.'

'Then we'll start our own record company. It's a thing I can't understand in an artiste like you Richie. You can afford to do anything you like, anything at all. And you stay tied to some pox-bottle record company. It's most disappointing.'

'What if "Gypsy Woman" isn't right for me?'

'It's right for you.'

'It sounds too low for me.'

'Nonsense. Paul was able to sing it before his voice broke.'

'Paul. . .'

'It was the first song he ever learned. Cannon taught him.'

'I didn't know. . . I didn't know he sang.'

'He had a lovely voice before it broke.'

'Look, if it's a tribute or whatever, there's no problem.'

Victor slams his fist down on the table. The two mugs roll over, spilling pools of hot tea. Victor tries to snatch the invitation before it gets flooded, but it's too late. He stands back from the table to avoid the tea dripping over the edge. Richie does likewise.

'It is not a tribute,' Victor says as calmly as he can. 'This is a professional decision on my part based on sound musical judgement.'

Richie braces himself for another explosion. 'Do I have any say?' he says.

'Of course.'

'Straight up, I know people are laughing at me already. Dee probably has all these fuckers gossiping. Fuckers who'll be at this party, they'll be thinking Richie Earls is gone mad. And if they see me doing a country song, they'll know I've gone mad.'

Victor considers this as though there's some sense in it.

'Dee might be at this, of course,' he says. 'It might be awkward.'

'Look, Victor, I don't mean to be smart here, but could I say something?'

'Sure thing.'

'You won't go apeshit?'

'Fire away.'

'You've been out of the business for a long time now, Victor. They're a different type these days, the type who'll be at this party. If they get landed with someone that isn't right, it can get a bit frosty.'

'Nothing new there, Richie. That's the way it is with the big stars.'

'It's different now. It's smarter than that at the top end of rock 'n' roll. It's like a science. It's like an art in itself. You probably think that Richie Earls decides who he likes and who he doesn't like, and then Johnny lets them in and lets them out. Is that right?'

'Johnny's a good judge.'

'I don't need Johnny now. Not for that. Not to let them in and let them out. Not to protect me. And you know why? Because people do it all themselves. They are so fucking grateful that they know me, and that I say hello to them and sit down with them in Lillie's Bordello and have a drink with them. . . they are so fucking grateful, they'll do anything to stop some other fucker getting in ahead of them. They'll do anything to stop some other clown smelling the power. You wouldn't believe how well it works.'

'So how do you meet anyone you haven't met already?'

'Maybe I know enough people.'

'True.'

'And anyway, if it's another big name, or a genius or something, we find each other eventually. We're just like the gentry. We meet no-one apart from people like us. And a few peasants that we're especially fond of. And we like it that way.'

'So I wouldn't be welcome at this here barn dance in Baltrudder House?'

'It doesn't quite work like that either. That wouldn't be. . . rock 'n' roll. I mean, if we showed up, if we made it past the crocodiles, they'd live with it. They'd probably treat us civil enough too, on the face of it. They like to think that they're very down-to-earth people. They really think that about themselves. They think they're very down to earth.'

'You are very down to earth, Richie.'

'Maybe I am. But I'm also protected. I am protected by money and power and the people I know. I am protected up to the tonsils. Or at least. . . I used to be.'

'So they'd give us the down-to-earth act, but they'd be thinking, there but for the grace of God?'

'Dee will have the word out. Richie has snapped.'

'You paint it black.'

'I'm busking it. But I'm not far wrong.'

'The rock 'n' roll music has gone to shit as well. Have you noticed?'

'No doubt you're going to tell me. . .'

'I was telling Johnny up in The Jester . . .'

'Ideally, we don't show up in the first place. That's how it works. We're supposed to know. . . that there's parts of us that some might find disturbing.'

'You mean, parts of me.' Victor goes over to the couch and picks up the Property Supplement cutting. He motions

220

to Richie to come over and share his pleasure.

'That's like Muscle Shoals,' Richie says. 'Nearly the same house exactly.'

'No two are exactly alike,' Victor says. 'Not up there.'

'Do you want it?'

'What's a Bossi fireplace?'

'I suppose. . . it's a fireplace made by Bossi.'

'I want it.'

'Have it.'

'I will.'

'I'll get on to Alexis Murphy's office,' Richie says. 'He'll release the funds.'

'He'll release the funds, will he?'

'Anything you want, I'll clear it.'

Victor holds his hand out to Richie and they shake on it.

'I appreciate it,' says Victor.

'I told you money is no problem.'

'I mean, I appreciate you marking my card about your rock 'n' roll chums.'

'No sweat.'

'It took bottle.'

'You might as well know.'

Victor squeezes Richie's hand affectionately. He speaks gently to him. 'It's a thing I like about you, Richie, in the few days we've known each other. You've got bottle. You're willing to say the unpopular thing at times. I like that. I reckon you're not like those people. The way you talk back to me sometimes, you remind me of someone far better than them. I think you know who.'

Victor lets go of Richie's hand and hold up his own hands like he is signalling the end of that particular subject.

'I'm only pissed off I can't talk like them,' Richie says. 'I sound like what I am. A gurrier from Dundalk.'

'A gurrier from Dundalk who doesn't know what a Bossi

221

fireplace is,' Victor adds.

Richie bursts out laughing. It's the first time that Victor has seen him even slightly merry.

Victor looks again at the cutting, and draws Richie's attention to it.

Richie keeps laughing until Victor shushes him.

Then Victor speaks, slowly, like he is giving directions to a tourist. 'Looking at this picture here, does it bring back memories of you running my son into the sea?'

Richie steps away from Victor as if he is dodging the swipe of a razor. He is full of helpless wrath.

Victor coolly offers him the cutting.

When Richie speaks, he is ripping.

'You know those people I was telling you about?' he says. 'They're the best people. I'm one of those people and I love it. Fucking love it.'

With the clatter of cuban heels on wood he sweeps out the door and storms away down the track.

'You're beautiful when you're angry,' Victor says. He rubs his hands together with satisfaction. That was the other line that the screenwriter hated.

'You're beautiful when you're angry.' Victor remembers it now.

Chapter 23

Drumbolus House, County Westmeath

Simon Bartley arrives at the big house with a bunch of twelve red roses for Dee Bellingham.

She opens the door to him and they embrace like two people mourning a shared misfortune. Dee is up and dressed after her night in Malone's with Nulty. She is hungover but in a pleasantly delirious sort of way. She can't recall feeling such a buzz about any man since she was introduced to Michael Stipe in the Clarence Hotel after the Supermodels bash for Bosnia at The Point.

'Shall we walk?' Simon says.

Dee fancies a stroll. 'Show me where Richie is going to play,' she says.

Simon closes the door behind them. It seems slightly odd to Dee that he is wearing a suit on a Saturday, but somehow normal that he is calling to Drumbolus House like a visitor. It's just like Simon to wait until everything is exactly right.

'It's round the other side,' he says.

'Show me,' she says.

Simon and she walk around the side of the old grey mansion, where the manicured lawns meet Westmeath in its natural autumn state, the land without purpose for a century looking suddenly like the perfect festival venue when you run your eye along it and up towards the hills, and imagine eighty thousand kids getting out of their heads, maybe a hundred thousand, maybe another Glastonbury here in the centre of Ireland, the centre of the old Celtic world according to Simon.

'I'm sorry I couldn't be here to welcome you,' he says.

'The bad manners are all mine,' she says. 'I suppose we toffs think we can drop in any time to the stately homes of Ireland.'

'I believe Nulty did the honours.'

'He's been an absolute angel.'

'He took you drinking,' Simon says.

'The other way round.'

'He said you came here when you were a child.'

'Is he really that good-looking or am I going completely barmy?'

'You must be shattered, now,' Simon says.

'Shattered.'

They stop walking at the spot where the stage will supposedly be. It is the obvious spot, when you look at the land inclining gently towards the hills, and visualise the kids pouring down, the ravers, the hippies, the bikers, the stoners, and the choppers flying in the people who matter to the sanctuary of the big house.

'This is breathtaking,' Dee says.

'Is it better than Slane?' Simon asks.

'I'm more shattered now that I've seen this,' she says. 'This is a special place.'

'There'll be no festival here,' Simon says. 'Not with Richie Earls anyway. Not the way he is.'

'Nulty told me. . . you signed a contract.'

'I signed a yoke with Victor to get him out of my face until we figure out how to get rid of him.'

Dee looks intently at Simon, impressed again that such a sharp mind could live behind those benign features.

'That yoke, as you call it, is still legal,' she says.

'Believe me,' he says, 'no court will find Victor in a fit state of mind to be signing contracts.'

'I have a feeling you don't see this ending up in court.'

'I want him put away. For good this time.'

'You're saying you want him committed?'

'This is my dream here. This is my dream.'

'Gosh.'

'Victor was drinking all night in Malone's for starters. He's not supposed to be drinking at all.'

'He'll be drugging as well, with Richie,' Dee says.

'If Richie is out of his head on drugs, or if he's had some sort of a breakdown. . . we can see him right the other end.'

'I'll be absolutely upfront with you here, Simon. The coke is not the whole story.'

'Drink, I suppose. . . these guys can drink. . .'

'I can hardly bear to say this, but what if I said it was more ghastly than you think?'

Simon sees Nulty in the distance, standing at the side of the house. He waves to Nulty. Nulty responds with a brief salute and then disappears around the front.

'In to work on Saturday morning,' says Simon. 'I've always said that when they get stuck in, the Irish are capable of anything.'

'You like Nulty, don't you?'

'I tolerate him.'

Simon starts to stroll back towards the house.

Dee figures she'll give him the full facts now. She doesn't doubt his resolve to take appropriate action.

'This is what the Irish are capable of,' she says. 'Are you ready?'

'Tell me,' he says.

'Richie killed your nephew. Victor's son. He was out of his head and he set the dogs on him up at Muscle Shoals. Paul Bartley was chased into the sea by Richie's dogs. I'm sorry, but you must be told.'

Simon stops walking. He seems to be adding it all up.

'Terrible way to go,' he says quietly.

'There is a tape,' says Dee. 'A video tape. The security cameras, right?'

'Right.'

'It seems that Victor was made aware of the tape. By Johnny, I guess.'

'Jesus,' says Simon.

'The rest we can imagine.'

'What a stroke.'

'Abracadabra,' Dee says.

'A hostile takeover, as we say.'

'I've seen the tape, but they don't know that I've seen it. Tell you about it later.'

'In a strange way,' says Simon, 'it makes sense to me now. It makes more sense than Victor showing up here as Richie Earls's new manager just because he's a great manager.'

'Maybe he is a great manager, when you're on drugs.'

'It must be shocking, Dee, to think of all your hard work turned to this.'

'Poor Richie. I had a feeling he was going to dump me anyway.'

'You've seen this tape with your own eyes?'

'It's a bloody freak show.'

'Richie is in great danger now, I feel,' Simon says. 'Victor can swing up and down at the best of times.'

'He must be quite mad now.'

'Dangerous.'

'He's had a big blow,' Dee says, 'and a big break.'

'Massive break for Victor. Massive.'

'So he'd want to protect the merchandise?'

'Ah, we're talking about Victor here,' Simon says. 'No guarantees.'

They stroll on back to the house.

'How well did you know Paul Bartley?' Dee says.

'Not well. But in fairness, Victor didn't know him all that well either. He wasn't around much when Paul was growing up. Then he was put away. I think they started to hit it off towards the end, but sure by then the damage is done.'

'I'd feel more for him if he'd been a good father.'

Simon laughs. 'No fear of that,' he says. 'And while he was at it, he robbed Paul of a perfectly good mother.'

'It's such a bloody shame,' Dee says. 'A few loose words from Richie . . . It's terrifying.'

'You don't want drawing Victor on you at all. That's how it happens. It starts small and it ends up big.'

They reach the front of the house. Dee wants to say something else before she goes in.

'Do we tell Nulty?' she says.

'I wouldn't,' Simon says. 'Not yet anyway.'

'I suppose when we settle on a strategy. . .'

'I think he likes Victor. People do.'

'Victor that we are going to. . . put away?' she says.

'Eradicate.'

'Gosh.'

They are at the door of the big house. They lower their voices so that Nulty inside can't hear. Simon feels like he has just moved to the next level of business almost subconsciously, like he was ready for it, and it came out just right, hitting the sweet spot, and evidently hitting Dee's sweet spot.

She smiles at him and shakes her head in wonder, like this guy is way out of her depth, but she's loving the trip.

'I've tried everything else,' says Simon.

'Eradicate?'

'Any other way. . . if you think about it, any other way is wrong for us. I could pick up the phone right now and tell the guards, but then Richie's up for manslaughter at least. No use in doing that. No Richie, no gig.'

Dee nods like Mary Robinson.

'Don't say any more now,' she says, glancing at the unseen Nulty.

'You like Nulty, don't you?' says Simon.

'It's just. . . I fancy I'll be spending some time with your Mr Nulty. If I may.'

'You don't need my permission.'

'I'd like you to know anyway,' Dee says.

'Lucky man.'

'I'm sorry I wasn't completely upfront on the phone last night,' Dee says. 'Still a bit spooked I guess. And a bit drunk.'

She kisses Simon on the forehead.

'It's lovely to have you here,' he says.

'You're a thoroughly decent man,' says Dee. 'I mean that.'

As Simon walks down the avenue of Drumbolus House he can hear Nulty and Dee laughing. He looks back at them standing at the door, like they're a couple already, waving goodbye to a guest. And poor Nulty, he looks as stiff as ever to Simon, like he can't figure out if her ladyship is just being friendly, or what. He's dropped Nulty in it now, landing him with a woman, as if becoming a businessman wasn't enough.

Simon has a funny feeling they're laughing at him, but it doesn't bother him. He doesn't let himself get caught up in negative thoughts. Victor is in his thoughts now, and how right it felt when he told Dee that Victor must be eradicated. The word just came to him on the spot. Eradicate, like eradicating bovine TB.

They are laughing at him too, laughing at his new lisp. Dee and Nulty have at least one thing in common, a strong suspicion that the further he gets in life, the more Simon is developing a lisp. The other thing they have in common is dread. The sick sweet dread of sex, dread that it might not happen, and that it might.

'This is going to get rather heavy,' Dee says.

And Nulty knows she's not talking about the show business.

Chapter 24

Kinsale, West Cork

The Late Late Show still has magic for Victor. He is about to take the Daimler up the road after Richie, and tell him to stop being such a thick bollocks, when the call comes. It's one of Pat Kenny's researchers saying that Pat would love to have Victor on the show next Friday, in the light of recent reports about the sensational improvement in his pay and conditions.

The old butterflies. Victor has to control the urge to say that if Pat wants him on the programme so bad, he can fucking well do the asking himself. Victor has nothing but bile for RTÉ. But then he sat rotting in Rathmines for years in which a call like this seemed totally out of the question. He fantasised about someone out there remembering that he was still alive, and asking him on to something, any old shite. So he controls the urge.

'What did you say your name was again?' he says.

'Linda Duffy,' the researcher says.

'Let me guess now, Linda. You want me to do that last item where Pat talks to some poor divil who has had his head chopped off and sewn back on again. Right?'

'That's not how we see it. We had Gerry Adams on last,

230

David Trimble. . .'

'I saw them. I've seen them all.'

'So it's a flexible spot. It's not like, here comes the dying man.'

'I know that, Linda. I know, deep down.'

'You could do a head-to-head with Pat, or maybe take questions from the audience?'

'I wouldn't want this to turn into an ambush now, Linda. I don't want punters hopping up out of the audience. . .'

'It's just . . . it could be terrific.'

'For who?'

'Look, we've spoken to Dee Bellingham. Just so you know we've nothing up our sleeves. We asked her on to give her side of the story but she says she's taking a complete break down the country. Down your way actually.'

'Kinsale?'

'Drumbolus.'

'You know your stuff, Linda.'

'She said you'd be brilliant on your own and it's all for the best. She said we should give you the top slot.'

'She won't suddenly appear on the phone? Caller on line one?'

'She wishes you well. She says that all things come to an end.'

'Drumbolus, you say?'

'I got the impression there was romance in the air.'

'In Drumbolus?'

'She said not to be bothering her. It's the first Saturday she's had off in ages, and she's really, really happy.'

'There's no romance down in Drumbolus.'

'Someone called Nulty?'

'What about him?'

'She said that Nulty makes her realise what's really important. She was just chatting really. No axe to grind.'

'Nulty?'

'She said he's organising some huge Richie Earls gig.'

'Unprofessional. There's no official announcement for a couple of weeks. Most unprofessional.'

'She really sounded in great form. It would make a terrific show, the two of you. . . if I got back to her . . .'

'I'd prefer to go solo. I'll go for the tragic chair.'

'Maybe some other time.'

'I understand what you're saying, Linda. But right now, Victor Bartley is . . . a bit raw.'

'Pat would love to have you on, full stop. Just Victor Bartley then, in person.'

'There was no harm in trying, Linda. I appreciate you're only doing your job.'

'We can organise the limo . . .'

'I'll talk it over with Richie. And then I'll get back to you. If that's all right with you, Linda.'

'That's brilliant.'

'Tell Pat. . . tell him not to mind the critics. They're a shower of cunts.'

'Thank you. He knows that.'

Victor is playing with a packet of Benson & Hedges. When he puts the phone down he sees that the packet of twenty has about ten cigarettes still in it, ten thick-rolled cigarettes that can only be one thing, made by one man.

'Johnny,' says Victor to himself, examining a particularly fine specimen of the joint-maker's art.

He shuffles over to his temporary bed and settles himself with the joint and a big box of kitchen matches and a full view of the lake through the big triangular windows on this crisp September afternoon. He lights the joint and takes five, six, seven hits on it like he did up at Muscle Shoals, partly to impress Johnny at the time it must be said, to reassure him that his dope wasn't wasted on Victor Bartley.

As the drug loosens up his brain, Victor figures that this is the first time he has ever sat on his own with a full joint. It makes him feel young, like the time has come to start buying his own dope, and hopefully meeting women willing to smoke it with him.

The smell makes Victor think of women, Johnny's kind of women, and how it doesn't really matter to them if you look like an ape as long as you're right inside. And maybe what makes a man right inside is knowing that he has a lodge in Kinsale or a place on Kilbrittan Hill with his name on it. Only a pure saint could tempt the likes of Greta with a hole in Rathmines, not because she minded it being a hole, but because you'd have to be wrong inside to be living so bad.

Victor takes in another lungful of Red Leb, and vows that marijuana will be his love-drug from now on, now that he's back in the love-drugging stakes. Drink used to be his love-drug, his everything. And apart from six months, probably less, when he had normal sex with Sheila, he can't recall one single ride that doesn't make him freeze with shame at the thought of all the drink that went into it, how it was totally out of the question for Victor Bartley to ride any woman without both of them polluted with drink. But no more of these drink-sodden regrets need detain him, now that he is back in the business, imagining already that there's a golden-hearted rock chick with an unbelievable body sitting on his lap and both of them in a very loving state thanks to this Red Leb and maybe, at the very maximum, a snipe or two of red wine.

As Victor sees it, a spot on the *Late Late* is still highly recommended for any man in need of love. That researcher sounded nice, but then she's in the business, so there's nothing special about Victor Bartley for her, unless by some huge stroke of luck she likes them meaty, beaty, big and bouncy, with a plate in the head, and sharing a birthday with Dickie Rock. For most women, no matter what they say, there's still a mystique about some fella who's sat in the tragic chair pouring out his guts to Pat, talking about Ireland. An aura that stays there long enough for the man to get his Nat King Cole. But he hears Paul now, talking about sick relationships, and how you're better off pulling your wire than getting into one of them. As if Victor ever had any other kind. In the past.

It would be easy now for Victor Bartley to go apeshit, now that he is a power in the land again. But Paul would want him to do the right thing, not the easy thing, and Paul put him here, with all this power flowing to him. One mad ride then, and one only, and not two, will get it out of his system.

Tonight? He fancies the pub tonight. One of those old Kinsale pubs with glass cases full of big fish where he could walk in with the great Richie Earls and have the women fighting over him.

He'll have to get used to this effect he is about to have on other people from now on, just by walking into a room. He must take care not to abuse this power flowing to him. Victor feels good about himself, thinking such considerate thoughts, but then that's the way with the top people. They feel nice about being nice.

I feel nice about being nice, thinks Victor. And after another couple of puffs on Johnny's finest, he figures it's time to hunt down the great Richie Earls and take him for a beer. And to tell him, when he's placid enough, that Dee has moved to Westmeath where she is riding another man.

Richie Earls likes a Saturday afternoon drink in Kinsale, but not today. He's too fucked up after the scene with Victor. He marches in the direction of town on the side of the main road like some broken-down hobo, rather than the poetic type that he imagines himself to be when reading Kerouac, who wrote that the only ones for him were the mad ones, but who might have written different if he had ever crossed Victor Bartley.

Richie always saw himself as the Kerouac type, a free man on the road chasing a rhapsody. But now it feels more like Hitchcock's road in *Psycho*, and Richie Earls has become the Janet Leigh type, because he made one big mistake, and panicked, and all the time all that was at the end of the road was the Victor Bartley motel.

He is gumming for drink as he nears town, but he can't face being with people who are suddenly far better off than he is. Even the kid who lifts the lobsters out of the tank in The Neptune has more shots in his locker these days, than Richie Earls.

The Harley. It feels almost like a lucky break when he remembers that the Harley was left up at Charles Fort the other night, and might still be up there for all he knows. It's not like he can make some great escape on it, it just gives him something to focus on apart from these sick mother-fucking games with Victor.

He starts to feel nervous marching down into Summer Cove and up the hill to Charles Fort, thinking about luck, thinking that if the bike is still up there, it will be a lucky omen, knowing that he is setting himself up for another knock, but unable to stop this stupid desire. He doesn't think so much about luck and destiny since he stopped doing all that Charlie. It's not a healthy subject when you're the one guy in a hundred thousand who gets wrecked out of his skull, and who winds up saddled with a dead man for all his days.

He is strongly tempted to throw away Jerry Lee's rattlesnake bracelet, but he thinks better of it. No matter how badly the balls are bouncing, you don't go messing with that shit.

He stops halfway up the hill to Charles Fort to get his breath back, and because he is afraid now that the Harley will be gone. He despises himself further for this. He imagines Dee despising him for it. He imagines that if he had told Dee everything as soon as she got back from Antibes, they might all be laughing now. But he held out because he needed to, because it was his idea of being a man. And he got it arseways. And now, as a man, he is glad of one thing. He is glad that it's over with Dee. He feels that he shouldn't feel like that, but it's undeniable.

Gasping, he lights a Marlboro. He readies himself for the last few steps up the hill and what awaits him at the top. He feels free in just one way. He feels that the world's women are available to him again after five years with Dee, available with just a small squeak of the old Dundalk guilt, but nothing like the few occasions when he went offside and Dee never let on whether she sussed it, nothing he can't handle now.

This freedom from Dee, the one thing that was barred to him in his pomp is his, all his now, until he uses up the dregs of it and they break up his last rat-arsed three-in-a-bed scene to carry him through the lobby of The Blue Haven hotel, hog-tied.

And in this state of raddled expectation, Richie Earls comes over the hill to see his Harley standing there.

The Daimler is next up the hill, giving Richie just two minutes to enjoy this small marvel, unrecognised with his helmet on by the scattering of tourists, reacquainting himself with the beautiful brute for two minutes of what seems almost like peace.

Victor steps out of the Daimler. He walks over to Richie

with his arms extended, giving the thumbs-up. He looks like Johnny Cash in a long black leather coat and black shirt and black jeans and black cowboy boots.

'What do you think?' he says.

'The man in black,' Richie says, removing his helmet.

'I mean the bike, I mean the bike,' Victor says.

'Great.'

'In this day and age, to think that you can leave your Harley Davidson out for the best part of a week . . . that sums up Ireland for me.'

'That sums it up all right.'

'Ireland. Pat will want me to talk about Ireland. On *The Late Late Show*.'

'Fuck's sake.'

'Next Friday, old son. What do you think?'

'What the fuck does it matter what I think?'

'It matters very much, Richie.'

'No it does not, Victor.'

'Didn't you steer me away from the barn dance next Saturday?'

'You have your mind made up,' Richie says.

'No way. I am acting under instructions.'

'Anything I say. . .' Richie says, 'you're just looking to get at me.'

'Fair enough. Fair enough so.'

'What so?'

'Fair enough,' Victor says. 'I will try not to get at you, as you put it. I will try to. . . I'm feeling a bit different today. Markedly different.'

Richie plucks a bit of shirt-plastic from under Victor's collar, and throws it away like a golfer testing the breeze. He still has no idea how Victor will react to what he says, but he's starting to feel that it's not worth worrying any more.

'You feel a bit different, do you?' Richie says.

'A new set of clothes without counting the pennies. . . *The Late Late Show*. . . Johnny's dope. . .'

With his eyes dancing, Victor takes the packet of Benson & Hedges out of the deep pocket of his new leather coat. Richie is quick on the draw with the Zippo. He sucks on the fat cigarette and blows the smoke towards the sea.

'Did you ever think we had something in common?' Richie says.

Victor studies the ground, rubbing his temples like he wants to be precise in his answer.

'I want us to have a good working relationship,' he says. 'And eventually, who knows?'

'I like the Johnny Cash thing you got going there, Victor. But you could do with a leather waistcoat. Like Johnny. Johnny Oregon, who sold me down the river.'

'I was hoping you wouldn't even notice the threads. A good image is the bare minimum of good management.'

'Did you ever see *Psycho*?'

'I did,' says Victor.

'It's like you were waiting out there for me all the time, like Anthony Perkins waiting for your one, just when she breaks free.'

'A bit harsh, chum.'

'I'm just riffing here, Victor. I'm having to think about my life these days.'

'Harsh, harsh words,' says Victor.

'But I still say that we have something else altogether in common. Think about it, Victor. Think hard about it now.'

'You're coming out of yourself at last, Richie. I respect that.'

'What did you do to your wife, Victor?'

'My wife Sheila?'

'Your wife Sheila. What did you do to her?'

Victor looks concerned that the tourists will suss the

238

dope. He takes the joint from Richie and stamps it out.

'Start her up there,' he says, nodding towards the spot where they were first introduced.

Richie revs up and rides the Harley straight over. Victor follows him, walking slowly towards the wall. The two men look back towards Kinsale.

'I'm going to buy a boat,' Richie says. 'And I'm going to keep it down there. And I'm going to take women out to it.'

'Very nice.'

'Did you ever do it in a boat?'

'Not exactly.'

'We've got a big one over in Antibes. But I want one here.'

'I must tell you about the bould Dee Bellingham above in Drumbolus. . .'

'You must tell me about Victor Bartley. And what he did to his wife.'

Victor scratches his itchy arm.

'I'm lucky to be alive you know,' he says. 'Looking at this lovely view. Picture postcard stuff.'

'What was she called again? Your wife?'

'My wife Sheila.'

'What did you do to her, boss?'

'You won't laugh will you?'

'Why the fuck would I laugh?' Richie says.

'You might laugh.'

'I don't think so.'

'It was up your way,' Victor starts. 'Carlingford. A Sunday afternoon drive. We came to the pier. And I just kept driving.'

'You put the boot down?'

'Not really. I just kept driving.'

'You snapped.'

'I just kept driving.'

'Suicide thing?'

'Not really. I mean, I was very down in myself. Me and Sheila were not hitting it off at all. I thought about killing the two of us, more than once. I thought about killing her, and I thought about killing myself, and I thought about killing the two of us together. But on that day, on that Sunday in Carlingford, I didn't feel like killing anyone.'

'Were you drunk?'

'No.'

'Hungover?'

'I was always hungover. Look, there was no big bang in my head, and we weren't having a row. What can I tell you, Richie, except I drove into the water because I was... drawn to it?'

'And Sheila?'

'That's enough now.'

'Did she scream?'

'She didn't know much about it.'

'And you got out of it, you hoor.'

'That's enough now.'

'You can swim?'

'I was saved.'

'So then, we're quits.'

'How's that?'

'You're as bad as me. Worse actually. I was on drugs.'

'We have something in common all right.'

'Except you have me by the balls,' Richie says. 'Do you think that's fair?'

'We have both made mistakes in our lives, it is true. And in recognition of this fact, I have stopped myself again and again from smashing your skull with a lump hammer.'

'You're drawn to that are you?' Richie says.

'The other thing is, I owned up straight away. Like a big fucking eejit, I owned up and they put me away to think about it for a while. That's something we don't have in common, you and me. Your kind never pay the price. Like you said, you're protected.'

'They're not my kind.'

'They were a couple of hours ago.'

'I didn't mean that. I lost the head.'

'You have some nerve, boy, raising your voice to me.'

'It's all I've got now, Victor. The voice.'

'I'll try not to get at you. I'll try.'

'Hop on to the bike and we'll go for a fucking pint.'

Richie kicks the Harley to life, but Victor hesitates. Over the growl of the engine he signals to Richie to switch it off. Victor studies the ground again, composing his thoughts.

'You are paying a heavy price,' he says. 'Your woman. . . your woman has left you for another man.'

'Who?' Richie asks.

'Nulty.'

'Get on the back of the bike,' Richie says.

Victor manoeuvres himself on to the pillion seat and holds on to Richie so that he feels the vibrations of Richie howling with delight over the noise of the engine as they race down the steep hill and up out of Summer Cove, Victor holding tighter and tighter to Richie as they gain speed on the narrow back road into Kinsale, Victor going mad with fright as the road flashes by underneath him, sickened by the thought of hitting the hard road a smack at sixty or seventy miles an hour, slowing down, thank Christ, as they reach the traffic in the town and Richie weaves through the cars at cruising speed before gunning her up again and racing along the quay with the water to the left and the water straight ahead.

Richie stops the bike maybe six feet from the edge. And he takes off his helmet and looks back at Victor who has turned green or yellow or some such nauseous hue.

'I'm definitely going to buy a boat,' Richie says.

Drumbolus House, County Westmeath.

'I steal things,' Nulty says to Dee Bellingham. 'I steal things from shops,' he says, limp after about twenty minutes of intense screwing on the sumptuous cushions of the Cream Room.

All the dread is gone now, laughable in the light of how quickly they got it together, and how it is still not entirely clear who started it when the smallest vibration between them blasts away all that tension.

'It's something I'm really, really good at, stealing,' Nulty says, like the first time he mentions this gift of his out in the hall, and Dee instantly knows that this is the signal, that he is telling her something vital about himself that he would not tell to anyone else, and that she must do something about it.

'I'd like to take you out for a day of it,' he says.

'You want to take me shoplifting?'

'Anywhere you like.'

'Athlone?'

'Anywhere.'

'I'd like that.'

She directs him inside her again and straight away they are welded together, they build it up slowly and then with a sudden dizzying shaft, they let it rip.

Kinsale, West Cork

Victor is getting his colour back after a few snipes of red wine in The Wolfhound pub. He and Richie are sitting up at the bar wondering whether to eat or keep drinking, and sticking with the drink as the Saturday night buzz is building.

There is a band setting up on a small stage at the other end of the lounge, a music venue in itself with a low roof for a sweaty, stomping atmosphere. 'Moondance' they call themselves. They test the PA, tinkering with guitars and drums and a sax and trumpet, evidently a bunch of West Cork musos having a blow for beer money, one more time with feeling.

Richie is hitting the Powers, going toe to toe with Victor and his snipes.

'I mean it,' Victor says. 'I don't like any of my artistes to ride motorbikes. You'll find that Paul McGuinness isn't exactly ecstatic about Bono and Larry doing the biker thing.'

'You're just windy. I put the shite up you.'

'As long as you're happy, Richie. The artiste has to be happy in himself.'

Richie turns away from the bar to face the stage and to be seen clearly by the punters, specifically the women. He is starting to get the recognition, the usual smiles and giggles and sniggers and those who come to the bar and order their drinks and simply pretend that he is not there. And of course it is not the lovely woman across the room who makes the first move, but a bloke with a beard and a Guinness T-shirt, an English bloke name of Gilly, who is the manager of Moondance, and who would be deeply honoured if Richie would get up with the boys and have a blast.

'I'd have to clear that with my manager,' Richie says.

'He'll do it,' Victor says. And then he winks at Richie. 'He'll do a little gypsy song.'

Victor is in control again after his turbulent afternoon, controlling the drink too, still on top of that aspect at least, sensing that the Saturday night buzz is buzzing an extra bit with Richie Earls in the house. And he is with Richie Earls. He dismisses Gilly and orders another Powers for Richie, intoxicated enough by the sight of so many women eyeing them.

'I'll have to hear these clowns first,' Richie says.

'Of course,' Victor says.

Moondance wander on, seven in all, two guitars, bass, drums, and a brass section, average age forty and rising. They doodle and strum and scratch out a lick or two, looking like all bar-bands as if tonight's set is for their own private amusement. One-two-three-four and the horns blow the opening bars of 'Real Real Gone' by Van Morrison, like they mean it.

The crowd is up for it straight away, the room seems to bounce and shake as the horns hit home, and Richie Earls feels something he has not felt for a long time, that shiver, that shiver down the backbone. The singer is no Van the Man but the band is kicking, pumping, delivering. Richie remembers how much he loves the sound of a decent bar-band, the rhythm section booming away in your gut and how the guitar wails always a bit too loud but just right, and the song grabs you by the heart, some Roy Orbison song belting through the echo-chamber while the booze makes you grin and grin and call for more.

'They're a Van Morrison cover band!' Victor yells over the applause. 'Hence the name Moondance!'

Richie doesn't need to be told this, but Victor needs to be seen talking to Richie, like he's the great man's best pal.

Richie seems to be in a trance. He keeps on clapping over the intro to the next number, 'Jackie Wilson Said'.

Victor beckons to Gilly to come hither.

'Now, Gilly,' he shouts. 'My man here will want to do a country-and-western number. "Gypsy Woman" No Van the Man. "Gypsy Woman".'

Gilly gives him the thumbs-up. He wants to confirm this

with Richie, but Richie is still entranced, concentrating on the band.

Victor is getting anxious about those faraway eyes. He wants to hear Richie performing before the whiskey takes the edge off his interpretation. He shouts at Gilly that now is as good a time as any.

The band polishes off 'Jackie Wilson' *a cappella* and the room rises to them, banging their bottles of Mexican beer and their extra-chilled Guinness, whistling like rowdy boyos just off the trawler, or maybe just stepped off the yacht.

'We have a very special man in with us tonight, and a fine musician too,' the singer says, to another round of banging and whistling. 'Put your hands together for the one and only Mr Richie Earls.'

Richie breaks out of his dreaming. He gives Victor's arm a friendly squeeze, seen by the watching punters, which Victor greatly appreciates, and he bounces up to the stage through a standing ovation. He consults with the musos and they seem to have it figured.

'This is for my good friend and manager, Victor Bartley, who's in here tonight,' he says. 'He's the old geezer up at the bar.'

The crowd roar and whistle and Victor takes a bow.

'He's a kind of a father figure,' Richie says. 'It's sick. He lets me have the odd fiver and he tells me what to do.'

Victor laughs uproariously. This is a happy, happy moment for him, with all these fine young things clapping and smiling at him, such smiles.

'I think he's kind of adopted me,' Richie says.

The yahoo-ing continues, and Victor keeps laughing, though he can feel a heaviness coming on him, with the strain.

'This number is for Victor, for leaving me with nothing

245

except the clothes I stand up in, and the voice I started with. It's a gypsy song.'

The piano rolls and the band kicks in to 'Caravan', a carbon copy of Van the Man's original but for Richie Earls taking the vocals and singing with such soul and conviction and grace that everyone in the room knows it, knows that they have not heard the like of this, that Richie Earls is giving it the full soul treatment and doing it in electrifying style. He tears the joint apart and the band stays with him all the way, kicking and sparking off his performance. He reaches places with his voice that he never got to even when he was loved by two critics and half-a-dozen Muscle Shoals aficionados. This is the voice he started with, this is what set him free, and what made him rich, but he never understood that freedom until he was driven back to the music, until there was nothing else for him but the music, this music that is so fine.

'Turn it up now!' he hollers, and he strides off the stage and through the crowd and out the door while the band kicks for home and the crowd goes apeshit.

Victor slips out after him and finds Richie around the corner leaning against the wall of The Wolfhound, lighting up a Marlboro.

Victor is sweating heavily. He leans against the wall to steady himself, coming down after the surge. 'I spoke to Van the Man once,' he says. 'I said, "Van, you might think sometimes that they all hate you, but you're wrong. They all love you."'

Richie takes a deep drag on his cigarette.

'Victor?' he says. 'Shut the fuck up.'

Chapter 25

Drumbolus, County Westmeath

The Fiesta is outside Malone's, an inflated swan in the back window giving the impression of a family returned from holiday. It is the most conspicuous sign of a day's shoplifting in Athlone which has yielded for Nulty and Dee Bellingham a litre of Teacher's scotch whiskey, a naggin of Vladivar vodka, eight packets of Orbit sugar-free gum, six Cream Eggs, one packet of Fig Rolls, two Gino Ginelli stone-oven pizzas, a mini-disc player, a hardback copy of *Angela's Ashes*, a cassette of the poetry of Tennyson read by Dame Sybil Thorndike, a Liverpool 'away' strip, newspapers and magazines including *The Irish Times*, *The Examiner*, *Vanity Fair*, *Magill*, *Hot Press*, *The Spectator* and *Men's Health*, the videos *There's Something about Mary* and *Fargo*, a fishing net, an identity bracelet, three John Rocha shirts, three John Rocha T-shirts, two pairs of John Rocha jeans, two John Rocha jackets, a game of Trivial Pursuit, swimming goggles, a snorkel, and the rubber swan. It all cost the price of getting the bracelet engraved with Dee's name at the jewellers' shop where Nulty lifted it an hour earlier.

'This is a bit special,' Dee says.

She takes the bracelet out of the top pocket of her new John Rocha shirt, the dark blue one to go with her new John Rocha jeans. She and Nulty are having pints of lager in Nulty's usual spot by the window of the lounge, like any two people tired after a day in town.

Dee raises her glass to Nulty. 'Teach me the ways of the Jedi,' she says.

'I was showing off a bit,' says Nulty. 'No need for it.'

'How was I?' says Dee.

'You were brilliant.'

'Thanks.'

'A bit jumpy in the newsagent's, but otherwise perfect.'

'I felt exposed all of a sudden. Starts you thinking.'

Simon comes in the door and sits with them. He keeps his hands buried in the pockets of a full-length grey mackintosh, worn over a dark three-piece suit. His skin looks especially soft and pink, like he is losing his stubble and regaining the fresh face of his youth.

'You're looking particularly well, Dee,' he says.

'Cheers, Simon. I lost all my old clobber. In a fire.'

'We burnt dungarees and a couple of old Aran jumpers and stuff on the side of the road,' Nulty says.

'Nulty is very traditional after all,' Dee says. 'He likes me to be well-dressed.'

'I'm so glad to hear that, Dee. John Rocha. Very nice stuff.'

'There's a very nice place in Athlone now,' Nulty says. 'A bit dear, mind you.'

It's Monday night, so Nulty leaves them to sort out his records for the evening. Simon calls for another drink for Dee. Simon sits closer to Dee, talking quietly, conspiring.

'We will need Nulty,' he says. 'If we are going to do what we need to do to Victor, Nulty's the man to set it up.'

'It's more a matter of when we are going to do it,' Dee says. 'Timing.'

'You're still strong?' Simon says.

'I run the slight risk of losing Nulty at the other end of it,' Dee says. 'The very thought of it breaks my heart.'

'I'll put it to him, what we need him to do. I'll take him out for a game of golf.'

'No, I must ask him myself,' Dee says decisively.

'We're still . . . eh . . . we're still leaving him out of the loop as to the actual . . . outcome', Simon says.

'When it's all eventually explained to him, he'll know it had to be done and there was really no decent alternative, none whatsoever,' Dee says, like she is rehearsing an official line.

Simon laughs.

'We're worrying about Nulty here. Are we forgetting the main man?' he says.

'Oh God, *The Late Late Show*.' Dee laughs. 'Listen, I tried to send a smoke signal to Victor through RTÉ, telling them we're all relaxez-vous down here and we wish him well. But really we have to assume that Victor is on red alert all the time, and if he's not, Johnny will be. And so we need a friendly face, and so we need Nulty.'

'It's lovely to have you here, Dee.'

She is getting to love these nights in this lounge in the middle of nowhere, and later she loves the way that Nulty picks the songs so that there's a bit of country, Patsy Cline maybe, a Pogues number and then something by Jimmy Durante, and they all seem to go together. She has big respect for Nulty for still clinging to socialism, and if it all works out, touch wood, Richie will dedicate the Drumbolus festival next summer to the protestors in Seattle who disrupted the world summit of capitalist pigs. Nulty is straight out of a David Bailey collection, she reckons, so slim and blond. She wonders if he is really aware of this, with his sombre polo-necks. She wonders how his life got so fucked up, how such a pretty boy could do so badly in the big shakeout until Simon saw all that potential, bless him. The more she drinks, the more beautiful he looks as he busies himself with his records, and Dee Bellingham gets blissfully hammered, thinking it was a lucky thing that he landed here in this hopeless place.

Kinsale, West Cork

Victor Bartley phones the *Late Late* office to confirm that he will be a guest on Friday's show. They offer to bring him up for an interview with one of the researchers, 'just to check a few facts,' but Victor suspects they are worried about him arriving at all, him being such a notorious wild man. So he says no, he'll take whatever Pat throws at him just like David Trimble. And anyway he fancies flying up from Cork, just because he can.

The early days of the week are quiet at the lodge, probably quieter than any days Victor has passed since the days of his years in front of the telly in Rathmines, rotting. Richie goes a bit thick on him again, drinking solidly and ordering pizzas biked up to the lodge to mark his liberation from Dee, and sleeping half the day, refusing all compliments about his soulful performance at The Wolfhound, muttering that it's Van Morrison's soul should be getting the compliments.

But Victor feels he is quietly chuffed, and that this is just the perfectionist in Richie Earls, the artiste. Their relationship is a more normal one now that certain issues have been aired, and Richie is saying some nice things, like that thing about Victor being a sort of father figure. That was nice. But the old butterflies are starting early, the palms are getting sweaty and it's only Monday.

The day after and the day after that he tries to calm down by drawing up some kind of career path for Richie, something on paper, but he can get nothing done except smoking Johnny's dope to ease the nerves, the old *hors d'oeuvres*. It's good to be nervous, he thinks, it's good to be on your toes, but it's wasting him at the same time, starting up so early, running Pat's questions back and forth until it tangles up his mind.

Thursday takes a long time to come, but it brings a tremendous relief. Victor's game plan is to fly up to Dublin a day in advance and stay overnight at the Shelbourne, do it in style, maybe even go on the razzle in a controlled fashion and then face the big day with all the refreshment that the Shelbourne can throw at him, maybe a bit of that Chinese massage first thing.

Destination: Dublin

Richie drives him to Cork Airport in the Daimler and promises to watch it in a pub, ideally with a woman perched on his knee.

'Good things are starting to happen to you, son,' Victor says. 'You've got a lot to offer any woman.'

Even the novelty of getting on a plane is giving Victor a little dart in the bowels. He has a quick snipe at the airport bar and another in the air, savouring the views of Ireland below, a country entirely under reconstruction, and Victor just one more of the men who have tasted success. He's still not used to it, reading the airline magazine and realising that he can actually buy a lot of this stuff now, and visit these countries and stay in these hotels. There is so much more to buy in Ireland than there was the last time he had money, long ago. It occurs to him that he can afford to have the plate looked at again, privately, in the Blackrock Clinic.

Would he hate someone like himself, if he was poor again? The question itself gives him a glow of well-being, descending into Dublin with the lovely prospect of more wine, and maybe more friends. Another swift snipe at Dublin Airport, the third of the day, the crucial third, sees him absolutely right for the taxi into the city and a load of shite-talk with the driver about the shocking traffic and the property prices, and then another first, when Victor Bartley steps out of the cab and into the Shelbourne to say, 'I have a reservation.'

The Horseshoe Bar is to his right and the sight of it quickens Victor's step as he bounces up the stairs and opens his room just to throw his gear into it, the Johnny Cash gear for tomorrow night, one of seven identical Johnny Cash suits that will comprise the Victor Bartley image. Late afternoon in the Horseshoe Bar and Victor is elbows down on the counter with a snipe of red wine in front of him, and a spot on *The Late Late Show* tomorrow night.

This is the best time of all, this quiet time when the Monday Club used to shift up a gear. This is what it's all about. Maybe a little tour of the pubs of Baggot Street, O'Donoghue's of course, maybe not Temple Bar and U2's place and the John Rocha hotel, because that's for the younger crowd. The old guard will stick to the traditional route, the old guard that is down now to just the one. Back in business, Mister, back in business.

They are sending the limo to the hotel tomorrow night, an hour before the show, more than two hours before he walks out and faces Pat. A lot of time to be arsing around in make-up and hospitality, and people sympathising with him about Paul, no doubt, because he was their colleague after all.

But he's ready. He's a professional. He can think on his feet and tell a story and he's relieved that it's Pat and not Gaybo, because Pat sticks to the facts, whereas Gaybo might ask you the size of your mickey just to speed things up a bit. One thing that Victor understands about the chat-show game, Victor who was with Ollie Reed the night that Ollie died on the *Late Late*, is that you don't just sit there answering questions. He always stresses this to up-and-coming acts. You can make yourself a star for all time on the *Late Late*, so you don't want to waste your half-an-hour of prime exposure answering stupid fucking questions. You must say exactly what you want to say, in exactly the way you want to say it, and so, as soon as is humanly possible, Victor plans to tell the story of the old-style republican who ate the money. Regardless of what Pat asks him. There's nothing like laughing and a big round of applause to chase away the butterflies.

The tea-time crowd is making him sweat up a bit. Strange, how trendy this joint has become, where once you'd have nobody in except the Monday Club types and a few horsy alcoholics. He must prepare a few ready-made lines in case Pat gets stuck into Ireland, the scandals, the tribunals, the traffic and the property prices, and the incredible success stories like the boy bands and the rock groups and *Riverdance*. What attitude to strike? He might get angry talking about the music scene, and on the telly that just makes you look like a lunatic. No, he doesn't want to get tangled up in some rant about the young people being codded and all the corporate cunts down at The Point at *Phantom of the Opera* and he really couldn't give a monkey's about the scandals.

So the line to take is, again, to tell a story. A story with a bit of music and a bit of scandal and a bit of history. Tell the story about Victor Bartley and the taxman, back when tax really was a laughing matter, and rightly so, and rightly so, ho-ho-ho.

And now that's enough brain damage. Victor realises he is at a delicate stage, with five or six snipes inside him. Above all, you need to be fresh for the *Late Late*. This is for the marbles, and Paul is watching, and he'd be very critical of a full-scale razzle down the Strip on the night before the show.

So Victor settles himself on the barstool, and orders a pint of Guinness, a slow pint of Guinness, because this is the night for slow pints, the better to revel in the good of it all, the deep satisfaction of being a top person, and the knowledge that all these young men and women with their money made, all of them can kiss Victor Bartley's ass now, because he is in the business, the business that beats all, and they're not, and they never will be.

Slow, slow, slow pints of Guinness and not a word to anyone below the stature of Ron Wood. Towards closing time, Victor increasingly expects Ron Wood to walk in, and is becoming a small bit disappointed as each new face fails to be that of the gaunt Rolling Stone, a sweet geezer according to Johnny, and a great painter.

Victor is definitely one over the eight, and rising, but the situation is so controlled that he still feels tranquil, like he's living right, like he's right inside, thinking as he steers himself up the stairs and not left in the direction of Lillie's Bordello that Paul was spot on again about the environment, how you have to control your environment if you want to beat the bottle.

Victor trips on the top step and as he is falling forward he can feel his full weight buckling his right ankle, and he howls with the pain. A shot of panic makes him howl again. The leg must be broken. He could feel something going. He looks up and Brad Pitt is looking down at him, his face full of concern. It's not the drink, or the pain, it is actually Brad Pitt.

'I'll get a doctor for you,' Brad says. And he skips down the stairs.

Victor is feeling the shame now, the shame of howling in front of Brad Pitt. A young man who looks too young to be a doctor is on the case quickly, but not before Victor suffers more shame, chatting to a receptionist who heard him howling and who undoubtedly takes him for some sad old fucker of a drunkard. Victor holds on to the doctor and hops towards his room. Stretched on the bed, the doctor tells him it's just ligament damage, nothing broken, no need for the hospital, a matter of strapping it up and icing it and painkillers. But nothing for the shame.

They have the painkillers brought to him. He takes a couple of capsules and lies back on the bed, but he needs something for his head as well, because he is gripped by the terror that he will get no sleep tonight. He needs something for his head, just to slow the bastard down, to get settled. He drags himself over to the mini-bar and grabs an armful of miniature bottles of gin, vodka, whiskey, martini, just to look at them anyway, to know that they're there if he needs them, to knock him out. The rumpus in his head dies down when he figures that this is another story for Pat, maybe the one to get him going, as he limps on and Pat asks him what's wrong with his foot, and he says that he tripped up in the Shelbourne and he looked up and there was Brad Pitt.

At least his head is still working. But he can't be letting it work all night. It's still working at four in the morning, and at that stage he loses hope. He is dosing himself with the miniatures, getting wound up about Pat going in hard over Sheila, getting wound up about twenty other potential black spots, when he should be conking out.

It's the painkillers. The painkillers won't let him sleep. He rings down for breakfast at five. The food might send him off. And he asks for a small bottle of champagne on the side, thinking that it might just do the trick. And anyway it's the Shelbourne, where they expect you to live a little.

Victor crawls over to the bin with the empty miniatures, getting rid of a dozen assorted spirits before the food arrives. There's fuck all in them, but people jump to conclusions. Jesus, he's a target for the tabloids now, and all. The full Irish breakfast is brought to him by a foreign girl. There's a full-size bottle of Moet & Chandon on the tray, and Victor is about to say that he ordered a small one, but he doesn't want to be annoying her arse. He's glad of it, actually, because if the full bottle of bubbly and a feed of sausages, rashers, eggs, tomatoes, mushrooms and black pudding doesn't land the knockout punch, nothing will. Victor pops open the champagne and it is good, it is so good to see the old foam gushing, when only a month ago he thought that nothing good would ever happen to him again.

He's still sitting up drinking at daybreak. The Irish breakfast doesn't really go with the champagne. But he is still in control of his environment. And while there's a lot of sound theory behind Paul's psychobabble, a man can have too much control over himself. He can forget to live altogether. And in a way that's worse than the few drinks.

Another attack of the butterflies and Victor realises it's decision time. If he's not going to get to sleep, then he has to stay awake in a way that has him well-oiled for tonight, without being overly oiled. Sleep mightn't be the best idea anyway, now that he's missed his natural sleep. He might end up shuffling on half-doped, and making no impression at all. And he has to keep taking the painkillers. So if they kept him awake all night, they'll hardly send him off in the middle of the morning to John O'Dreams.

Victor slides off the bed and hops on one leg over to the shower. He turns it on and gets down on all fours with his right foot sticking out to miss the blast of hot water on the bandage. He notes another improvement in his lot, as the last time he knelt in the shower, he was bleeding to death. You can hardly even see the scars now, thanks to Greta, better than any doctor.

And while he's at it, he must call Johnny in Antibes, for a briefing. He crawls out of the shower and with a fresh Johnny Cash suit to slip into, and a long black Johnny Cash leather coat, Victor is getting a second wind. It feels less like a sleepless night and more like a touch of jet-lag. But he knows of old that you have to maintain a certain level of alcohol in your system once you've started or else it seems to go bad inside you, and you suddenly feel so weary as the day wears on, and weariness on television makes you look sick. Whatever you do, you must sparkle.

So it is that Victor Bartley limps across the road and enters the darkened bar of O'Donoghue's around noon, six or seven more miniatures of various kinds maintaining his alcohol level, just maintaining, rather than adding greatly to it, still spruce and cheerful at noon, intoxicated if at all by the smell of pub lemons that, like the bunch of thyme, brings all things to his mind. He met Sheila here. But with a pint of white wine and soda in front of him, a splitzer as Barney McKenna of the Dubliners calls it, it strikes him as just amazing that three decades later, Victor Bartley is at the sharp end of the business after all those years of creative frustration.

Because, you know, the manager is an artiste too, and something inside of him dies when his sensibilities are offended by everyone in his stable. A good line there, for Pat. These splitzers, they're not drink at all. More like sweets. Victor is keeping an eye on his appearance by limping into the jakes and studying himself in the mirror, and he's sparkling all right, it's definitely Victor of the dancing eyes, but then people have had enough of these poker-up-the-hole rock managers with their toney accents measuring every word like they're drawing up a fucking contract, like they need it in writing before they give you the time of day or the steam off their piss. Victor wants to come across more natural.

The splitzers are a happy drink, a refreshing drink, and six more pints with oodles of ice see the afternoon sailing by most agreeably, maintaining, just maintaining, and slipping the barman a few words of small-talk about the fucking traffic and the fucking property prices and Charlie Fucking Haughey just to check that the yapping gear is in mint condition.

Fuck's sake, will Brad Pitt be out there? Ah no, it's well past the stage when anyone famous who comes to Ireland has to be wheeled on to the box in case they never come back. They're all over here now.

The painkillers are supposed to be strong but the ankle is at him, so he figures it's time to leave this grand old spot and heave himself over to the Shelbourne so he can get a seat before the Friday evening rush. Victor starts sweating up the moment he hobbles through the swing doors of the Shelbourne.

It's like the eve of Prohibition in there now, punters roaring with pleasure as the first drink hits the sweet spot, punters spilling out of the Horseshoe Bar and standing in the lobby belting back the booze while Victor manoeuvres his way past them, brushing up against all that expensive tailoring, smiling at the tanned women. He's sweating up, looking for a seat in the jammed bar, wondering if a man could faint in this crush, thinking he'd be better off retiring to his room, but drawn back to the roaring crowd, fearing that with his luck he'd probably fall asleep in the quiet of the room and leave Pat with a no-show.

He catches sight of himself in the big mirror, looking

flustered, sweating up, getting angry that he didn't just fuck off out of O'Donoghue's five minutes earlier.

He barges back out through the lobby and hobbles out on to the pavement because he's afraid that something inside his head will go off and he'll hit one of the bad-mannered selfish bastards and they're not worth it.

Still, the room seems like such a lonely place to be at this time. But with the bitterness brewing up in him, he takes a huge deep breath and remembers that nothing, but nothing, must come between him and a good show tonight. So he wades back in, giving a couple of the braying punters a dirty elbow in the ribs and a big phoney apology, and he makes it back to his room.

The solitude is hard to take with the roaring below, but it still feels like the professional choice, to just sit it out on the bed until the limo arrives, composing his thoughts with the aid of a few nips from the mini-bar. Which is freshly stocked, after all.

Victor picks out a rake of the little buggers and downs a gin straight off to stabilise him after that buffeting by the beautiful people. He is tempted to have a right go at these cunts on the show, but that would only be going down to their level.

The trick now is to remember that it's his show as much as Pat's when he walks out to do his thing, and that it's important to enjoy yourself as well, to go out there and enjoy yourself like it's the All-Ireland Final, because you might never get another chance.

He puts his face right up against the mirror, his nose touching the glass. Looking a bit flushed, but that's a job for the make-up ladies. Victor unscrews a cool vodka and whatever way he does it, he cuts his finger. He is possessed by a gale-force fury watching the blood flowing out of the stupid bastard cut, because it's always the small things that get you in the end, it's always this kind of thing that drives you spare.

And he feels so proud that at this moment of supreme provocation, he remembers Paul and the psychobabble and instead of bashing the mirror or putting his shoe through the television, which he is totally entitled to do, he crawls on to the bed and takes the pillow between his teeth and rips it open so that he gets a mouth full of feathers but he's made his point.

Victor is thinking that you get a good quality of feather at the Shelbourne too, when the bedside phone rings and it's a car for Mr Bartley to go to RTÉ. All righty.

He rolls off the bed and selects his last drink from the mini-bar with an eeny-meeny-miny-mo, and the mo gives him a vodka, which seems like the perfect choice to cool him down, all sharp and clean and fresh from Siberia.

It's showtime. He feels like a man apart from the baying hordes in the lobby, the golden boys who are looking a bit shook now, a bit wild, while the mature man is off to address the nation, drawing on his stamina when attacked by the gremlins, under a bit of strain from the drink it is true, and only a fool would deny it, but still very much on top of that aspect, still in the pink. And it's a most pleasant sensation too, cruising out to Donnybrook in the back of the long black Merc, to swig another wee-fella of the old Vladivar, maintaining, maintaining, maintaining.

Is Pat nervous? Maybe he should be. And Victor laughs out loud at his internal dialogue, while the driver smiles and shakes his head philosophically. Getting out at the TV Centre, Victor gives the driver a twenty-pound note enclosed in a vice-like handshake. He hops through the swing-doors and over to reception and he is directed up to hospitality, the first room at the top of the stairs. The woman at reception avoids his dancing eyes. She says that

Linda will be along soon to take him to make-up. Victor limps over to the statue of Eamonn Andrews.

'Hello, Eamonn,' he says quietly. 'I'm not like the others.'

Climbing the stairs to hospitality, Victor's antennae are up for RTÉ who might construe him to be a bit squiffy by their miserable standards. He aims to be jolly without being boisterous, so as not to give them the pleasure.

He offers a cursory greeting to the other guests and their aides in hospitality, no-one he recognises apart from some mickey-dodger who's always on about the poor. There was a mickey-dodger once in St Fachtna's who insisted that Victor had a wet brain, and he never fancied them much after that.

He can feel their eyes on him, but then there's something in the natural order of things that lets the other guests know who's top of the bill. A certain swagger.

The way the business is going now, looking around the room Victor wouldn't know who's on the show tonight and who's just along for the ride. You're supposed to be able to tell the difference between the artiste and the aides. It looks like they're all shitting bricks. You can smell the fear. Time for the top dog to stay cool.

The girl behind the counter asks him what'll he have.

'I'll have a glass of white wine please,' he says.

Linda Duffy is steering him out the door to make-up before he can take a sip, all a-flurry and a nice-looking woman to boot, but clearly het up in that way that women get when they've been told that the star guest was speaking to a statue in reception.

She's yammering away while they work on him in make-up, bringing down his colour somewhat. She's telling him he's got his own dressing-room, and now Victor's antennae are twitching uncontrollably, because he knows she's keeping him away from the drink in hospitality. He just

261

knows. She shows him into a little dressing-room and asks him if he would like that glass of wine brought to him, the way that professional people talk to Hannibal Lecter when they are introduced.

'I'll have that glass of wine now,' he says, with total poise.

Linda seems slightly relieved at this, though perhaps she hears his laughter down the corridor. I'll have that glass of wine now. I'll have that cup of tea now. She returns with the glass of wine and a big plate of sandwiches. She seems more human now.

'I can get you another glass of wine,' she says. 'Two glasses are perfect to settle the nerves, anything more and you're pushing it. The lights, you know.'

'Thank you, Linda,' Victor says. 'Thank you very much. But no thank you. This will suffice.'

'You can have all you want afterwards.'

'I know.'

'You'll be great.'

'I'll be. . . honest.'

You know what this place is like? You know what it's like? To Victor it's exactly like a cell. The little jakes and the telly and not much else, and the hooch too that fills the large inside pocket of his long black leather Johnny Cash coat.

It's a matter of principle now, unscrewing a small gin and supping it, a matter of refusing to go under the yoke.

The nine o'clock news is just started when Pat pops in and touches base and makes no remarks whatsoever about how much white wine a man should have before he goes under the lights, none of that shit because Pat is a professional and from one professional to another, these things go without saying.

Pat tells him to roam willy-nilly around RTÉ if that is his bag, but that the top guests usually like the bit of privacy to gather their thoughts. And there's no agenda, they'll just kick off with Brad Pitt and play it like it lays and hopefully spark off one another and nothing is on the table and everything is on the table except the plate. Richie doesn't know about the plate yet.

Victor is finding the news very depressing. The drop of gin has that effect on him, since time immemorial. The foot is at him too. He pops another painkiller, but he doesn't believe in them.

The Late Late starts and Victor turns the sound down so that he can keep thinking straight, so that he doesn't get caught up in another man's misery. In the silence he can see Pat looking solemn talking to the mickey-dodger about the widening gap between rich and poor at this time of boom and bloom. What else could they be talking about? He opts for one last vodka because the vodka has been good to him today, keeping him up without sending him mental, cutting through the crap.

It stimulates the memory too, because Victor remembers that he never rang Johnny after all for a briefing. He could try calling the South of France right now a mere fifteen minutes before kick-off. But he drains the vodka instead, and tries to imagine what Johnny would say to him. Just go out there and enjoy it, mate, he'd say.

Linda is here now to lead him up to the studio. He takes her by the hand, for balance. Perhaps he is harsh on her, with his antennae up so high. She's just a busy media lady making sure that everyone reaches Pat in peak condition, and while Victor most definitely is not drunk by any reasonable international standards, he may at this stage be smelling of drink.

Linda stands with him all the way, holding his hand as he hears Pat announcing his next guest, a man who's been to the highest highs and the lowest lows and the highest highs again, and it seems like he must be talking about someone else until Linda gives Victor a little shove and he's on, limping across to Pat and shaking him by the hand and not forgetting a little wave to the crowd, who are clapping him now just because he's alive, but who will rise to him later if he plays them right, like they did for Salman Rushdie.

'The tragic chair,' Victor says, sitting down.

What the fuck did he say that for? What the fuck? No problem. Pat is looking downwards with a puzzled expression, working on the gammy leg. Just enjoy it, Victor. And sparkle.

Victor delivers a word-perfect description of the Brad Pitt incident. The audience likes him. He can feel that they want him to do well. But fucking hell it's hot with the long leather coat, a classic case of image coming before comfort, a cardinal error of judgement not to be repeated. He's started well, but now he needs to seize the day.

'I'll tell you something about this country,' Victor says, leaning towards Pat like he's confiding in him, like he's going to be a terrific guest. 'And Brad Pitt should know this too, if you're watching, Brad. We hear a lot about the so-called Celtic Tiger these days, but I have my ear to the ground too, and I hear things that the Dublin Four media would prefer to ignore.'

Victor smiles, signalling like a true pro that there's a laugh in this, that he's not going to go shiting on about rural Ireland without a punchline.

'It concerns an old-style republican up in Monaghan whose daughter wanted to marry a Protestant gentleman. Up with this the old-style republican would not put. Up with his he absolutely would not put. And when the poor man died, they found that he'd eaten no less than fourteen grand.'

The ten laugh-less seconds which follow are to Victor hideous. He's lost it. And he keeps talking.

'Of course he was eating twenty-pound notes every day. For his tea. Over a long period of time.'

'Total intransigence,' Pat says, in a sympathetic sort of way.

Victor looks into Pat's eyes, feeling this weird intimacy that passes between chat-show host and guest. He would love if the two of them were alone now, back in the cell, and not on television, this very second, with the top story mangled and the man in the tragic chair pulverised with the certain knowledge that he is drunk. On live television. And everyone knows it.

'Tell us about the Monday Club,' Pat says.

The Monday Club. Victor has this searing sensation of being totally alone, but for the fact that he is on *The Late Late Show*, scuttered. It's like his brain is sliced in two, split open for inspection, and there's not much left in there except this thought that he is in the process, this instant, of committing the blackest of all war-crimes in the show business, that of being pissed on television. There is nothing more unprofessional than that. Nothing. And there's not a chance now of talking about Paul with a shred of dignity. Don't even think about it, Victor, you sweaty asshole.

'Tell us about the Monday Club.' Pat says it again with a more forceful tone, but Victor is looking deep into his eyes, and Pat can be under no illusions. Victor Bartley has had his chips.

There's something way back at the base of his skull connecting the Monday Club with tax, but the wires are all snapped.

'And that was only Monday,' Victor says quietly. 'And that was only Monday.'

His shoulders start to shake like Ted Heath laughing, and at first a few punters laugh along, and a light comes into Pat's eye like this has all been some big wind-up. But any relief is destroyed when everyone in the studio and at home realises that Victor Bartley is weeping. Drunk and weeping. And Linda comes on and wheels him away and Pat calls for an ad-break.

Rathmines

The papers are unsparing the next day, front page pics of Victor Bartley weeping, talk of a new low. Victor stands in the doorway of his old flat. He expected the mauling, but he got the papers early anyway. It's funny, but the best career move a man can make these days is to cry on television. Unfortunately, drunk doesn't count.

He limps over to the shower and picks up the broken bottle that he used to slash his wrist. There is something appealing about the jagged edges, an elegance.

He takes one last look at the place where he lived for so long. This is no place to live or die.

A few hours later, he gets a flight to the South of France.

Chapter 26

Antibes

For Johnny Oregon, Picasso qualifies as a friend of the vibe. In fact he's right up there. Graham Greene lived in Antibes and Maupassant and Old Rubber Lips is always saying that you got the best birds on the Cote d'Azur, but what makes Antibes magic for Johnny is the Picasso museum. He comes here nearly every day with Greta, when she tells him the sun is getting too heavy out on the yacht. They stroll up to the gaffe hanging out over the sea, the Chateau Grimaldi as it was when old Pablo got it on here in 1946, leaving behind him a bunch of canvasses and ceramics and a chateau-full of the vibe. And there's the guitars, a heavy metal sculpture thingy like old Pablo went scavenging backstage at Knebworth for all these acoustic axes and did a Pete Townshend on it, smashing 'em up and forging them into a tower of flamenco power.

Johnny turns to it now for healing, because Victor Bartley is here, and he needs more healing now than he ever needed before. But it's clear too what Victor needs to do, and it's strange how a catastrophe can lead you to the truth, weeping and wailing at first, but then gently by the hand. He's certain of his next move, is Victor, he's hip to it after a night of reasoning on the yacht, with the warm wind in from Africa.

He's got a gun, a little thing they keep on the yacht. Dee taught Richie how to use it, and Richie taught Johnny, and Johnny is teaching Victor. He's got the hang of it now.

And tomorrow, he's going to take that pistol home with him, and take it up to Kilbrittan Hill, and finish this business with one shot. Finish it up where it started, where the spirit of Paul Bartley mingles with the glitterati, waiting for his tormented father to return.

That one shot should do it. One for the road.

There'll be a sentimental supper on the yacht tonight. Greta will set up the camcorder, and some sentimental things will be said into it, about the way it all happened for Victor Bartley. They will record over that bastard tape that brought them to this. They will wipe the obscene contents of *Richie Earls Unplugged* once and for all and put something in its place that honours the dead man, instead of using his last desperate minutes as a bargaining tool.

The games are over for Victor Bartley. It is time for the gun.

It is Johnny Oregon who has something to say today, about the end of something, and maybe the start of something else, like some cowboy bidding farewell to the old West, figuring at last that there is right and there is wrong, and this is judgement day, and after all these years, he's earned the right to call it.

He introduces Victor to the Picasso guitars in the museum yard. They stand there admiring the work, and then Johnny asks Victor and Greta to listen up. And Greta knows well that when a man like Johnny asks you to listen up, it must be important, Johnny who has said so many important things under his breath in case Lazzer McGeegan or the Sensational Alex Harveys should feel under any obligation.

When Johnny asks you to listen up, usually he is the top dog telling the crew that the gendarmes will be stopping them down the road, and everyone better get smoking so there's nothing left for the fuzz except to slash up the flight cases. Important stuff.

'This geezer had it all figured out,' Johnny says. 'Pablo Picasso was rockin' and rollin' for ninety odd years.'

A couple of visitors to the museum stop to listen, thinking that Johnny is some kind of tour guide, his red mane and the leather waistcoat perhaps lending a dash of bohemian cred.

'Not now, folks,' he says. 'You'll find the brochures at the front of the house.'

They wander off and Johnny starts again.

'I came here with Jagger many years ago,' he starts. 'We used to knock around Villefranche. All along this Riviera I have memories of fantastic times and great, great people. So we came up here one day and I said I don't want to be still rocking when I'm fifty years old. This geezer Picasso did it for ninety, but he's a one off. And Jagger just kept looking at all these plates and ceramics and stuff because he has a really good eye for art and he says that the art brings him to the South of France quite apart from the glamour and the French birds that we all love. But Johnny Oregon is standing here now and he's fifty years old and that world is all gone now. We'd only be fooling ourselves if geezers like me thought we were still bringing something to the party. When Johnny Oregon started coming down here, he couldn't be mistaken for no tour guide, because he'd be hanging with Keef and Anita Pallenberg.

'You see, the world used to look at us and know we were different. We were hairy-bollocked rockers and we lived by our own rules. Now we're just businessmen with a bit of attitude.

'Did my eyes deceive me or was that the man Iggy himself

getting down at the MTV Awards? Sometimes I think it's a shame I should live to see such things. I see Keef from time to time. I say, "Keef, we're at the crossroads, mate."'

Victor raises his hand. He wants to say something.

'Keef has been down to the crossroads,' Victor says. 'I can tell.'

'A very nice man, too,' Johnny says. 'It breaks my heart to think what it was like down here, with Keef and Anita and Dee Bellingham too. But that's all over now, and we don't matter anymore. We bring nothing with us that Celine Fucking Dion isn't delivering up there in Monte Carlo. We're all bread-heads now. And we were supposed to be the good guys.

'You were right, Victor, you were so right, mate. And tomorrow we go back to Ireland where the people who say that rock 'n' roll is alive and well, are the same people who didn't get it when it was really happening. There was a few of us who knew about it, some of the top blokes who ever lived, like my mate Bill Graham who checked out.

'OK, so the men of 1916 didn't die so that Johnny Oregon could rock and Johnny Oregon could roll, but they didn't not die for it either, mate. They didn't not die for it either. They would have looked at Philo and Rory and Van the Man and the Horslips, and Richie Earls too when he had it, and they would have said, these geezers are bringing something to the table.

'And now? They'd see nothing but dudes dabbling in real estate. Dudes who set the dogs on a geezer when he makes the wrong move. They'd see corporate entertainment. And they would call on the kids to rise up again, like they did in seventy-seven.

'One more time for rock 'n' roll, the *Titanic* sails at dawn.'

A long tall French punk rocker who has been listening to

Johnny's soliloquy applauds like this is the most brilliant thing he has ever heard. He is all sign language now, no-speaka-de-English and beseeching them, it seems, to come with him because he has something to show them.

They follow him out of the chateau, Johnny in the middle with an arm around Greta and an arm around Victor. The punk signals to them to stop at a wall where he points delightedly to the graffiti in huge purple letters: THE VIRGIN PRUNES. It seems like the right thing to do, to return the punk's round of applause.

Cork Airport

Nulty feels like a man these days, and maybe that's all he ever wanted to feel like. A man halfway on his own terms, even if it takes Simon annoying him and Dee Bellingham loving him to shoot him out of the low responsibility league. Into this, a drive down to Cork Airport in Simon's big silver car, with Titus in the front seat and Phil in the back, ready for what has to be done.

It has to be done like this, according to Dee, and Nulty trusts Dee because trusting her makes him feel terrific, like she is teaching him how to use the trust-muscles along with all the other muscles she is bringing back to life.

It has to be done like this, because Dee opens up to him and he knows the whole story now, he knows all about Richie and Paul Bartley and the tape. And after *The Late Late* debacle, the whole country knows that Victor Bartley needs to lie down for a while and rest.

It has to be done like this or, as Simon put it, the Richie Earls product will die of embarrassment, and Richie himself will get a whack of a shovel.

Dee phoned up Richie the day after the *Late Late* to try

to talk him down from the cocaine, she says, to try to talk him back to this planet, she says. But he just shouts at her, she says, tells her he's happy, and at least now he has a human being for a manager, a man who can cry.

Nulty reaches Cork Airport now with Dee's words guiding him all the way: 'I want you to steal something for me,' Dee says to Nulty. 'I want you to steal Victor Bartley.'

Here they come, Victor and Johnny and Greta walking through Arrivals. Nulty gets up to meet them, as they have arranged it, because they have no quarrel with Nulty, and still some business to discuss. That's the idea.

Nulty ushers them into the back of the big silver beauty, and when they are seated, they are joined by Titus and Phil. Titus takes the front seat, and Phil squeezes into the back. Titus takes out a shooter.

'It'll be all right,' Nulty says calmly to Victor and Johnny and Greta. 'We'll be keeping you somewhere safe.'

Nulty thinks the hard part is over. Victor is sweating some, but no-one is throwing a fit. Driving towards Kinsale he explains that Dee is telling Richie what is happening at this minute, and obviously Richie will give the word and then the three of them can go. But Richie will have to agree to treatment. And Victor will have to agree to treatment too, and Dee will take over again. It's a pity, but there's no other way of getting through to Richie, to any of them.

'We understand,' Victor says. 'We're professionals.'

Near Kinsale, Nulty stops at the top of the lane leading to the lodge. Titus and Phil shepherd everyone through the trees to the safe place, probably the safest place in Europe, the bunker that Johnny told Victor about in Goggin's, the place where Ireland's rockstars and their selected friends hope to see out the nuclear winter, the ultimate VIP enclosure for which no laminates or lanyards exist, even on Johnny's laminate-maker.

Johnny is able to assist Titus and Phil with the precise location, kicking away some leaves until the manhole cover can be seen. Phil unscrews it and they climb one by one down the ladder and into the bunker. Victor laughs.

'So be it, boys. So be it.'

'The only other one is under the barracks in Athlone,' Nulty says. 'For the government.'

'This is better than the one in Athlone,' says Johnny. 'Much better.'

It is no dungeon, for sure, but a series of rooms with superb design which seems to be modelled on the clean lines of Dublin's fashionable Morrison Hotel, using natural materials such as wood and stone, with dyed velvet throws and oriental vases.

Titus points the gun at Victor. There is a tremendous noise and Victor goes flying backwards. Johnny and Greta are with him immediately as he lies stretched, only this time the blood is pouring out of his head, and not even Greta can bring him back from that.

Titus raises the gun again. Phil shouts at him to wait. A video tape has fallen out of Victor's pocket. Phil picks it up.

'*Richie Earls Unplugged*,' he says to Titus. 'This is the one.'

'Come over here,' Titus snaps. 'We're not finished yet.'

Phil walks quickly to stand beside Titus, but Greta is quick too, and she goes for that gun in the inside breast pocket of Victor's long black Johnny Cash coat, the gun they taught him to use in Antibes. And she has it pointing at Titus before Titus can finish anything.

'Go away,' she shouts. 'Fuck off.'

Titus takes maybe a minute to make his mind up. Then he starts to walk backwards, pointing the gun at Greta, a stalemate. Phil walks backwards beside him, still holding the tape. With a sudden spurt they are up the ladder one after the other and out.

Nulty puts his hands up and walks slowly towards Greta and Johnny and Victor. He opens his mouth to speak but no words come to him. Greta keeps the gun pointed at him.

He'd like to tell her he knew nothing about this, that there wasn't supposed to be any shooting, that he has been betrayed by Dee Bellingham and by Simon, shafted.

He wants to tell them over and over that this was supposed to be a simple deal, a short trip underground to concentrate the mind, some damage limitation as Dee put it when she was shafting him. He wants to say all that. But he feels more like screaming, and he can hear himself screaming inside, but nothing comes out.

He kneels beside Victor. Ignoring the gun, he presses his mouth against Victor's, and starts to give him the kiss of life. But Victor is stirring anyway. Nulty withdraws his mouth and his eyes meet Victor's and Victor's eyes are alive.

'The fucking plate,' Johnny shouts. 'The fucking plate. The bullet went flying off the fucking plate.'

Victor gives the faintest smile. He is desperately trying to say something. Greta and Johnny lift him into a sitting position. Victor whispers to Nulty. He touches Nulty's hand.

'Go now,' he says. 'Go now.'

Nulty, speechless, stands up. He starts to cry, but that doesn't happen for him either. He turns around and walks.

Nulty hears the explosion of the gunshot and he freezes, waiting for death. But death does not come to him.

Nulty looks back. There's a big hole in the side of Victor Bartley's head and he put it there himself with that one shot.

Like a professional.

Chapter 27

Dublin

The showbiz reporters troop into the conference room of the Bartley Hotel in Camden Street, not the most fashionable Dublin joint but Simon has just bought it. Victor Bartley is dead a week now, a decent enough interval, in Simon's view, to hold a press conference announcing details of Richie Earls at Drumbolus House next July.

At noon, the reporters will be treated to a ten-minute video hailing the birth of a sensational new festival venue in a natural amphitheatre at the centre of the ancient Celtic world, according to Simon. With the co-operation of all present, who see this as a vital national interest, no other matter will be discussed. No unhappy men on *The Late Late Show*, unhappy, and dead to boot.

Dee Bellingham and Simon and then Richie Earls take their seats at the top table, Richie still a prisoner with a new pair of jailers. Dee asks the reporters to hold their questions until they see the video. They are already sampling the free drink and the triangular sandwiches, so this is no hardship.

Nulty switches off the lights. Nulty is in charge of the projector. For the first time in his life, he possesses a cold clarity of purpose, and the means to make it count. He will

275

tell Dee Bellingham later that there's no point in her trying to repair their relationship, because she's an alcoholic and she needs help, and she probably fell for him and he for her because he's an addict too, a kleptomaniac.

It is not only the right thing, it is the compassionate thing, the just thing. But he wouldn't be a full human if he didn't thirst for the vengeance thing as well, that thing they don't have in the Hare Krishnas, the you-fuck-with-me-and-I'll-fuck-with-you thing.

Last night, he indulged his addiction for what he trusts will be the last time. After a long session in Malone's, with Dee stroking him on one side and Simon lisping on the other, telling him there was no other option, that Victor had to be eradicated, he swallows it all and concedes that they might have a point, and yes, this is what must be done when you're playing by the big boys' rules.

When they are satisfied that he is cool about it, unhindered by a skinful of rum-and-blacks, he slips upstairs. He swipes *Richie Earls Unplugged* from Simon's safe and replaces it with a dud.

They can fool all the people, all the time, but they don't fool him this time. He even walks with Dee with the stolen tape stuck down the front of his trousers all the way out to Drumbolus House, where in the fever of drunken sex, he figures he could get to like this you-fuck-with-me-and-I'll-fuck-with-you thing.

So on this morning after this demented night, in the conference room of the Bartley Hotel in Camden Street, instead of the corporate video, Nulty is going to play *Richie Earls Unplugged*. He believes Dee on this at least, that it is the tape of Richie Earls and his dogs chasing Paul Bartley into the sea. He is going to see for himself anyway.

He is going to play it for the edification of the assembled media, on the big screen. He slides the tape into the machine, the tape that has been from Kilbrittan Hill to Kinsale and over to the South of France and back to Drumbolus and up here to Dublin, with a short trip underground to Ireland's most exclusive venue.

There, in the moments after it is blasted out of Victor Bartley's coat, it passes to the hitmen and from them to Dee Bellingham. Moments that keep Greta and Johnny alive, but that rip the heart out of Nulty.

Twelve bells. Nulty presses the Play button, and, inexplicably to him, the big screen fills with the face of Victor Bartley. He is sitting on a yacht with a lot of other yachts in the background. The yachts fade out of the picture as the camera concentrates on Victor's face. Then Victor Bartley speaks.

'By the time you see this, I will be dead,' he begins. 'I don't wish to make a big issue of this, because the world will not be mourning Victor Bartley. But for the sake of posterity, let me suggest the reasons for my. . . my checking out, as my good friend Johnny Oregon would put it.

'True, I am here in the South of France on a beautiful boat. I am the manager of Richie Earls, who I believe to be a brilliant talent about to enter the most rewarding phase of his career. And Richie, I wish you all the best. You are free now. I know you'll be able to handle this.

'But I have lost my son. And I have tried to live with this and all the other people and everything I have lost and squandered. But it seems there is something inside Victor Bartley that will not be healed.

'Many of you probably witnessed my performance on *The Late Late Show*, when, on the biggest night of my career, I was found wanting. There are no excuses for such a total lack of professionalism. Except to say that, for too long, I have been in too much pain, and I have tried to control it with alcohol, and then I have tried to control

277

alcohol, sometimes with. . . hilarious results.

'I can't do it any more, folks. I just can't do it. I have these patches of remembering what it was like to be a well man, but it's too little. My son tried valiantly to help me understand this pain deep down inside of me. But I couldn't do it. I can't do it.

'And maybe it's no big thing that's causing this pain, but one of those little things, some song on the jukebox on the summer breeze, gone forever.

'I will miss the music.

'Music is my life.'

Dee Bellingham and Simon Bartley play it cool in the middle of the media uproar. Richie Earls slips through with the light step of a man free at last.

On his way out the door he sees Nulty sitting at the back of the room, still staring up at the blank screen, but beginning to understand.

Richie beckons Nulty, and the two men leave the hotel together, walking, marching, running with the adrenaline all the way down Camden Street and into Wicklow Street, to the International Bar.

They drink all day and all night, to the repose of the soul of Victor Bartley.

Epilogue

Dublin

Richie Earls, Johnny Oregon and Greta stand at the graveside. They are admiring the new headstone, with an inscription which they jointly agreed:

VICTOR BARTLEY AND HIS WIFE SHEILA AND SON PAUL

IT'S A MIGHTY LONG WAY DOWN ROCK 'N' ROLL

Richie says something, but he is drowned out by an Aer Lingus jet coming in to land. He tries again.

'You're from out this way, Johnny, aren't you? Out near the airport?'

Johnny thinks about it.

'Kinda,' he says. 'And kinda not.'

They stroll away to the gate. Richie puts his arm around Greta, and Johnny instinctively takes a step away, like he's giving them space.

He's from out this way, all right. And before the jumbos were coming in every day from America, another sound from America came to him somehow, the sound of Maurice Williams and the Zodiacs.

Stay.

Just a little bit longer.